ANGEL/PEARL

天使／真珠

by **Friction Press**

Yaoi Novel

ANGEL PEARL

ISBN 979-8999001306 (paperback edition)
First printing 2025

Cover art by Roo Fiction
Gallery art by Puck and Cyborg Nachte
Editing by Beleghir
Formatting and proofreading by subvertebra

friction-press.itch.io
subscribestar.adult/friction-press

Thank you to all the BL mangaka in the world who create hilarious, beautiful, emotionally poignant, deeply sexy work which taught me that you really can have it all in one story if you're willing to put in the time.

ANGEL

Bram's knuckles steadily turn white on the steering wheel. The roaring of the engine is starting to sound like the car is preparing to take flight. He knows he's going to get pulled over in the next ten minutes if he doesn't slow down, but he's also certain that if he starts going the speed limit again, he'll get the urge to rear-end the next car in front of him, and really, a speeding ticket is less trouble to disappear than an accident outside his turf.

Lips curled, Bram turns the radio up as loud as he can stand, and forces himself to take the next exit in a feat of remarkable self-restraint. He can hear Chel's voice in his head. *Fucking slow down, christ, nobody can see your dick from here.*

Bram wonders if there are any drag races outside the city. That kind of sport fell out of his gang's purview before his time. Maybe if he had the mental permission to drive as fast as he could, he wouldn't feel like clawing his eyes out every time he was forced to play nice on the highway. Chel may not be here to browbeat him into submission, but his newfound reputation as the laughingstock of the Outerridge criminal underworld just barely manages to keep him in check.

If he's going to fuck up, it can't be a matter of public record.

Bram Stoker: alias for the (newly appointed) boss of the Southside Vampires, a gang that traffics in stolen goods. Shortly after his promotion, Bram got dumped by his former girlfriend Chelsea

Richardson in a very well-known debacle that surely has nothing to do with Bram's sudden interest in crashing his car at very high velocities. Despite the name of his gang, Bram is only human.

For two weeks, Bram was the biggest man in the city—boss of the biggest gang, with the heiress and daughter of a *very* influential politician on his arm. It seemed like he had everything in place to finally relax and delegate all the heavy lifting *he'd* been doing for so many years leading up to the former boss's passing.

It started when the owner of a particularly well-loved brothel refused to join Bram's territory. A hearty blow on its own, but not devastating. Shortly after, Bram lost a spectacular bet on a boxing match when his favorite fighter got mauled in one round. He could have recovered if he hadn't come home earlier than promised from that fight to find Chel fucking one his own men—Reese, who didn't just have his dick in Bram's girlfriend, but his fingers in every one of Bram's pockets leeching money from the gang in an attempt to run away with Chel. Now, Reese has ten broken fingers and several more problems in the ICU at St. Helena's. The worst part of it *would* have been Bram being forced to pay Reese's medical bills just to keep him from going to the cops and turning on all of them—but then Chel herself started the very flammable rumor that Bram couldn't get it up for her anymore and *that's* why she fucked his lieutenant.

That's about when Bram's new habit of driving through the upper neighborhoods began. Every time he enters his own apartment, he's sure he's about to hear the telltale sounds of two people fucking in his own bed. Now, his gang thinks they have to take care of him, and he can't even convince one goddamn brothel to fold into their territory.

At least in the residential neighborhoods, Bram knows he won't run into anyone he doesn't want to see. He rarely left his own territory before all of this, but nowadays, the only place he can stand to be is way the hell out in suburbs like Beechwood where people are too polite to draw attention to their vices.

Driving by a seemingly endless loop of townhouses with perfectly measured squares of lawns, Bram sees him. A boy, much too young to know what he's doing, standing on a street corner with his bare legs out on a forty-degree spring night. He wears nothing but a large, black sweater, much too big for his gangly body, and a pair of white sneakers. There's no avoiding him right next to the stop sign, and he visibly perks up when Bram's car rolls to a stop beside him.

The boy raises his hand up to wave with his fingers at Bram in the driver's seat of his SUV. He's got legs like a pony, a thick wave of brown hair licking off his forehead, his face all round features and soft cheeks—impossible to tell if he's *too* young to be out here by himself, or just blessed with youthful features. Either way, when he holds his hands behind his back and bats his eyes at Bram, it's obvious what he wants.

Or, obvious what he thinks *Bram* wants.

Bram throws the car into park, his thoughts finally calming from their angry tempest. He lowers the volume of his music and rolls the window down, letting in the light of the nearest street lamp. This is exactly what he needed: a dumb kid to teach a lesson to.

The boy bounds over to his car, leaning his hands on the windowsill—the sleeves of the sweater cover his palms, leaving only the tips of pale brown fingers showing. He smiles at Bram through dark, thick lashes, the chill turning his round cheeks pink.

"Do you know what you're doing out here, kid?" Bram asks.

The boy chews on his bottom lip, turning his smile into a cheeky grin, and he nods.

"You sure about that?" Bram presses, letting his voice drop as deep as he can get it.

The boy's eyes flick up, and his irises look entirely black. His breath seems to suck up into his lungs, and for a minute, Bram prepares for the satisfying victory of fear bleeding into this boy's gaze when he finally realizes he is talking to someone three times his size.

The boy grips the windowsill, and Bram can see the swell of excitement passing through his body as his wide-eyed gaze roves over Bram. He nods again, faster and shorter, and Bram's footing falters.

So maybe he *can't* scare a boy just by looking at him. He has other tactics.

"Your parents know you're out here?" Bram asks.

The boy is bubbling with enthusiasm, on the verge of giggling as he shakes his head. He doesn't once look away from Bram, and suddenly Bram's face is heating up. He didn't expect the kid to be so dogged.

"What's your name?" Bram tries.

The kid blushes and shakes his head again, a soft hum emitting from his throat. Hiding his sigh, Bram shifts in his seat, realizing he has fully fallen into the trap of playing this boy's game.

"Come on kid, you know you shouldn't be out here by yourself in the middle of the night."

The boy sinks down, leaning his chin on the windowsill like a puppy, those wide, black eyes fixed on Bram like searchlights. It seems as though nothing will deter him, and for a brief moment, Bram gets an electric stirring in his belly at being pursued by someone so brazenly—before he remembers he has no idea how old this boy is.

"How far away do you live?" Bram asks.

The boy leans further into the car, holding out his hands to indicate the number two and the number zero, then points toward the cluster of large buildings that make up the heart of the city. Right in the direction Bram was already headed.

"Alright get in," Bram says, unlocking the door.

The boy wastes no time jumping into Bram's car, even going so far as to start rolling up the window for him. Bram pops his phone off the grip on his dashboard and passes it to the boy.

"Put your address in. I'm taking you home."

This is not exactly the show of masculine force Bram had intended it to be, but maybe the walk of shame back into his own house will finally put the fear in this boy and he'll break character.

The boy types something in and starts up the map for Bram before handing the phone back. Exactly twenty minutes away from them. Bram switches gears and starts following the directions, glancing over at the boy in his passenger seat, disconcerted by the unbroken stare of this boy's black eyes.

"You really think it's a good idea to be out here fishing for johns in the middle of the night?" Bram asks. "Do you even know who runs this neighborhood?"

His gaze flicks over to the boy, who seems to be hanging off his words.

Bram puffs up, sure he's onto something here. "The Eels patrol the blocks out here. They're not nearly as organized or structured as the city gangs are. They're bikers. You don't want to fuck with bikers, I promise. They're a lot meaner to their boys."

Bram settles into his spiel, relaxing into the driver's seat as he revels in his own knowledge of this area. Finally, a chance to flaunt for someone, even if he is just some dumb kid in need of a good scare. Bram rolls his shoulders, some of the tension starting to melt away. He drives with one hand on the wheel, control coming back to him after the worst month of his life.

Bram doesn't notice the boy unbuckling his own seatbelt. It's much too late for Bram to do anything about it when the boy pops up with his hands on the console between their seats, his face suddenly close enough to catch warm breath on Bram's cheek.

"Hey, what are you—?"

Bram doesn't get to finish asking before he gets an answer. The boy presses his lips to Bram's cheek and Bram startles so badly, the car veers into the lane of oncoming traffic. A tiny white car slams on the horn as Bram quickly jerks the wheel back into the right lane, his heart slamming in his chest.

The boy's lips seem to linger on his cheek even after he breaks the kiss, and a wild bit of unwelcome heat sinks into Bram's blood. Lord help him, if this were *anyone else*, Bram would be hard as a rock but when he glares at his passenger, all he can see is a face too youthful to trust.

"What the fuck do you think you're doing?" Bram tries to snarl but it comes out too breathless.

The boy is blushing, eyes lowered, lips parted. He looks *starving* in exactly the way Bram wishes a woman would look at him. It takes a strange amount of effort for Bram to tear his gaze off the boy's mouth and focus back on the road as they roll up to a stoplight. As soon as the car comes to a complete stop, Bram takes a breath to scold this idiot boy at the same time that the boy's hand lands on Bram's chest.

Bram freezes up, that little bit of contact enough to remind him just how long it's been since someone felt him up. His breath slowly builds in his lungs while the boy draws his fingers down the length of Bram's torso, a feather-soft touch through the fabric of his gym t-shirt.

Bram's gaze cuts back to the boy's black eyes. The way this boy smiles, the kid thing *must* be an act. Bram tries to make his expression look angry, distrustful, a silent warning in his eyes that people *used* to tell him was intimidating.

The boy makes a pleased sound in the back of his throat and kisses Bram again, his lips pillowing against the hollow of Bram's cheek as his thin fingers graze the pounding lump in Bram's pants.

The sound of the car behind them laying on the horn shoots through Bram's spine and he lurches forward to grab the wheel with both hands, staring down the green light he'd been ignoring. The car rockets forward, much too fast, and the boy gives a wheezing laugh in Bram's ear, almost no sound at all.

"Jesus fucking Christ," Bram whispers, blood pressure shooting through the roof.

The boy is gripping Bram's cock through his sweatpants, his breath tickling Bram's ear.

"This isn't what I let you in here for!" Bram snaps, but there is no anger in his voice, only a manic sort of overwhelm as his heart slams against his ribs.

He's only getting harder as more and more cars populate the road. It's not yet late enough for the streets to be truly empty, and they're only getting deeper into the city as this reckless pretty boy slowly rubs Bram's cock to full attention. Again, he presses a kiss to Bram face, closer and closer to Bram's mouth each time, and every time Bram tells himself that he needs to shut this down ASAP, yet more blood empties from his head and goes straight to his dick. He can't even bring himself to close his damn thighs with those slender fingers drawing tantalizing circles on his criminally unloved cock.

Fuck him, it's been *weeks*. Chel was giving him the cold shoulder even before they split up, and she never touched him like this—reckless and desperate.

When the boy's tongue crests over the apple of Bram's cheek, Bram loses his grip.

"*Fuck.*"

Ignoring his phone entirely, he scans the streets, orienting himself in the neighborhood. It's hard to think with a boy latched onto him like a barnacle and his dick stealing all his oxygen but eventually he figures out where they are. Near the north branch of the library, not far from the park, perfect.

Bram slams on the gas while the boy plucks the waist of Bram's sweatpants and slips his fingers down to trace the length of Bram's cock through his briefs.

"*Fuck fuck fuck, just hold on.*" Bram grinds the words out between clenched teeth, unable to stop his hips from pressing into the boy's soft grip. A drop of fluid melts into the fabric of his underwear.

Blessedly, the parking lot outside the entrance to Piccolo Park is devoid of all life, save for the same broken-down Subaru that's been stranded there for the last six months. Bram shoves his car into the spot furthest from the road, blocked by a few anemic trees, and kills the engine.

"Fucking calm *down*." Bram breathes. He's scared to touch the boy, scared he won't really be able to stop him from touching Bram.

The boy inhales sharply, planting another kiss on Bram's cheek before he suddenly scrambles into the backseat in a flurry of limbs. Bram cranes around to glare at him, watching in horror as the gangly boy begins removing his white sneakers.

"Whoa, whoa, whoa!" Bram reaches out his hand as if to stop him, but the boy is too far away, his back pressed to the opposite door. "Fucking fuck fuck."

Bram quickly gets out of the driver's seat and opens the door to the backseat right in time to see the boy pick up his legs and hold them apart to reveal that he is not even wearing underwear. Bram stares, slack-jawed, at the boy's hairless thighs while he parts them wide open for Bram to see right to the center of his body. A sweaty shiver runs up Bram's spine as he remembers he's holding the car door just as wide open as those smooth thighs, and he throws himself into the backseat just so he can close the door behind him.

Turning to face the boy, Bram leans on the seat between them and holds his hand up to block the sight of whatever is between the boy's legs.

"You can't be doing this," Bram says, but even he can hear how desperate his voice sounds.

His pulse throbs under every inch of his skin as the boy gives a muted giggle, his smile turning wicked.

"You didn't even ask for money," Bram says, voice strained. "The hell kind of business are you running?"

The boy pulls his large sweater over his head, revealing his reedy body, and a pair of tiny tits that Bram's gaze instantly zeroes in on.

"Christing fuck," Bram whispers.

The only thing he likes more than huge, round breasts he can grab onto are...tiny little cupcake tits that turn puffy and cute and red when he plays with them long enough. Not that he would tell anyone that.

"Wait a second, I thought you were a—" Forgetting himself, Bram lowers his hand and sees the darkened folds of the boy's cunt, and the proportionally biggest clit he's ever seen peeking out at him. "Holy shit."

The boy (?) springs forward, wrapping his arms around Bram's neck and catching him off guard in a kiss that instantly gives Bram a fever. His hind brain howls its pleasure at the needy body pressed up against him, how desperate this little thing is to get in Bram's pants. Surely that means Bram *is* desirable, that he's not just some limp-dick coward who makes terrible business decisions and loses the respect of his men?

Not that he would ever tell *anyone* about this dubiously youthful, questionably gendered kid pressing his needy hole against Bram's cock.

Bram's better judgment vanishes for a minute as he slips his tongue past small but full lips, cradling the back of this fluffy head to return such a desperate kiss. Bram feels like a teenager as he trails his hand down the soft curve of a spine, and the slightest heft of a squeezable ass, too curious and hard not to run his fingers across the mouth of a slicked-up cunt.

The boy moans in a strange, wheezing muffled way, and Bram snaps back to himself, breaking their kiss with a hand in that dense wave of hair.

"Are you a girl or what?" Bram asks, breathing hard. His dick still twitches insistently against the naked hips in his lap.

The boy's eyes widen and he gives a demure shrug.

"You...but..."

The boy's gaze instantly brightens, like he's heard this joke a hundred times and it never gets old. Bram immediately regrets asking, his skin prickling with embarrassed heat as he tries to figure out why he assumed anything at all. That youthful face says *boy*, but strangely, even looking right at those little tits doesn't make Bram think *girl*.

"Look, we have to establish some things 'cause I don't fuck boys," Bram says. "I like girls—*women*, I only fuck women. Do you hear me?"

Instantly, the boy's expression melts back into low-lidded hunger as he leans back into Bram's hands, drawing his fingers off of Bram's neck and onto his own chest. He pushes the small swell of his barely A-cup breasts up for Bram to admire, ruddy nipples gone hard. The edges of Bram's vision are starting to go black as he stares at the cutest boobs he's ever seen, his tongue getting heavier in his head, his hands prickling with heat.

"This isn't..." Bram wants to suck on his tits more than anything. "Isn't, uh..." Just a little wouldn't hurt. As long as they don't have sex, it's probably fine. "Not gonna..." How did his mouth get so close? "*Mmhh.*"

Bram moans when his lips brush over the button of the boy's left nipple, his cock jumping in his sweatpants. He laps at the boy's chest like a hungry dog. The boy didn't ask for money. That must mean he just wanted to fuck, right? He's way too good at this to be a kid, but not good enough to be a pro. A perfect little mistake just for Bram to suck on.

Which he does, with breathless, reckless abandon as the boy holds Bram's head against his chest, encouraging Bram with his strange little muted moans that give the impression that his voice is somehow being suppressed. Not that Bram cares. It's obvious the boy likes it or else he wouldn't be rutting the knob of his clit against Bram's chest like he's trying to start a fire.

Bram is so distracted with the dollop of flesh in his mouth, he barely notices when his sweatpants are pushed down his thighs. All of a sudden, his cock is straining against the inside of his briefs, tantalizingly close to fresh air, and it's driving him crazy how hot the fabric is on his skin, so he shoves his underwear down his thighs just to make himself more comfortable.

He doesn't *mean* to invite the boy to rub his hips against the tip of Bram's dick. He doesn't say anything at all when the boy reaches down to steady Bram's length underneath him. All Bram can manage are throaty moans and curses as the boy sinks down onto his cock with shockingly little resistance. The boy's eyes flutter shut, his skin covered in a sheen of sweat and a fierce flush and that's the last thing Bram remembers before he's definitely fucking the boy he said he wasn't going to fuck, completely mesmerized by the way his tits bounce and oddly turned on by those wheezing, breathy moans as he clings to Bram's neck.

The most delicious haze sets into Bram's muscles, tugging at his nerves, so much better than speeding down the highway and waiting for an accident. This boy no longer looks like a barely legal idiot trying to piss off his parents by riding a stranger's cock, but a fucking angel sent to give Bram the best orgasm of his life.

It rips through Bram, his eyes slamming shut as he grinds his cock as deep as he can get it into his angel's cunt, the delirious spill of his own cum making him dizzy as his head falls back onto the car seat. Bram's entire body buzzes, dancing on the edge of numbness as he crashes back from the breathless high. His hands grasp at his angel's hips as he gets another kiss pressed to his mouth, then his neck. Slender hands graze over Bram's chest, the slight tease over his nipples making Bram shudder with a last twinge of pleasure before the boy crawls out of his lap.

All too soon, Bram hears fabric rustling, and then the car door opening. Bram picks himself up a minute too late, confronted with an empty car, and his angel's silhouette disappearing through the tinted window.

The first thing Bram does is check his wallet—nothing stolen.

The second thing Bram does is grip the edge of the driver's seat and try not to hyperventilate as he assures himself that fucking a boy doesn't make him gay. He just likes pussy too much, doesn't matter what it's attached to. He was too horny and desperate to care. None of this means anything at all.

By the time Bram manages to crawl back into the front seat, he rips his phone off the dashboard grip and checks to see the address that the boy put in, only to find that the directions he was following were for Piccolo Park the whole time.

▷▷▷

Bram does not think about the little demon who seduced him every second of the day for the next three days. He does not think about a *next time* where he could be sure to get the boy to come on him just to prove he can. It is a coincidence when he lowers all the seats in the back of his car after it suddenly occurs to him that he can make the trunk way more spacious if he wants. And it's only sensible to keep some blankets in the back, in case of an emergency. His mother always did that, claiming they could get trapped in freezing temperatures and it's always good to keep blankets on hand. The pillows are just to make it more comfortable—in case of a sudden spring blizzard, and not because he wants to fuck a lithe pony-boy who doesn't wear underwear in the backseat of his car.

"Boss."

Lee cocks his head to the side as Bram slams back into his body behind his desk.

"Huh?" Bram looks at him, hoping it wasn't obvious that he tuned out ten minutes ago.

"We were talking about the Dandelion," Lee says, posture straight, green eyes betraying some of his concern behind his thick-rimmed glasses. "Are you getting enough sleep?"

Leandro "Lee" Baladin: recently appointed lieutenant to Bram Stoker, as of the hospitalization of former lieutenant, Reese. Lee is now the second most important member of the Southside Vampires, and takes his station very seriously.

"We're always talking about the goddamn Dandelion," Bram says, trying to match Lee's perfect posture. "And yes, I'm fine."

He snaps that last little lie a little too loudly, but Lee graciously ignores it.

"I think it's time we put the Dandelion on ice," Lee says. "The owner made his point very clear, and trying to split our focus between the Spiders, the Boars *and* this place is just going to weaken things even further."

Bram flicks the pen on his desk, watching it spin out of control and veer dangerously close to the edge. "This guy is pissing me off. How does he make so much goddamn money sitting outside everyone's territory? I assume the Spiders already made their offer."

"As far as I'm aware, yes. The owner didn't take it. No word from the Boars, but I suspect they're not interested in...well..."

Bram shakes his head. "That's what kills me. How does a *gay* brothel do that well? He's got to have someone in his pocket, and I want to know who it is."

"We're not actually sure it *is* a brothel, sir," Lee responds.

Bram shakes his head. "There's no other explanation for it. You said it yourself, it's a lot of fucking money."

Lee clears his throat, adjusting his straight-backed posture a little to the left. "Boss."

"Hm?" Bram gears up to give the pen another spin, flicking the end with his finger too hard. The pen shoots across his desk, flying several feet through the room in a blink.

Lee lets out a sigh. "I don't know how else to say this other than bluntly. If you spend any more time trying to court the owner of a gay club, people are going to talk even more than they already are."

Bram grips the edge of his desk, a swell of rage passing through him like a tornado. "Money is money! Who gives a shit if it's from gay boys or girls?"

"Listen, you know that I know that," Lee says, hands raised to calm Bram. "But you *also* know how bad the rumors can get when you're not around. We're already gearing up to chase the Spiders out of the corners of our territory. Now is not the time to make people think that you're...not the same man they thought you were."

Bram's lip curls, but the cool look on Lee's face takes the wind out of his sails. "I know, I know, christ, I know how this works."

"Lay off the Dandelion until we fix our own house," Lee says.

Bram nods. "I know you're right. I'm sorry I didn't promote you sooner, you're way better at this than Reese ever was."

Lee's black brows pinch for a split second, and he rubs the back of his shorn neck. "Uh, thanks boss."

Bram leans his arms on his desk and rubs his eyes. "I'm going fucking crazy in this office."

"I know," Lee says, his face finally breaking out of his business-calm. "You're used to breaking noses, not sitting back. It's going to take some getting used to. But hey, maybe if we clean up shop, the Dandelion will come to us."

"That's the hope," Bram mutters, pinching the bridge of his nose. "Fuck me, I need a drink."

"Just don't go too crazy," Lee says, rising from his chair and twitching his black tie a centimeter to the right. "Did you delete Chel's number from your phone yet?"

Rolling his eyes, Bram slides his phone across the desk for Lee to check. "See for yourself. She's dead and buried."

Lee's eyes flash, and Bram throws his hands up. "Not literally, jesus."

"Just checking," Lee says.

Bram doesn't need to tell Lee that his thoughts have been deeply buried inside someone's else cunt for the last few days. A boy's cunt, to make matters even worse. Exactly the goddamn press he doesn't need.

Bram manages to stay away for nearly a week before he cracks and finds himself cruising though Beechwood at an ungodly hour, hoping against hope that he'll find himself face to face with a set of knobbly knees. He finds the exact same stop sign where he found his angel before, and turns the car off. He's about to light a cigarette when there comes a soft knock on the passenger side window.

Bram's stomach clenches, his spine tingling as he slowly turns to look at who it is. A lanky man in a bathrobe looks in on him, eyes narrowed as he tries to peer inside the tinted windows. Rolling his eyes, Bram slams the button to slide the window down.

"Can I help you?" Bram asks.

The man continues staring at him with narrowed eyes, as if he took his glasses off too early. "We have a neighborhood watch out here, you know?"

Bram quirks his eyebrow. "Yeah, and?"

"So..." The man gestures to Bram's car. "We don't tolerate, uhm, suspicious figures."

Bram stares at the middle-aged, white man in his blue bathrobe and white undershirt for an aching five seconds before he says, "I'm an undercover cop, sir. Why do you think I'm here?"

The man's eyes pop open and he gives an overenthusiastic nod. "*Ooh,* oh, oh, oh." Dropping his voice to a whisper, he leans his face into the car and says, "I understand now, thank you, sir. Apologies. We've just been dealing with a recent...issue. It's got us all on edge."

"Let me guess," Bram says. "You suspect there's a young man selling himself out here?"

The man in the bathrobe raises his clasped hands up to Bram, a relived smile on his lips. "You *are* good. Yes, that's the one. We just don't want that kind of thing happening in our neighborhood."

"Understandable," Bram says, his body ice-cold. "If you don't mind, talking to you is only going to scare him away so..."

"Oh, yes, of course, duh." The man laughs and backs away from the car, muttering some kind of thanks as Bram rolls the window back up.

He takes the car up one block further and kills the engine again, trying to figure out what he's going to do with himself for the rest of the evening because he is surely not going to run into the boy after that. Nobody would be dumb enough to approach his car after seeing one of the neighborhood dads at his window.

Knock knock.

Bram jumps out of his skin at the soft rapping on the driver's side window. He turns, the breath punched from his chest as he see two wide black eyes peering in, his angel's hands cupped around his face.

Bram panics, trying to act as quickly as possible so he doesn't lose his moment, which results in opening his own car door for some stupid reason.

His angel doesn't care. As soon as he has room, he squeezes through and hops into Bram's lap, looping his reedy arms around Bram's neck with a smile.

"You scared the shit out of me," Bram says.

The boy gives him a delighted smirk, pushing his hand up into Bram's black hair, his head lolling to the side. Bram's breath quickens, his pulse already accelerating into a roar as he sets his tanned fingers against the boy's neck.

"Fuck me," Bram mutters, already getting hard as the boy shifts his hips and leans his back against the steering wheel. Today, he's only wearing a long button-down shirt that shows his nipples through the fabric. When he lifts his slender leg up to prop his foot against the car door, Bram can see his pussy peeking out from under the shirt.

All the blood drains straight to Bram's cock.

"Come here, Angel," Bram whispers, pulling the boy against his chest. "Is it okay if I call you Angel?"

His answer comes with a hungry kiss that sends gooseflesh rippling down Bram's body. Soft lips on his, soft fingers on his face, soft hips pressing into his cock—Bram moans into Angel's mouth and grips those lean hips with both hands.

"I gotta take us somewhere else." Bram breathes the words between hungry kisses. He's barely able to stop himself, but he manages to peel his lips off of Angel's mouth long enough to get his car in drive.

"Please don't make me crash," Bram whispers as he starts driving with his little angel seated in his lap.

Angel turns his attention to Bram's chest, trailing his fingers over the swell of muscle and the beads of Bram's nipples. Bram's hips push up into

Angel's body without his permission, the unexpected, spiraling pleasure of that light touch making him mad as he accidentally starts down the road at double the speed limit.

"What are you doing down there," Bram murmurs.

Angel snakes his hand under Bram's t-shirt, leaning forward to kiss Bram's jaw while he lightly rubs his fingers into Bram's nipples.

"*Jesus.*" Bram grips the wheel in both hands. Chel never touched him like this—Angel lightly flicking the pad of his thumbs over Bram's hardening buds.

Angel licks Bram's jaw and gives a wheezing little giggle that travels across Bram's skin like lightning.

"Gonna make me come before I can even get inside you," Bram whispers, voice strained. "Ease up a little, huh?"

Angel does *not* ease up—lifting Bram's shirt high enough that he can readjust his legs and latch his mouth onto Bram's nipple.

"Nnn, *fuck.*" Bram drives them into the nearest office parking lot, hitting the brakes much too hard just to get his hands back on Angel's body. "There's more room in the back," Bram says.

Angel leans his head to the side, looking over the flattened trunk, and gives Bram a knowing smile, just a bit of smugness tinting those black eyes.

Bram breaks into a fresh sweat. "I just...had to move some things so, you know..."

With another quick kiss, Angel crawls into the back and Bram wastes no time following after him. Angel tugs his shirt off without any prompting, and much to Bram's surprise, takes a moment to fold it neatly and set it on the passenger seat. Bram kisses the curve of Angel's ass when he leans into the front of the car, Bram's pulse throbbing as he waits for Angel to wriggle back over to him and sit on his chest, forcing Bram to lay down across the newly spacious trunk.

Any hesitation Bram might have felt instantly vanishes as Angel leans his hands on either side of Bram's head to smile at him with such an obvious lust. Bram is certain it's only a product of his own hungry mind, but it seems like Angel's tits are just a little big bigger than they were before. The arc of his clit looks bigger too, and Bram can't help but touch, reveling in the way Angel leans into his fingers, his back curving.

"Come back to my place," Bram blurts out. "I got a spare room if you wanna stay."

Angel's eyes flick open and he gives a soft laugh.

"I'm serious," Bram says, swirling his thumb over Angel's clit—it's practically a little cock for how big it is. "I could do this for you whenever you want."

Angel pouts at him and draws his fingers over Bram's chest. It takes Bram a moment to realize he is spelling a word over Bram's t-shirt. Bram shoves his hand into pants pocket, pulling his phone out and hastily opening up a notepad for Angel to use.

"You really can't talk, can you?" Bram muses as Angel quickly types out a sentence and holds the phone back out to Bram.

I have a home!

Bram squeezes Angel's hip, enjoying the slight squish of his flesh.

"You sure you're not just saying that so I don't worry?" Bram asks.

Angel laughs with no sound and types out more, presenting the phone back to him.

I can prove it.

Bram nods at him. "Alright, alright, then give me your real address. We'll go over together and I'll see for myself that you're well cared for. And if not..."

He reaches up to take Angel's round face, admiring the look of his deep tan against Angel's light skin, gently pulling him closer to kiss him again. In the thrill of those lips pressing into his own, Bram almost forgets what he was saying, but he pulls himself back from the brink of his own raging erection and whispers to Angel.

"If you're lying to me, I might have to steal you for myself."

Angel meets his gaze, unflinching, and nods at him.

"*After,*" Bram rushes to add, holding Angel right where he sits. "We'll go after..."

Angel pulls Bram's lip between his teeth in a painless nip. Of course, they're on the same page about the order of operations.

Bram's skin still buzzes with a deep pleasure as he gets back into the driver's seat with Angel seated beside him. Watching Angel wipe his cunt off on a towel was entirely too satisfying, and Bram had to stop himself from just kidnapping the boy right then and there. He settled for licking Angel's pussy clean until he was half-hard again, not caring at all about his own taste mixed with Angel's slick. With Angel's address in his phone, they set off toward the edges of Bram's territory.

Bram isn't sure what he hopes for. Part of him would like to believe that Angel *is* well taken care of, and that he just does this because he likes it—because he likes *Bram*. But the louder, more selfish part of him wishes he'll get an excuse to rescue this perfect creature and give him a life of spoiled luxury.

As they draw nearer to a hotspot of commercial business, Bram's stomach twists with anticipation. There aren't a ton of places to live near here. Maybe they're building toward Angel admitting he has nowhere to live, or that he ran away from terrible parents, or that he just didn't want to admit that he really *does* want to live with Bram.

Angel only stares out the windows with the same little smirk on his lips.

When a familiar neon sign looms in the distance, Bram's mouth instantly falls into a frown. Now is the last time he wants to think about the fucking Dandelion, but at least he's not here to mingle with any of the business owners.

Or, so he thinks.

"Are you...sure this is right?" Bram asks, dread ballooning in his gut at the directions on his phone.

Angel turns to him with a smile and points right at the yellow neon lettering.

THE DANDELION CLUB: *Dance, drinks, delights.*

"Sonuva..." Bram bites back the curse and looks over at Angel, who stares brightly at the looming strip club. His hair is still messed up from Bram running his fingers through it, and it has doubled in volume, framing his round face in a halo of fluff.

"Angel," Bram says sharply as they wait at the red light. "Did someone send you to me?"

Angel cocks his head to the side. He shakes his head *no*, genuine confusion painting his features. He pouts at Bram and mouths, *angry?*

Bram schools his voice back into something more controlled. "Nah, 'course not."

Angel perks up again as Bram guides them into the very back of the parking lot. Bram's joints ache as he sits there debating his options. Before he can do anything else, Angel slips his shoes on and exits the car, running around to Bram's side to beckon him in.

If this is some kind of trap laid by the owner of the Dandelion, Bram isn't sure his ego will survive. He digs into his glove box and pulls out a black mask, fitting it over his mouth before he gets out of the car. Angel immediately takes his hand and begins leading Bram to the back door of the Dandelion club without a hint of hesitation.

He fishes a small key out of the breast pocket of his too-large button up shirt and unlocks the door. Bram feels like he's going to pass out as they cross the threshold and Angel takes his hand again—they could easily be mistaken for father and son with Angel a whole head shorter than Bram. As soon as they enter into a narrow hallway, a huge man, even bigger than Bram, gives Bram a death stare before he sees Angel and lets his breath out.

"Go on, then."

Angel pulls Bram into a red-painted hall, passing a series of dressing room doors, some of them open, some of them closed, and several tantalizing photographs of men's legs, thighs, and chests. A couple of guys in tight shorts and fishnets pass them by, giving funny looks to Bram, and little smirks at Angel. No one is surprised to see Angel roaming these corridors. The dread in Bram's stomach is evolving into all-out nausea as Angel knocks three times on a closed door at the end of the hall.

"It's open!"

The door reveals a large office. Two couches face each other in front of a thick, wooden desk where a red-headed man sits, a similar black mask to Bram's secured over his mouth. His eyes light up when he sees Angel.

"Pearl! Where you been?"

His gaze lands on Bram like the sights of a sniper rifle.

"You brought a friend."

Rohan: alias for the owner and operator of the Dandelion Club, the most profitable brothel in Outerridge, and current thorn in the Vampires' side. Despite offers coming in from multiple gangs across the region, Rohan has refused to be folded into any gang's territory, opting to maintain his independence and eschewing all protection from the larger gangs.

The quality of Rohan's voice carries an almost imperceptible blade when he addresses Bram. His eyes narrow above the black mask, and he tilts his head, his long red ponytail trailing behind him.

"I swear I've seen your face before," Rohan says.

Angel darts over to Rohan as the door swings shut, and leans his hands into Rohan's lap, beaming up at him.

When Rohan turns to smile at Angel—Pearl?—there is obvious

affection in his face that digs into Bram's skin like nails. He sweeps Angel's fluffed up hair away from his forehead and narrows his eyes.

"You know this place isn't for outsiders, Pearl."

Angel nods at him and runs back over to grab Bram's hand, forcing him closer. Bram has never met Rohan himself, but everything he's ever heard about the man has painted a sharp and unpleasant picture. When he rises from his chair to greet Bram face to face, Bram is instantly furious that this man is markedly taller than him. A cluster of freckles spans the bridge of his nose, just visible above the edge of his mask. He has unsettlingly bright hazel eyes that Bram wishes he didn't have to look directly at. They make his milk skin look even paler.

"Seems you met my ward," Rohan says, putting his hand on Angel's shoulder. "Thanks for bringing him back."

Bram lets go of Angel's hand, anger and jealousy brewing into a nasty storm in the pit of his stomach.

"I know what this place is," Bram says.

Rohan's red brows jump up. "Perfectly legal strip club, last time the police checked. Why do you ask?"

Bram swallows, trying to rein in his mood. He takes a step closer, lowering his voice as he tries to get a measure of Rohan's character.

"I sure hope all your dancers are legal," Bram says.

"Perfectly," Rohan says, not missing a beat. "You looking for a new career? I'm sure plenty of people would pay to see your ass in some fishnets."

Bram's hands clench into fists and he lurches forward, closing the distance between him and Rohan. "Is your *ward* working for you too?"

Rohan meets Bram's gaze, unflinching. "He doesn't work. He just lives here. Why, did you fuck him?"

Bram's heart is going to shatter his ribs for how hard it's beating. "I know you run a brothel out of this place."

"I know you from somewhere," Rohan says, ignoring the accusation entirely. "Feel like I've seen your picture online. Something about not being able to get it up for your girlfriend."

"Don't know what the fuck you're talking about," Bram snarls through the mask.

"Yeah, you're right," Rohan says, arms folded, hooded eyes shining with obvious glee. "Mistook you for a vampire, but I'm pretty sure you don't have any teeth in there. Is that why you wore the mask?"

Bram grabs the front of Rohan's nice suit jacket and runs Rohan's back into the wall, all his pent up anger jumping into his hands as he growls, "You using kids to pass favors for you?"

"Pearl doesn't work for me," Rohan snaps back, his hands clasping Bram's wrists. "All my employees are legal. You don't have fuck all on me."

"Then what the fuck is your *ward* doing out on a corner?" Bram demands.

"He does whatever he wants!" Rohan snaps. "He's his own person. Who the fuck are you?"

Bram wants to throttle this smug bastard's pale neck. "I'm a concerned citizen."

Rohan's eyes shift, the brightness returning in a wicked glint like light on the edge of a knife. "I can see now why that little heiress wasn't getting you hard. She too old for ya?"

Before he even feels it, Bram's arm is reeled back ready to cave Rohan's skull in—until he feels small fists beating against his back in an utterly useless assault. Bram blinks, and then turns to look behind him at Angel who desperately tries to pull Bram away from Rohan.

Shame ignites through Bram's entire body and he shoves Rohan away from himself, stalking across the room to get a breather. Out of the corner of his eye, he can see Angel tugging on Rohan's jacket, concern bleeding through his gaze.

Rohan shrugs it off, smiling for Angel. "I'm alright, don't worry. We're just getting to know each other. Isn't that right, stranger?"

Bram turns back around. "Right, yeah."

"Besides," Rohan says, letting his breath out. "Sounds like we're in the same boat."

Bram frowns as Rohan crosses the room, locks the door to this office, and then takes a seat on one of the red couches. He gestures for Bram to sit across from him, and Angel crawls into Rohan's lap—salt on the wound.

Angel tugs harshly on Rohan's lapels, and Rohan tucks some of Angel's hair behind his ear. "I'll play nice, I promise."

Satisfied, Angel darts over to Bram, pouting as he takes Bram's hand in his own. "I won't do that again," Bram mumbles, feeling like a child in the principal's office. "Sorry."

Angel perches on the dark, wooden table between them, his gangly legs folded beneath him.

"Alright, stranger, I can only assume Pearl brought you here for one reason," Rohan says. "He likes you."

Some of the jealousy cools as Bram gives a small shrug. "Seems like it."

Angel turns to him, a slight smile tugging at the corner of his mouth.

"So," Rohan says. "Did you fuck him?"

"No comment," Bram says back immediately. "Did *you*?"

"No," Rohan responds just as quick. "He's go no ID, no legal records, nothing. I don't know where he came from or who his parents are. He won't tell me anything except that he ran away from home. What'd he tell you?"

Bram tries to hide his embarrassment as he realizes he didn't bother trying to wring *any* info out of Angel.

"He's been pretty tight-lipped about, uh, everything," Bram says, nerves prickling down his neck. "I thought he was mute."

"Yeah, I haven't heard a peep out of him, save for the wheezing."

"Same here," Bram says.

Angel smiles at both of them, no comment of his own.

Rohan shakes his head and pulls his phone out to give to Angel. "What do you want, Pearl?"

Angel takes the phone up and types out a quick message, showing it to Rohan who fixes him with the kind of look that Bram can't quite decipher with the black mask over his mouth.

"I'm not your keeper," Rohan says quietly, hazel eyes softening. "You can go wherever you like."

Angel beams at him, jumping up to give Rohan a kiss on the temple, which Rohan receives like some kind of king accepting a most precious gift. Quickly, Angel types something else out and shows it to Rohan who barely glances at it before scoffing.

"I appreciate the offer, handsome, but that's not gonna work."

"What-what are you talking about?" Bram asks.

Rohan erases whatever was on the phone and says, "Looks like Pearl just wanted to let me know that he plans to spend a night with you sometime. Consider yourself lucky, stranger."

Pride threatens to leech back into his skin as Bram looks at Angel. "You know you can spend more than one night if you want. I got a whole spare room. It's a nice place. Probably nicer than this."

Angel gives him a cherubic smile as he saunters over and types out another message for him to see.

If you let Rohan come with us, I'll stay longer.

"Yeah, no, sorry, Angel," Bram says, stomaching the pout fixed to Angel's face. "Let's start with one night for now."

Angel sighs, mouthing the word, *fine,* and Bram's thighs finally manage to unclench. Bram looks over at Rohan again, scrutinizing his easy posture, the casual way he seems to communicate with Angel.

"How long has he been here?" Bram asks quietly.

Rohan waves his hand in the air. "I don't know, a few weeks? I don't keep track. Kinda feels like he's always been here."

Angel smiles brightly at that, drifting back over to Rohan so he can curl up in Rohan's lap like a cat. Rohan immediately starts running his fingers through Angel's hair, tracing the shell of his ear. Angel stretches his arms above his head, arching his back over Rohan's legs, his nipples pressing into the fabric of his too-long shirt.

"He's wearing *your* clothes, isn't he?" Bram asks.

Rohan laughs. "He doesn't have any of his own. If I start buying clothes in his size, people are gonna talk. And if there's one thing this city loves more than money, it's talk."

Bram grunts, pissed all over again as he realizes the two of them are in a stalemate. Nothing good with come of throwing either of them under the bus, but worst of all, Angel will get pissed at whichever one of them fucks up first.

"What day are you gonna take him?" Rohan asks, glancing over at Bram with his fingers massaging the back of a blissed-out Angel's head. Angel's eyes flutter shut, his body going slack.

It seems impossible that these two *don't* have some kind of relationship, but Rohan is obviously too smart to admit to that here.

"Not sure," Bram says. "Figured he'd tell me when he wants to go."

Angel raises his hand up and gestures twice, as if to push something away.

"Monday?" Rohan asks.

Angel nods, and then looks over at Bram with an expectant, albeit sleepy, expression.

Bram suddenly feels like he's wearing a suit one size too small, packed tight into someone else's shell. "I'll, uh, pick you...up...here?"

Angel looks over at Rohan who smiles beneath his mask, his eyes crinkling at the edges. "I'll drop him off myself, thank you. Gotta make sure you're not taking him somewhere dangerous."

Bram barely holds back from rolling his eyes. "Yeah, yeah, fine, whatever. Just don't be bringing anyone with you. My address is not public knowledge."

"Great," Rohan says. "He has a burner phone, by the way. He just conveniently forgets to bring it with him whenever he leaves, despite my numerous and very *reasonable* requests."

Angel's lips tug into a smirk.

"I'll give you the number," Rohan says to Bram.

Bram digs around for his phone, nearly dropping it as he comes to grips with this incredibly mundane conclusion to meeting the man who fucked him over a month ago. Once he has Angel's number logged, Bram rises to his feet again.

"I, uh, I guess I'll just...head out?"

"I'm sure you can find your way from here," Rohan says, making no move to send Bram off himself.

Bram has never felt more awkward in his life as Rohan slouches back on the couch, and Angel jumps up to say goodbye. He stands in front of Bram and raises his arms up, clearly expecting to be lifted. Bram kneels down and scoops Angel into his arms, heart beating faster as he waits to see what Angel will do in front of Rohan. His slender arms wrap around Bram's neck and he plants a kiss between Bram's eyes, squeezing him tight. Bram can't stop himself from hugging Angel back, praying that he doesn't look too needy in front of his rival business owner.

Setting Angel back on his feet, Bram glances back at Rohan and his freckles, embarrassed heat coursing through him. He shoves his hands in his pockets as Angel sits back down in Rohan's lap, picking Rohan's hand up to place those long, pale fingers back on his head.

Swallowing his pride and his spit, Bram clears his throat. "Sorry I got heated. I'm trying not to be like that anymore."

As soon as the words are out of his mouth, Bram hears how very *un-boss-like* he sounds and he straightens his back. "If you tell anyone I was here, you're dead."

And with that, he flees the Dandelion like someone's chasing him. Back in his car, Bram sits with the engine idling, staring at the chain-link fence surrounding the parking lot of the club, picking apart every interaction between Rohan and Angel—Pearl, as he called the boy. Bram tries to pull up all his mental notes that he's gathered over the last few months on this guy, but he comes up shockingly short. Rohan is good at protecting his own image and the details of his life, but it seems even a man like that is susceptible to Angel's charm.

One thing Bram's men could never ascertain was whether Rohan himself was gay or not. All of the guys working at the Dandelion are incredibly tight-lipped, and strangely, so are their former clients. Bram is well aware that one's business pursuits don't necessarily dictate one's personal interests, but Bram had always assumed that Rohan was at least an omnivore. Talking to him didn't answer that question. Maybe he's not interested in Angel because he isn't built like other men—then again, there seemed to be no question that Rohan sees Angel as a boy.

Maybe Rohan *is* interested in Angel and just doesn't want to admit to it.

For all Bram knows, they've been fucking for weeks. The thought depresses him for a moment, until he reminds himself that Angel likes him enough to spend a night with him in his own home. That's not nothing. That's a very big *something.*

Bram will have to prove that he's the better match.

Rohan stares down at Pearl dozing in his lap. He looks happy, sated, like he's sleeping off a big meal. Rohan buries his fingers in Pearl's shaggy brown hair, loosed from its usual tight waves. Mr. Bram Stoker must be handsy. Considering how quick he was to grab Rohan, it doesn't come as much of a surprise. No, the only thing that *did* surprise Rohan was that pathetic little apology right at the end. It almost sounded sincere, and Rohan has to remind himself that it's a bad idea to trust gang boys even when they look like kicked puppies.

"What are you planning, Pearl?" Rohan asks.

The boy's lips pull wider into a smile.

"You should know, that man's dangerous," Rohan tells him, pulling the black mask from his face. "Don't let his awkward charm fool you. He does bloody work."

Pearl's lids slide open, and he reaches his hands up to take Rohan's face. Rohan holds his black gaze, feeling the same pull he always does to sink into deep, dark water that he may never be able to crawl back out of.

"You don't care at all, do you?" Rohan asks.

Pearl runs his thumbs over Rohan's cheekbones, the same pretty look on his face, beckoning trouble.

"Be safe," Rohan says, pulling out of his soft grip. "And use your damn phone."

Pearl only giggles, muted as it is.

Early Monday evening, Rohan gets into his car with Pearl in the passenger seat wearing one of Rohan's favorite long-sleeved shirts and the pair of white sneakers he got from one of Rohan's dancers. Pearl leans over the center console to tug on Rohan's jacket and mimes like he's spraying a bottle.

"You're really trying to wine and dine this guy, huh?" Rohan shoos Pearl off the console and pops it open to pull out a bottle of cologne. "Here, put it on your chest."

Pearl lifts up his shirt with both hands, and Rohan's temples pound. "You think you're clever, don't you? Fine, fine."

He sprays once in the center of Pearl's chest, right between the little drops of flesh that make up his breasts. Rohan's gaze flicks down between Pearl's thighs once, the head of his small cock budding up between lips of ruddy skin, and then tugs the shirt back down.

"Maybe your new sugar daddy can buy you some fancy underwear," Rohan jokes.

Pearl's eyes light up, and Rohan laughs.

"Milk him for all he's worth, that's what I say," Rohan announces, hoping his jovial voice can disguise his discontent.

If someone had told Rohan two months ago that he would soon be housing a young boy entirely on his own dime, that would have been crazy enough. But to say, *hey yeah so that boy? You would pretty much do anything for him. Congrats, asshole, you have a new cat that scares the shit out of you. And now you have to drive him to a bloody mobster's house so he can probably have sex with Pearl just to restore his own wounded ego.*

Rohan gets vertigo every time he thinks about Pearl holding out his phone with the single sentence typed out.

play with us

Goosebumps riddle Rohan's arms and chest as he drives the speed limit downtown to the high-rise where none other than Bram Stoker, newly appointed leader of the Southside Vampires, lives. The very same Bram Stoker who's been trying to get Rohan to fold into his gang and split profits with him. The very same Bram Stoker who recently got his ass absolutely handed to him by his ex-girlfriend who managed to emasculate him on a citywide scale.

Rohan almost feels bad for the guy, except every time he looks at Pearl making wide, hopeful eyes at him, he shakes the feeling off. Bram is a desperate man, in need of a rebound that restores his masculinity. He's probably telling himself that Pearl doesn't count as a boy and it's not gay at all to fuck him. To his credit, Rohan isn't even really sure that Pearl *is* a boy, but Pearl has never corrected anyone for calling him one.

Smirking to himself, Rohan turns the radio on and lets Pearl pick the station until some barely tolerable pop music fills the car. Pearl kisses Rohan on the cheek three times between the Dandelion and the parking garage beneath Bram Stoker's building. He exudes giddy energy, and it's spilling over into Rohan as he guides them into the temporary visitor parking spot.

"Damn, you are relentless," Rohan whispers as Pearl loops his arms around Rohan's neck, settling into his lap.

Rohan carries Pearl into the elevator, checking his phone again for the forwarded directions to the vampire's apartment. He's close to the top floor, which doesn't surprise Rohan at all. Pearl practically vibrates in his arms, suddenly pulling Rohan's face toward his, fixing Rohan with the most imploring, desperately needy look that Rohan has ever seen on him. For a moment, Rohan feels his balance tilting away. He doesn't want to leave Pearl here. He *wants* to stay with this boy, he wants to see what Pearl does with his awkward slab of meat who raises his fists and murmurs apologies like a rowdy teenager. Rohan wants to be part of whatever the fuck goes on with Pearl when *he's* not around.

Rohan's gaze snags on Pearl's pouting lips, full and round and delirious when they're pressed against his face. Heat flashes down his back as he pictures that mouth on Bram Stoker's massive chest. There's more than one way to milk a vampire, and Rohan's pulse throbs for a dangerous moment before the elevator dings, announcing they've arrived.

"God, this place is fucking nice," Rohan mutters as they cross into an ornate entry hall. A gilded mirror reflects the two of them as they step onto a long, dark rug, passing potted plants and various paintings. There's only a handful of doors on this floor, and Rohan easily locates apartment C. Pearl reaches out to knock for them, beating his fists with enthusiasm against the door.

When Bram opens up, his black mask is fixed back over his mouth, light brown gaze narrowed. He eyes Rohan up with suspicion, his thick black hair looking like he slicked it back four hours ago and never bothered fixing it. Finally, he steps aside to let them both in.

"Take your shoes off," he mutters, closing to the door behind them.

Rohan releases a bouncing Pearl from his arms and unzips his black boots as Pearl goes tearing into a massive living room.

Rohan whistles. "I figured you were in another tax bracket, but this is crazy."

"It's not really my place," Bram says, arms folded. "I, uh, inherited it, so to speak."

Rohan gives Bram a smirking stare and sidles over to him as Pearl presses his face to the huge glass window overlooking the city. It's only just begun to spill black night over the sky, and the lights are pretty stunning from way up there.

Rohan asks in a whisper, "Are we really going to keep pretending we don't know each other?"

Bram glares, holding a murderous gaze for exactly two seconds before he rips the mask off and tosses it onto the nearby kitchen counter. Bram's face doesn't exactly relax, but it does make Rohan feel better to get the full view of his wide jaw and his rounded cheeks—even more puppy-like than before.

He has an island kitchen that butts up against the huge open living room. It's the kind of place Rohan used to picture living in before he had any idea of how much they cost.

"This place is way too nice for a guy who cracks skulls for a living," Rohan says.

"I don't crack skulls anymore," Bram says, obviously defensive. "I can though, if the situation calls for it."

He's trying to flex his width and heft over Rohan, from six inches beneath him.

Rohan smiles back, holding Bram's warning gaze. "Good to know Pearl is with someone who's so eager to get into a fight."

"*Not* eager," Bram responds, clipped and huffy. "Angel's safe with me. No one comes in here but me and my lieutenant."

"And me," Rohan adds, smile widening. "Did you want to make me another offer while I'm here? It's been a while since I turned you down, I could use a refresh."

The muscles around Bram's nose twitch. He's got thick skin, rich golden brown that makes Rohan look like a ghost next to him. Rohan knows his height is a fluke, but Bram isn't small by any means. He could have had a career in the ring if he wanted it, but apparently the former leader of the Vampires saw something in him worth promoting to leadership.

Bram looks like he's seriously considering ramming his head into Rohan's as he says, "You made yourself very clear. It would be stupid to go knocking on your door this soon after you thoroughly rejected us.

Besides, we have more important shit to deal with than some smug pimp."

"Can't prove I'm a pimp," Rohan says quickly. "My business is legal."

"Don't need to prove it," Bram whispers back, his voice rising to a hiss. "It's fucking obvious, no run-of-the-mill strip club could possibly pull in what you do."

"Is that why you're so horny for me to join your turf?" Rohan asks. "Or do you just want more boys to look at?"

"Motherfuck—" Bram seethes, rising to the bait immediately. As soon as Rohan recognizes his own unfurling pleasure at pissing off this bull of a man, Pearl slips in close, taking each of them by the hand.

Rohan drops down to one knee, smiling up at him. "Sorry, Pearl, old habits and all that. I'll leave you to it."

Pearl squeezes his hand, pulling him closer so he can give Rohan one more kiss goodbye. His lips press in against Rohan's cheek, dangerously close to the corner of his mouth. The satisfaction of this display being seen by Bram sinks into Rohan's skin like a fever, and he gives Pearl's hip a squeeze before detaching.

"Later," he says. "Pearl, call me if the scary man starts touching you inappropriately."

"Alright, get the fuck out," Bram deadpans.

Rohan leaves with a smile and a wave. As soon as the door closes behind him, his mind becomes an infinite slide show of depraved images of Bram fucking Pearl all over that nice apartment. Bram doesn't deserve any of this in the slightest, but if it makes Pearl happy, Rohan supposes he can live with it.

Maybe he should have stayed. He doesn't need to be *part* of it, but if Pearl asked him...

"Fuck me," Rohan mutters, gripping his own biceps too tightly in the elevator.

Pearl asked him to stay. This is the first time Rohan has ever denied him. He tells himself it's for the obvious reason—the same reason Rohan has refused every offer for gang affiliation for the last five years. He will not get into bed with any more dangerous men.

Bram thought the nerves would finally leave him when was alone with Angel, but even when he's stripped down in his bed with Angel riding his dick, he is terrified that something will break the spell and Angel will suddenly call this whole thing off and ask to be rescued by Rohan. Bram would simply rather die.

At least Angel needs no encouragement. He plants his feet on the sheets beside Bram's hips and rocks up and down, chasing the high like he's been starving for it. Bram is quickly hypnotized by the flushed head of Angel's clit bobbing up and down, his chest swaying with every drop of his hips. Bram's mouth waters, his balls tightening. He barely remembers to touch Pearl—*Angel,* fuck him—as his body gives in at light speed. He comes in Angel with his palms glued to Angel's chest, his hips jolting up off the bed as he spills in the tight heat of Angel's body.

"Good fucking god," Bram breathes, his pulse throbbing twice as loud while he settles into buzzing, blissful numbness.

Angel's skin practically *shines* as he gives Bram's softening cock another squeeze. It's probably just a trick of the light and Bram's dwindling brain cells, but Angel really looks like he's glowing for a split second before he crawls off of Bram, their bodies separating with a rush of fluid. *Bram* asked *him* about condoms, even showed him the wrappers, but Angel pushed them away, and Bram couldn't stop thinking about how good it felt in the back of his car with only skin.

When Angel pulls Bram's face against his chest, the scent of his skin makes Bram's brain turn off, and his dick turn back on. He rubs his mouth over each of Angel's nipples, breathing in a smoky, rich scent that suits Angel perfectly.

"I just need a minute..." Bram says as Angel leans down to kiss a line across his face. "You want food? I could use some food. Let's get some food."

Angel laughs, hushed and scratchy, and crawls over to the edge of the bed to fish Bram's phone out of his pants pocket. He holds it out and Bram sees the notification of a text from Lee.

"Ah, fuck, I gotta talk to him," Bram says, taking the phone from Angel's hands. "If I set you up with my laptop, do you know how to order delivery?"

Angel nods enthusiastically, and Bram wills himself up and out of bed, digging his briefs out of the pile of his clothes—the nice briefs that Chel bought him a few months ago that she's formally never allowed to appreciate ever again. He gets the laptop, opening up the right page, and leaves Angel, naked, on his couch with the remote and his computer before shutting himself off in his office.

Leaning his chair back, Bram rests his bare feet on the desk and calls Lee.

"Boss." Less picks up on the first ring.

"This better be important," Bram says.

Lee hesitates, then says, "Do you need a minute?"

"You have my minute right now," Bram says. "Talk."

Lee updates him on the intruder they caught sneaking into their west warehouse.

"We chased him out before he could get anything, but nobody got good eyes on him. Not to mention, the security footage was corrupted, so I can't pin him down."

"Didn't steal anything?" Bram asks.

"And he made a mess," Lee says.

"Sounds like a Boar to me," Bram says. "But the security footage being fucked up sounds like a Spider."

"You see the dilemma," Lee sighs. "Someone is making a move, but I can't figure out who."

"I don't like anyone making moves," Bram says. "Move up the raid. I'm sick of waiting around for things to get worse. Even if it's not the Spiders, we can't look weak right now."

"I agree, it makes us look like sitting ducks not to retaliate," Lee says. "We'll gear up, but we might need to spend a little extra. It's either going to mean more men or more weapons."

"Dealer's choice," Bram says, looking out the window. "I trust you to pick a good team, if you think we need more, I'll take your word on it."

"Sometimes I think you're too trusting, sir," Lee says.

"Nah, I just know you're not gonna fuck me over," Bram tells him. "You're a good man, Lee."

The TV sounds in the living room, strange music that Bram doesn't recognize blaring over his speakers.

"That's...very kind of you, sir," Lee mutters.

"Should I go with you guys?" Bram asks, brows furrowing as the music stops and starts, as if someone is pausing it and skipping around. He walks over to the office door, hand on the door knob. "You know I'm one of the most experienced—"

"Boss, you can't," Lee says immediately. "If you want people to respect you as the boss, you can't be going on every raid and holding our hands. Trust goes both ways."

Rolling his eyes, Bram pops the door open. Two incredibly ripped men fill up the TV screen, looming over a lithe boy who kneels in front of them, buck naked. Bram's eyes widen.

"You gotta let us fight for you," Lee says.

Bram's pulse ricochets down his throat and through his spine as he realizes Angel is watching porn on his television.

"You're absolutely right, Lee. I gotta go," Bram says.

"Thanks, Boss," Lee says, his voice far too earnest as Bram hangs up the phone.

Angel wiggles on the couch, remote in hand. Bram walks over to him, heat in his face.

"I see you found some...entertainment," Bram says.

Angel grins at him and then points at the TV as the two muscular guys lift the little guy—nope, that's a woman—up in their arms.

"You'll have to share me," the woman drawls. "Since the fight was a tie."

Bram's pulse skyrockets. "That's uh, yeah, jesus are they really gonna fit?"

He is drawn like a moth to a light bulb as he sits on the couch beside Angel while the two male actors both get their fingers inside the woman's cunt, stretching her wider.

"Holy shit," Bram mutters, in awe.

Angel jumps up in front of him, pointing enthusiastically at the television. His face is stained red, and Bram can tell he's getting worked up.

"Yeah I see it, it's crazy," Bram says, gaze flicking between the screen and Angel's bright face. "I don't think most people can do that."

Angel pauses the video as the two dicks line up in front of the girl's slit. He runs over and points at the bigger guy who is holding the girl up against his chest, and then points at Bram.

Bram feels a little drunk as he smiles at Angel. "I'm flattered you think I'm hot enough for porn."

Angel points at the girl held up between the two men and then points at himself.

Bram's cheeks are getting hotter. "Are you saying...you want to do this?"

Angel nods.

Bram rubs his neck. "I'm sure there's, like, sex toys we could get to try and—"

Angel shakes his head and points to the third guy who has both their dicks in hand, pressing them into the same hole.

Bram's heart thuds loudly in his chest. "You want...another guy?"

Angel walks over to him, plucking Bram's phone out of his hand so he can type. With a sinking feeling, Bram braces himself for what he is already sure he will see typed out. Angel flips the phone around.

you + rohan + me = :)

Bram can't stop his lips from pulling into a frown. "I don't know if that's a good idea..."

Angel pouts at him, then steps over to pool his legs over Bram's lap.

"Look, I just..." Bram sighs, rubbing his hands over his face. "Rohan and I don't exactly get along, alright? He insulted my gang, and me, I can't just roll over and start sharing you with him right now. I already feel like I'm going fucking crazy, the entire city thinks I'm a limp-dick failure."

As soon the words are out, Bram deflates onto the couch, all the fight leaving him. Angel leans up against him, chest to chest, and presses a kiss to Bram's cheek.

"I can't fucking win," Bram says. "I don't want people thinking I'm weak, but it feels worse every time I get angry. I shouldn't have threatened Rohan, that was stupid, now he's definitely not going to do any business with us. *Ahh.*"

He lets out a groan, and Angel plucks Bram's hand off the couch, methodically folding three out of five of Bram's fingers to his palm. Gently, Angel twists Bram's middle and ring finger together. Bram's gaze flicks up, and he watches Angel push Bram's two fingers deep into his cunt.

"Why are you so fuckin' pretty," Bram mumbles, his gaze hollowing as he feels Angel clenching down on his two fingers, slick heat coating his skin.

Angel snatches up the remote again, pressing play on the video and filling the apartment with bellowing moans and squelching flesh. Before Bram can lose himself in the sight of Angel's swollen clit, Angel pulls Bram's hand out of him, turns around and plants himself in Bram's lap so he's no longer blocking the television. Head lolling back onto Bram's shoulder, Angel slips Bram's fingers back inside him, bending his legs up to his chest just like the girl on screen, and starts to fuck himself on Bram's hand while Bram's brain steadily melts.

"Holy fuck," Bram murmurs as the two cocks slip into the girl's body, flushed dark and covered in fluid as they slide up against each other. The girl gives a hiccuping moan as her eyes roll back, and Bram can't help but slot Angel's face over hers, wondering how he'd look stretched out that wide, stuffed full.

He slips another finger inside Angel, rewarded with a harsh breath and Angel's arms looping around Bram's neck. His cock is waking up again, stirred by all the stimuli, and offers of pleasure he's never considered before.

"You really think you could fit two guys in you?" Bram asks. "No offense, but you're pretty little."

Angel—*Pearl*—no, *fuck*, Angel—licks the side of Bram's face and fits Bram's fourth finger inside him, opening himself up even wider. Bram shudders at the slick press of skin, no pain at all on Angel's body or in his breath, only a delirious hunger that infects Bram with brutal efficiency.

Could he *really* fit two guys at once? Not that Bram wants to share Angel, but fuck him, that'd be a sight to see. He's never done anything like that in real life. Chel certainly never got adventurous like this. Not that Bram ever complained, of course. *He* never thought to push things either. He was fairly happy with a more typical relationship. Or, at least, he was satisfied. Or, well, he was glad to get the chance to fuck somebody fairly regularly, and Chel was good for appearances, even if she had no trouble complaining about everything Bram did in front of anyone who would listen.

Maybe she was more adventurous with Reese...

As soon as Bram pictures Rohan's smug face staring at him over top of Angel's body, the fantasy goes off the rails. If Bram has to be the one holding Angel up, he'll *only* be able to see Rohan, his eight mile long torso and his stupid fucking smirk, and his long, silky red hair and all that goddamn milk skin—does he have freckles everywhere? Or just his face?

"I don't want to see that guy naked," Bram says, refocusing on the body in his lap. He grabs Angel's chest with his other hand, massaging the swell of his breast. He's starting to get obsessed with the way Angel's legs frog up into triangles at his sides when he wants to show off his hole. "Just wanna see you. Is it just me or do you feel bigger? I must be crazy."

He can't stop staring at Angel's nipple between his fingers. His gaze drifts down to Angel's cunt, and he slips his hand over Angel's fluttering belly to rub Angel's clit with a thumb. Maybe he's just getting better at turning Angel on, but the head of his clit looks more and more like the head of a cock.

Bram's wounded pride settles down once more as he lets himself enjoy the scene overwhelming his senses. Angel might be a little strange, but Bram is sure he's never been this crazy about someone. To even consider sharing his gi—Angel's not a girl. Bram's brain seems to split in two as he realizes that Angel couldn't be *his girl*. But he could still be *Bram's*.

Maybe Lee would do it instead, but, no, Bram doesn't want to ruin his image with anyone in the gang, least of all his number two. Besides, Lee has never once discussed his sex life. Really, of all the people in the world to do something this wild, it would make some amount of sense to do it with the one guy who can't afford to badmouth Bram any more than he already has.

So as long as Angel is strung between Bram and Rohan, they're locked in mutually assured destruction.

Well, not necessarily *strung between them.*

Bram looks at the TV again, the way the actress's boobs jiggle with the constant motion of the two guys railing her. He looks down at Angel's pudding cup tits and his cock thickens in his briefs. In the safety of his mind, Bram tests out the way it sounds to call Angel *my boy.*

It would be a hell of a sight to see him so overwhelmed...with anyone *except* Rohan.

▶▷▷

The most delirious and pleasurable night that Bram has ever lived passes much too quickly. Even when he's not fucking Angel, Bram can't stop staring at him. He's delighted and surprised when some sushi shows up for them, and Angel lets Bram feed him a piece of ginger. Angel barely eats anything, but when Bram tries to offer him more food, Angel expertly makes Bram forget he'd ever thought about it in the first place, turning the tables and feeding Bram the rest of his platter before letting Bram suck on his massive clit.

The sight of Angel wearing one of Bram's sleeveless shirts to bed makes Bram feel ten feet tall. Angels flops backward onto Bram's pillows, spread eagle over the gray sheets, a little smile stuck to his lips. Bram is the one to crawl over top of him, drawing his fingers over the front of the dark blue fabric, down the hard line of Angel's breast bone. The shirt barely covers Angel's hips from sight, and when he bends his leg, Bram can see a hint of flushed skin.

"Think I'd kill for you," Bram murmurs, sliding his shirt up over Angel's hips.

Angel's hands circle Bram's face, drawing Bram's eyes up to his endless gaze. His warm hands slip down over Bram's chest, his fingers playing with Bram's nipples again.

"F...fuck." Bram huffs at the unfamiliar pleasure, reminding himself that Angel already asked him for something much wilder than this. His breath catches, thighs tensing, and he rubs the heated lump of his cock against Angel's cunt through his underwear.

Angel's grinning at him as he squeezes Bram's chest. A dark and buried feeling in Bram's brain tells him he should be offended, but it feels far too good to heed the words.

"*Keep doing that,*" Bram whispers, sinking down on his knees to press their hips together.

No one but Angel needs to know something like this makes him wet.

"*Let me fuck you again,*" Bram quietly pleads, his nerve-endings rewiring themselves around Angel's hands.

He doesn't need to ask twice. As soon as Angel lets him sink back inside, Bram melts into some new kind of animal.

▶▷▷

The call to come into the office so Bram can personally approve the raid sets his teeth on edge, but Bram can't exactly say no. Not when they're about to do something important, and this is the first chance Bram has had in weeks to address his men with anything other than an apology. Still, his mind is suddenly split.

If he starts a fight now, what will that mean for them? Constant threats, higher tension for everyone, and worst of all, places like the Dandelion that have rejected formal protection will be at an even higher risk of getting caught in the crossfire when one gang decides they don't want to fight on their own turf.

For the entire drive over, Bram can only think about Angel eating at the kitchen counter. The way Angel smiled at him, picking apart the edges of a pancake, and half of one egg. One day wasn't enough. Spending a week apart is going to kill Bram.

Every other minute that Bram is out of the house, his mind plays out scenarios where he comes home and finds Angel fucking someone else in his bed. He *knows* Angel isn't bothered by sharing, and there's no way for Bram to know if Angel is the kind of boy who doesn't care about permission. In the middle of Lee explaining their raid strategy out loud to Bram, Bram's eye twitches as he realizes he never asked Angel *not* to fuck another guy, and maybe they should have laid out those ground rules first.

Is Bram even allowed to ask him that if he knows Angel wants to have a threesome?

Bram feels like he's doing high-level calculus, and has to let it go as soon as he notices the entire room is staring at him, waiting for his word.

"Go over it one more time," Bram says, waving his hand in the air. "Need to make sure all the details line up."

He scrapes up all the attention he can muster for Lee until the plan actually makes sense, and he can hold onto the information for more than five seconds. As the guys are filtering back out of the room, Lee snags Bram and lowers his voice to a whisper.

"Is something bothering you about the plan?"

Bram grabs him by the arm and leads Lee away from everyone else. "Why do you ask?"

"I don't mean anything by it," Lee says, shaking his head. "You just seem...distracted."

Bram's mouth contorts into an incomprehensible shape as he slaps Lee on the back and says, "I went on a date yesterday."

Lee blinks, taking his glasses off and gripping Bram's arm in return.

"I wish you and her the best," Lee says, letting him go with a small, yet undeniably proud smile. "So the plan sounds solid?"

"There's nothing wrong with the *plan*," Bram says.

"But?" Lee prompts.

Frowning, Bram folds his arms over his chest. "I'm just...a little hesitant. We still don't know for sure where that guy came from, right? What if we start a fight with someone who didn't have anything to do with that?"

Lee catches his meaning with a nod. "It's definitely a risk. The boys are eager for another win, but if you're not a hundred percent on board with this, we should hold off."

It sounds like weakness, but Bram can't shake the feeling that if they go through with it now, everything will get worse in an instant. "Just tell the boys we're delaying it..."

"They'll want to know why," Lee tells him.

Bram chews on the inside of his cheek for a second before catching himself, Chel's voice rearing up in his brain once more. *Stop chewing like that, it's gross.*

"Tell them we got an invite to talk quietly or something," Bram rushes to say.

Lee nods again, then gently nudges Bram. "You going to see the girl again?"

"Ahah!" Bram barks out a startled laugh. "If I'm lucky! I'll talk to you soon, man, I have to get out of here."

Bram hurries out of the room as quickly as he can, feeling like the sights of a gun are tracking up his spine. He doesn't know how to balance the desire to brag about Angel and his perfect cunt and his hungry smile and the maddening lust he puts in Bram, with the crushing embarrassment of trying to tell the guys who kill for him that he met a cute boy on a fucking street corner and he *still* doesn't know how old Angel is.

But he practically glows after Bram comes in him and that's worth lying over.

▶▷▷

Bram manages to wait until a Friday night to text Angel on the number Rohan gave him.

It's B. Can I see you again?

It's a cruel few hours before he gets a message back.

tomorrow?

Sparks go off in Bram's thighs.

Bram [8:03 pm]: *Anytime you want.*
Angel [8:03 pm]: *we'll come after dark.*
Bram [8:03 pm]: *What are you up to tonight?*
Angel [8:04 pm]: *I like watching the boys dance*

Bram feels a bit like he's been punched, even while his cock comes back to life with a desperate pulse. Angel is watching the guys at Rohan's club dance. Does Angel like to dance? Is watching strippers anything like cheating? It doesn't really matter if they haven't even had a single conversation about it.

Does Bram even care?

Bram [8:06 pm]: *Didn't know you liked watching boys dance so much*
Angel [8:06 pm]: *it's fun :)*
Bram [8:06 pm]: *does it turn you on?*
Angel [8:06 pm]: *maybe :)*
Bram [8:07 pm]: *If you want to come by sooner I'll pick you up. You could show me how they dance*

Angel [8:07 pm]: *come here! we can watch boys dance together*
Bram [8:07 pm]: *sorry angel, I can't be seen in that club*
Angel [8:07 pm]: *then we'll see you tomorrow :P*

Bram fights the urge to push harder, remembering what Rohan said in his office.

He's his own person. Who the fuck are you?

Sighing, Bram tells Angel goodnight and puts on a movie to take his mind off raids and boys of any kind. It doesn't take long before he's sinking back into the memory of Angel's body draped over his own. It would be easy, really, to hold Angel up in his arms like that and get Bram's cock inside him. Or even to sit just like they were on the couch. And then Angel would practically be on display, an open invitation for someone else to press inside.

Would it feel even better? Or would it just dull the sensation for Bram? Another cock pressed in against his, slick and hot, Angel squeezing them both together. It would be *so tight*. And Angel wouldn't have to move a finger.

His hushed voice would be like a pounding rain in his ear.

Bram is hard before he knows it, debating the likelihood of getting recognized at the Dandelion with the prospect of jerking off in a warm shower. Remembering Lee's warning, he takes the shower and rereads Angel's messages with a growing hunger scratching at the door. The only thing worse than Bram's own men finding out he went to a gay club would be the intolerable smugness on Rohan's face if he ever found Bram as a patron at his club.

Thinking about Angel watching a bunch of male strippers turns out to be a pretty cute image. Pretty hot. Very hot to think about Angel watching a bunch of strippers and touching himself in the back of the club.

Bram drifts off to sleep, knowing he's fucking hopeless.

In his dream, he takes Angel to a concert. They're mashed into the crowd together, waiting for the headliner to come on. Rohan struts on stage in an open leather jacket and Bram remembers that, yeah, he agreed to take Pearl out to this show. He lifts Pearl up on his shoulders, because he knows how close those two are, and he wants Pearl to be happy.

When Rohan holds his hand out to invite a member of the audience on stage, Bram wastes no time helping Pearl get close enough. Rohan plucks Pearl onto the stage, taking Pearl into his arms in front of everyone. The crowd continues in their soft cheering as Rohan and Pearl stare deeply into each other's eyes. The way they kiss is so natural, it's easy to forget it's part of the show. Bram's cock throbs as he watches Rohan tongue deep into Pearl's mouth, obvious arousal shivering through them both.

As they start taking each other's clothes off, Bram aches. They look good together. They know how to communicate without talking. When Rohan bends Pearl over an amp and starts fucking him with that goddamn smirk on his face, looking at Pearl's ass like a prideful shark, probably admiring his own dick in the process, Bram remembers he *was supposed to be part of the fucking performance and he forgot his damn cue to get on stage with them.*

▶▷▷

When the club finally shuts down for the night, Rohan finds Pearl curled up on the couch in his office, his face flushed and his skin doing that thing it does when it seems like he's reflecting the light. Sometimes Rohan wonders if Pearl is like one of those fish whose scales can change color.

"You good?" Rohan asks, sitting on the edge of the table.

Pearl makes a low sound in his throat that seems an awful lot like a satisfied moan.

"Did'ya jerk off on my couch you little freak?" Rohan asks, half his mouth pulling into a smirk as his skin heats up.

Pearl smiles to himself and shakes his head.

"Not sure I believe you," Rohan stage whispers. "You've been twice as rowdy since you brought that vampire back here."

When Pearl rolls onto his back to give Rohan an utterly intoxicated look, the long button-up he took from Rohan hanging half-open over his lean torso, Rohan's breath deepens. He fights not to let his face show any of the thirst taking hold of him.

"If you want me to take you to him again, you just have to ask," Rohan reminds Pearl, his voice gone soft for no other reason than he likes how close they are.

Pearl mouths, *tomorrow.*

"Alright, alright." Rohan sighs and brushes Pearl's hair aside, letting himself enjoy the way Pearl pushes into his hand. "You're gonna drive me crazy, you know that?"

Pearl rests his cheek in Rohan's hand, looking sweet as can be, until he bites the meat of Rohan's palm with a wicked glint in his black eyes.

"Little demon," Rohan whispers, barely any pressure behind Pearl's jaw. "I'll be glad to get the break from you."

Pearl springs up and throws his arms around Rohan's neck. Rohan was expecting another little kiss on the cheek, but Pearl presses his face against the side of Rohan's head and whispers to him, his strange and ruined voice pushing at the edges of its limits.

Rohan has to strain to hear the words in the wheezing.

"Play with us."

Rohan shivers at the thought of finally giving into that lewd look on Pearl's face. To give Pearl whatever he asked for, to really share everything with him, nothing would compare to that.

Bram's face pops into his head, that suspicious gaze carving into Rohan, practically huffing like a bull at a matador. If Rohan got what he *really* wanted, he'd take Bram down a peg. A guy like that probably fucks everyone the same exact way. No doubt he's got Pearl acting as submissive as possible. As soon as Rohan remembers the way Bram ran him into the wall, his heart clenches in his chest. There is no trusting a guy like that, even if he did apologize.

"No way you'd get that slab of meat to agree to a threesome," Rohan says. "Guys like him can't stand to share."

Pearl catches Rohan's gaze and that wicked glint returns to his eye. Pearl's tenacity is admirable, and for a moment, Rohan lets himself imagine what would it be like. Building Bram's living room in the theater of his mind, Rohan dresses the stage and sets Bram and Pearl on the couch. Bram seems like the kind of guy who likes to get things going on the couch, a little background noise to ease into the foreplay.

He can easily slot Pearl into Bram's lap, Pearl's back to Bram's chest, his face tilted back to kiss Bram while Bram feels him up with those thick fingers. That's probably *exactly* how Bram does things. In the darkened stage of Rohan's mind, he pictures the two of them panting softly into each other's mouths, equally worked up just from a little bit of touching. Bram's thick fingers press into the soft squish of Pearl's hips. Right when it's clear they could take things further, the two of them turn to Rohan, mouths open, Pearl's face all flushed, and Bram gripping Pearl like a shield to hide how turned on he is. The two of them slowly opening their legs, Bram's dark tan peeking out from beneath Pearl's lighter, sandy shade. Bram hides his face in Pearl's hair while Pearl teases him with another ki—

Rohan shakes his head, the pulsing in his hips getting louder as he banishes the imaginary play with the firm reminder that Bram almost punched him in his own office.

"Do you need anything before I head home?"

Pearl makes a show like he's thinking really hard and then taps his own cheek. Rohan frowns at him, knowing damn well he can never make himself look angry when it comes to Pearl. It's a pathetic attempt to be clinical when he takes Pearl's face and holds it in place so he can press a kiss to Pearl's round cheek. Pulling away from Pearl is getting more difficult by the hour.

▶▷▷

Pearl is disquietingly polite on the drive to Bram's building the next evening. He puts on Rohan's preferred music at a reasonable volume, buckles his seatbelt, and does not try to kiss Rohan once. Fear percolates in Rohan's gut as they drive, silently, through the sunset-orange city.

"What are you and Bram up to you today?" Rohan asks, wanting to take it back as soon as the question leaves his mouth.

Hey, is your boyfriend planning to fuck you in any interesting ways today?

When he glances at Pearl in the passenger seat, Pearl holds his gaze with alarming intensity, as if he expects Rohan to know the answer already.

"Right..." Rohan mutters. "I hope he's good to you at least."

He doesn't look at Pearl, instead fixing his gaze on the yellow car in front of them. It has a vanity plate that reads 22TANGO.

"He may not be a good business man or a good person but as long as he's good to you and you don't feel scared or upset and he treats you right, that's all that matters," Rohan says, losing control of his words at an alarming rate.

Why is his throat so goddamn dry?

"I just don't want to see you get hurt, is all," Rohan blurts out, both his hands on the wheel. He feels himself leaning too far forward in the seat and tries to relax.

"Sorry, I don't know why I'm talking so much."

He sighs, adjusts the volume of the music, and shuts the fuck up for the rest of the drive to the parking garage. Both of the temporary visitor spots are taken up by a huge, red pickup truck that has been jammed in the wrong direction over the white lines. Glaring at the truck, Rohan drives two floors down to find the next open parking spot, his mood thoroughly trashed by the time he cuts the engine.

"Do you need help getting—" Before he can finish asking, Pearl is out the door.

He circles the car and opens Rohan's door for him, tugging on his blue jacket.

Rohan feels like a husk as he gets out, locks the car, and takes Pearl's hand. He thought it would be easier to keep dropping Pearl off for these dates, but being here for the second time to hand Pearl off like a baton is making him crazy.

"Maybe next time, your vampire can come get you at the club," Rohan says miserably, leaning up against the elevator. The reflective bronze-colored walls show Rohan's ghoulish expression glowering back at him, and he instantly fixes his face. He can't show weakness in front of Bram now. He'll just rub Rohan's nose in it.

Pearl squeezes Rohan's hand as they step off on Bram's floor. He's leading Rohan behind him to the door, confident as always. It was that confidence that Rohan was so charmed by when they first met each other. After identifying the initial signs that someone had broken into the club, it took a few days to finally figure out that they had a pest in their walls. When Rohan finally caught the boy who had weaseled into his club, he'd thought, *damn if I wouldn't have done the same stupid thing.* Pearl may not always have the best survival instincts, but when he wants something, he won't stop until he gets it. Rohan admires that about Pearl. There seemed to be no trouble at all communicating between them. Rohan felt like he understood this runaway who insisted on his own independence, sneaking into a gay club to watch the dancers with stars in his eyes.

Standing outside the vampire's front door, Rohan realizes that he and Pearl seem to share a questionable taste in men.

When Pearl knocks on the door, Bram shouts from somewhere in the apartment, "Coming!"

His voice is nails on a chalkboard. Rohan stiffens, entirely unprepared for the mental stamina of pretending everything's fine in front of the leader of the Vampires. Rohan can't even really pinpoint what exactly is making him so testy. It felt fine yesterday. He could make his peace with this arrangement even after Bram threatened him. But now Rohan doesn't even feel any anger toward Bram. He just wishes he could slip away and not be seen.

The door opens, and Bram looks a little out of breath. "Hey, sorry. You didn't say you were on your way."

His black hair is damp from the shower, no product in it, obviously just combed through with his fingers thirty seconds ago. He's wearing a muscle tank and, well, he's got muscle. Rohan's gaze snaps to Bram's thick arms, the wide shoulders, the broad chest—his nipples stand out against the faded gray fabric of his shirt, and Rohan is instantly struck by the thought that Bram might have been jerking off before they got here. He smells like the kind of soap that straight men buy—warm and earthy, a bit chemical around the edges. Rohan looks directly into his bright brown eyes.

"Brought your jail sentence," Rohan says, lifting up Pearl's hand.

"Jesus fucking—come inside before you say that shit," Bram mutters, his gaze darting away as he holds the door open wider.

Rohan suddenly doesn't feel so bad as he lets Pearl pull him into the vampire's den. They both slip their shoes off in the small foyer and Pearl starts dragging Rohan further into the house.

"Hold on, hold on," Rohan tells him, only a small bit of guilt in his stomach as Pearl stages Rohan in front of the huge glass windows so he can see the view.

"Yeah, yeah, I get it," Rohan teases, ruffling Pearl's hair. "You live like a prince, very nice."

It *is* nice, especially when the sun is still setting. The city looks like a candy shop, all twinkling lights against the orange-and-pink sky. Rohan can see Bram in the reflection of the glass standing behind them, his thick arms folded across his chest, looking like his dad just told him to play nice and he's still feeling the sting of a hand across his face. It's exactly the kind of discomfort that Rohan can clock at his bar from a mile away— exactly the kind of trouble that Rohan has been avoiding for the last decade.

Bram bothered to put on a pair of black jeans to go with his ratty t-shirt.

Pearl lets Rohan's hand go and darts over to Bram, tapping Bram's pants pockets until he prompts Bram to hand over the phone.

Rohan slowly turns to look at them, Pearl typing out a quick message and showing it to Bram.

"Angel." Bram says the name with a sigh, an unspoken denial somewhere in his breath.

Pearl points at Rohan insistently, and then points at the TV, and then locks his hand together and silently pleads. Bram looks like he's been socked in the gut by this skinny boy a whole head shorter than him.

"What's going on?" Rohan asks, hands in his pockets as he approaches the two of them.

Rohan didn't think it was possible, but Bram looks even more embarrassed than he did while apologizing. His cheeks are turning an alcohol-red as he lowers his gaze, his posture stiff as a board. Rohan swears he feels himself getting taller as he draws closer.

"Angel has it in his head that, uh."

As Bram sweatily flounders for words, Angel—*Pearl*—shows Rohan the same message.

I want to play with both of you and take all our clothes off!

"Christ, Angel." Bram sighs when Pearl shows Rohan the phone.

"So he's asking you too," Rohan says, leveling his gaze at Bram.

Bram shifts his weight between his feet, admitting with a defeated sigh, "Yes..."

Rohan's heart kicks up his throat, beating dangerously fast as he tries to maintain his cool. Bram looks like a wet dog, standing there and holding himself protectively. In a shocking turn of events, Bram *doesn't* look angry, just mildly distressed, like he's been cornered by wolves and he knows he's done for. Studying the guarded shame radiating from Bram's entire body, Rohan knows he hasn't heard his own pulse pounding this loudly in years. Rohan's tongue presses into the point of his incisor.

At the same exact time that Bram begins to say, "We need to explain to him that this isn't going to work."

Rohan sighs, "I'm gonna need weed for this."

They two of them startle at their overlapping voices and look at each other. Bram's mouth falls open, brows cinched together.

"Wait, are you actually *considering* it?" Bram demands.

Rohan throws his hand out toward Pearl. "Of course I'm considering it! He asked, didn't he? I'm not gonna let my pride get in the way."

Bram's eyes spark with animal fear, and he angles his face away. "It's not that easy, alright? I'm not..." He gestures with both hands at the empty space in front of him, his cheeks getting redder. "I don't do this kind of shit!"

Rohan cocks his head. "Look man, if Pearl is too much for you—"

"That's *not* what I said," Bram snaps.

He tries to look Rohan in the eye, but there's obvious embarrassment deeply rooted in him that makes Rohan's pulse roar. Rohan takes another step closer to Bram, lowering his voice as Pearl approaches on his heels, his black eyes wide and hopeful.

As Bram fights the knot of shame currently choking him, Rohan says, "You know Pearl could probably have anyone he wanted in this town, but for whatever fucking reason, he picked you and me. It's not about *us*, it's about him. Maybe you can at least appreciate that."

Bram's lip twitches, his fingers crushing his own biceps. Rohan can feel the crackling tension that could very easily end with Bram's fist in his face as he stares Bram down, waiting to see if he'll cave or not. Rohan can practically see the red flags waving around them, matador and bull, only it's the bull who's clearly eyeing up the exits and trying to flee.

Finally, Bram's shoulders hunch and he mutters, "How much weed do you have?"

"Enough," Rohan tells him. "It's in the car."

Bram's gaze flicks up. "Don't keep weed in your car, man."

Rohan smirks. "If a cop's searching my car, I have bigger problems than a little weed. Sit tight, I'll be right back."

As he puts his shoes on, Rohan steals a glance at Pearl. He slips in beside Bram, taking one of Bram's hands in both of his own and leaning his face against the cap of Bram's shoulder. His black eyes flick over to Rohan where he zips up his boots, and Pearl smiles at him as he presses Bram's knuckles between his legs.

"Easy," Bram whispers, his neck turning red now too.

Rohan's pulse throbs in his dick and he stands up so fast, his vision almost blackens. "Don't lock me out or you're dead."

"Quit whining," Bram snaps, so jumpy he can barely hide it.

The elevator feels twice as slow as Rohan descends back into the bowels of the parking garage. It stops at least four times, letting in increasingly loud people and crying babies until the elevator is completely full and Rohan's leg is bouncing up and down at light speed.

Bram's too nervous to touch him. They're going to have to keep this as tame as possible. Rohan will be lucky if Bram lets him hold Pearl's hand fully clothed while Bram fucks Pearl in his bed. It's not quite what Rohan wants—not at fucking all—but it's probably best to take it slow at first. If Bram can stand to have another guy see him while he's hard, that'll be impressive enough.

As soon as he thinks it, Rohan clutches his arms, distress building in his chest like steam. *What the fuck is wrong with me?* He rattles the question around in his head. Wasn't he *just* promising he would never get into bed with gang boys? He should be protecting Pearl from idiots like Bram, not offering to smoke him out so they can have the most ill-advised threesome Rohan's ever conceived of.

When the elevator stops on the lowest floor of the garage, Rohan holds the doors open for an agonizing ten seconds for the parents with a broken stroller while their baby screams bloody murder. Rohan is completely flaccid as he slowly walks faster and faster back to his car, frantically shoving his hand under the driver's seat to get the plastic first-aid kit and scraping his fingers on the hard edge.

Back in the elevator, Rohan clutches the hard case and tries to remember that he's doing this for Pearl. It's not about Rohan or how long it's been since he fucked another person or how good Bram looks with his arms out and an embarrassed, rosy tint to his face. Not a single soul gets in the elevator with Rohan as he rockets back up to Bram's apartment at what feels like twice the speed. Rohan is faced with his own manic reflection in the bronze doors, frowning at his outfit—the usual silky, bright blue jacket, a boring, white v-neck, and gray jeans he's worn so many times, they practically mold to his thighs.

It's been a long time since Rohan got the full workout he *used* to get before he took over the club, but at least he still goes to the gym with the other boys. Rohan is nowhere near as thickly built as Bram is, but he's been far too vain to let himself lose his precious muscle tone. Still, if he'd known he was going to be having sex tonight, he might have put a little more effort into his hair or clothes.

The door is still unlocked when he gets back to the apartment, and as Rohan goes to flip the deadbolt, he can't help but picture himself crawling into an enclosure with two wild animals and no protection. Bram is seated on the couch with Pearl stood in front of him with the remote in his hand, wiggling his hips back and forth like a metronome. Bram is too distracted to see, staring at the ceiling like he's just been told he's got one night to live.

He barely stirs when Rohan sits down on the couch, enough space for Pearl to sit comfortably between them, and opens the kit. Digging through band-aids and alcohol wipes, he fishes out the black pen and immediately takes a deep and selfish breath. Smoke fills his mouth and lungs, and Rohan holds onto it like a security blanket for much longer than he needs to before exhaling.

He holds the pen out to Bram, tapping him on the shoulder with it. "Come on."

Bram rouses again and takes the pen with a glare. "I thought you meant, you know...real weed."

"Do you know much more time it takes to roll a joint? Just fucking smoke and be grateful," Rohan scolds.

Face fixed in a pout, Bram takes a suspicious hit off the pen and blows the smoke away from Pearl. "How long does it take to do anything?"

Rohan leans over and snatches the pen out of his hand. "Longer when you're being a cop about it."

"Lay off it," Bram mutters, though his voice doesn't have the same bite as before. "Last time I smoked weed it was...analog."

Rohan snorts and takes another deep breath, careful to turn his head away from Pearl as he lets the smoke out. "Long as it gets the job done, I don't give a shit. Make yourself a drink if you're so antsy."

Bram shrugs, answering softly, "Booze isn't the same."

"Then *you're welcome*," Rohan says, passing the pen back to him.

Bram shakes his head as he takes the pen and for a split second, it almost looks like he's trying not to smile. He puts the pen to his lips like it might bite him, and Rohan slaps his arm.

"Do it like you mean it, man, Pearl's waiting."

Bram smacks his hand away and sucks in a deep breath.

Pearl turns around to face them and holds his hand out. Bram blinks at him, smoke billowing out of his mouth as he asks, "You sure?"

Nodding, Pearl beckons for the pen with his fingers and Bram passes it off to him. They both watch as Pearl flips the pen around a few times, and then holds it to his mouth like a musical instrument. His shoulders rise as he breathes in deep, his brows pinching in concentration. Bram and Rohan both slouch down lower on the couch as Pearl blows smoke as hard as he can between them like a dragon.

"Too goddamn cute," Bram mutters.

Rohan glances over at him and catches a heated look brewing in Bram's eyes, his fingers inching over his mouth. Rohan looks over at Pearl, who sticks his tongue out in protest of the taste. Rohan's gaze flicks rapidly between Bram, an anxious brick of ruddy-gold muscle and fat slowly sinking into his couch, and Pearl, a soft bundle of long, supple limbs with nothing but a halfway-buttoned shirt hanging open over his torso.

Rohan's heart *thumps* louder, and he shifts his legs as his cock starts to swell.

"So," Bram says. He turns his head where it lays on the back of the couch to look at Rohan. "You two really never..." He gestures between Rohan and Pearl.

Pearl leans onto the couch to hand Rohan the pen back, his shirt falling forward, giving Rohan a look straight down his bare torso, his puffy nipples and naked hips. Rohan takes the pen with buzzing fingertips, wanting to reach down Pearl's shirt, wondering if he's allowed to do that now.

The only reason he hasn't before was because of his own damn rules.

"No, never." Rohan shakes his head, feeling dumber by the minute.

"Why not?" Bram asks.

Pearl stares at him too, and Rohan breaks into a sweat.

"Fuck, I don't know," Rohan says. "It's bad to mix business and pleasure."

Bram lurches toward him, pointing at Rohan. "You *said* he didn't work for you."

"He doesn't!" Rohan snaps, face heating up. "But he lives at the club and that's where I do business and, fuck me, I don't know! It didn't seem like a good idea. I didn't think he'd stay with me this long and besides..."

The silence stretches as Rohan avoids putting this thought to words, something too big and too nebulous that's been living in his chest for far too long.

Pearl slowly furrows his thin brows.

"What?" Bram prompts.

Rohan takes another impossibly long hit, feeling Pearl's and Bram's eyes on him like heated stage lights. He lets his breath out in a massive sigh and tosses the pen toward Bram.

"It just didn't seem right," Rohan mutters. "Pearl's got his whole life ahead of him and I'm just some asshole who runs a strip club. We both know that guys like me are either headed for jail, or an early grave. I don't want to put that on anyone."

Bram rips the pen out of Rohan's limp fingers, his heated skin sparking against Rohan's like a match.

"That's a bullshit excuse," Bram says, inhaling with more confidence before he points the pen with accusatory sharpness back at Rohan. "If he wants it and you want it, what the fuck else matters?"

Pearl nods and points at Bram, black eyes imploring. Rohan tips his head back and sighs.

"*Ugh*, whatever. I'm here now, aren't I?" Rohan takes the pen from Bram, letting himself touch Bram's hand a little more directly, testing to see how quickly Bram pulls away from him—slower each time. "I took less convincing for this than *you* did."

Bram gives a half-hearted grunt. "You had a point. He obviously wants us to get along."

Rohan takes a hit while staring at Pearl who smiles back at him so easily. With smoke pouring out of his mouth, Rohan says, "He wants two dicks. That doesn't necessarily mean we have to get along."

Pearl pouts at him, hands on hips.

Bram sets his foot on the edge on the coffee table, clearing his throat. "He's, uh, adventurous."

"Maybe you're just not big enough for him," Rohan says, staring at Bram.

Bram's brown eyes narrow, not anger but something else rising up in him. "I'm plenty big."

"Prove it," Rohan says.

Bram's expression freezes, and Rohan takes another hit as his pulse slowly migrates through his cock. Pearl straightens like an arrow, his gaze zipping back and forth between them.

"*Fine*," Bram snaps, his hand darting to his waist before he goes still again. "You gotta do it too, though."

"Fine by me," Rohan says. "That's what we're here for, isn't it?"

Bram's face is steeping red as Pearl jumps to his feet on top of the table, sheds his oversized shirt in one motion, and sits back down on the table, buck naked with fire in his eyes. He nods at them both, his body suddenly taking up twice as much space as it did.

Rohan simmers in his own crackling nerves, not wanting to show any fear as he starts unbuttoning his pants. With a wayward glance in Rohan's direction, Bram starts doing the same. They go at roughly the same pace, shucking their pants down their thighs to reveal their underwear—Bram's black briefs, Rohan's dark blue. Pearl raises his hands up and gestures for the two of them to get closer, his eyes wider than ever.

"What?" Bram asks with a sigh.

Pearl puts his thumb and forefinger together, slowly widening the gap between them as if to measure.

"Just do it," Rohan says, shucking his pants all the way off and sliding over toward the center of the couch.

With a grumble, Bram takes his black jeans off and kicks them aside, forcing himself closer to Rohan, but oh-so-careful not to touch him. They sit in front of Pearl, hands on the waistbands on their briefs. Pearl leans his hand on the couch between them, smirking as he pointedly touches the label on Bram's underwear, and then the same label on Rohan's.

"My ex bought these, technically," Bram mutters.

"Well, she obviously knows more about clothing than you do," Rohan says. "Alright, nut up. Let's go."

Rohan slips his fingers down under the fabric and, much to his surprise, Bram does the same. Rohan's pale thighs jump up at the same time as Bram's tanned ones, and then they are both sitting bare-ass on the black, fabric couch.

Jumping to his feet, Pearl leans down to inspect Bram's cock, his face finally starting to show a little blush. His fingers gently trace the trunk, and the head, and Bram shifts his hips, his breath coming out in a huff. As Pearl's lips purse, Bram tries to make it look casual as he leans his arm on the back of the couch and presses his hand against his face as if to cover his expression. Pearl kisses the skin of his uncut dick with a soft smile, and Bram's breath sucks up into his chest, his eyes fixed on Pearl.

Is *this* what it's like for them? Rohan quickly rewrites his vision of Pearl and Bram's relationship as he watches Pearl give Bram a smug little look on his way back to standing. When he turns to Rohan, he bats his eyes like he does when he wants Rohan to do something for him. Suddenly all that smoke is behind his eyes as Rohan gestures at his lap.

"Do I pass inspection?"

The blush deepens on Pearl's face and he leans down to touch, the heat of his fingertips going straight through Rohan like sunlight. Pearl's eyes flick back to Rohan's, a little less certain than he was before as he lowers his mouth to kiss Rohan's cock in roughly the same place as Bram's, though Rohan is no doubt thinner than Bram. The contact has him stiffening up, and he's sure Pearl can feel him twitching. Rohan's breath is going haywire as Pearl stands back up, hands behind his back, and gives a very firm nod.

"What does that mean?" Bram asks, barely a whisper.

"I think it's a tie," Rohan mutters. "Although it's pretty obvious I got more inches than you."

"Mine's thicker," Bram says immediately, but neither of them even sound like they're arguing anymore. It's obvious anyway. Rohan may be longer, but Bram's cock is like a fucking beer can resting on his thigh.

"Okay, now we get a look at *your* dick," Rohan says, leaning toward Pearl.

Pearl's mouth curls into a wide smile which he tries to bite down on, and he shuffles his feet just a little bit, sticking his hips out. His skin fills with goosebumps as Rohan sets a hand on Pearl's thigh, but before he can touch, Pearl tugs on the sleeve of Rohan's shirt.

"What?" Bram looks between the two of them.

Rohan looks over at him, his tongue starting to feel a little looser, his body suffused with smoke. "He wants us naked."

"Oh." Bram stares back, his eyes utterly blank for a moment, and then he tears his shirt off. "Sorry."

Rohan laughs at his sudden eagerness to obey, and peels his jacket and t-shirt off, adding them to the pile of fabric on the floor. Without wasting another second, he takes Pearl's hips in his hands and pulls him closer.

"Let's really get a good look at you," Rohan says, his blood singing as Pearl immediately jumps in front of him, eager to show his own body off.

"Don't hog him," Bram mutters, crawling closer across the couch.

"You already fucked him god knows how many times, give me a minute," Rohan says, but he doesn't complain when he feels the heat of Bram's skin so close to his own. The two of them are glued to the sight of Pearl's dick, and Rohan savors the opportunity to slip his fingers into the flushed folds of skin, nudging Pearl's cock into full view.

Pearl's hand circles Rohan's ear, skirting over his scalp until he can tug the black tie free and shake Rohan's ponytail loose down his back. Such a simple touch that runs Rohan through with need. All that's left to do is press his mouth to Pearl's reddened cock and wait to see if Bram starts swinging.

No punches land, only Pearl giving a soft, wheezing gasp that shivers down Rohan's skin as he tries to suck the morsel of Pearl's dick past his lips. He feels Pearl leaning into him, the slight press of his hips into Rohan's mouth, and Rohan's cock jumps against his thigh. Any nerves about Bram's presence quickly drain away as Rohan flicks his tongue over Pearl's cock and watches Pearl twitch with pleasure.

"L-Let me." Bram's voice is cut with his husky breath and he puts his hands on Pearl's hips. "Let me hold him."

Rohan pulls back, eyeing Bram up, his flushed skin and dilated pupils and the fact that he doesn't seem to care that his arm is touching Rohan's. "You want his tits?"

Bram nods, his lips already parting.

"We doing this here on your couch or what?" Rohan asks, knowing he's on the brink of forgetting where he is.

"G-Got a guest, there's a bed, there's another guest, there's *one guest bed, it's in the loft*," Bram chokes out.

Rohan smiles, knowing full well he must look like a shark with blood in the water.

Bram just *had* to be his fucking type.

"Why don't you lead the way, Romeo?" Rohan asks. "Don't want you dropping Pearl with all the blood going to your dick."

"Shut up," Bram mumbles. His fucking nipples are hard as he gets to his feet, and Rohan looks up at Pearl, all sense of competition and jealousy gone out the window.

Pearl stares down the length of his own torso to meet Rohan's eyes, his chest swelling with a deep breath. He licks his full lips, and Rohan knows he's the dumbest guy in the world for denying himself this kind of fun for the last few months. He rushes to his feet, scooping Pearl up into his arms as he goes, and the two of them follow Bram toward the spiral staircase that leads to the loft over the kitchen. For some reason, Bram has put his underwear back on, and Rohan shamelessly stares at the black fabric cinching into the meat of Bram's hips the entire way up the steps.

Pearl's arms loop around Rohan's neck, his breath deep and his body red-hot. When he kisses Rohan's cheek again, he does it with a blatant hunger, his hands slipping down Rohan's neck. All those weeks of chaste kisses feel like nothing when Pearl touches him with permissive desire radiating from every inch of his skin.

The loft is a simple little square of carpet with a neatly made bed laying right on the floor, and a short end table with a generic lamp. Despite the lack of a bed frame, there's a hotel cleanliness to it that makes Rohan suspect that no one has ever been up here. He doesn't care to interrogate it as Bram turns to him with a hazy look in his eyes.

"Here, let me...uh. I'll hold him." Bram sticks his arms out.

"Will you now?" Rohan asks, smirking with glee.

"I...wanna hold him," Bram says. "I'll hold his chest. You can. Have his. Bottom half. For now."

Rohan doesn't know if it's the drugs or Bram's nerves grinding him to a stuttering halt, but Rohan feels himself getting harder the less composed Bram acts. Pearl reaches for Bram with a smile, and easily folds into his arms. Bram's grip is protective as he settles Pearl against his hip and steps onto the bed, but it's not *Pearl* he seems to want to protect. Rohan can't help but think that Bram is using Pearl as a shield while he sinks down to lean his back against the wall. When Pearl kisses Bram on the mouth, Bram looks grateful to sink into something familiar, hiding behind Pearl's gangly body.

Watching Pearl lean into Bram, filling Bram's mouth with his tongue, Rohan suddenly knows *exactly* what he wants to do with these boys.

▶▷▷

Bram knows he's panicking a little bit, but the fear is cut through with strange, goading excitement that he blames squarely on the drugs and the way he reacts to Angel's hands roving over his skin. It's the same kind of fear that nips at his heels whenever he enters a dangerous situation that he knows he can't back out of. He is hyper-alert as Rohan steps onto the bed with them, knowing full well where this is going. As Pearl peels off his chest and smiles over his shoulder at Rohan, Bram breaks into a fresh sweat. The image of Rohan's tongue swirling over Angel's clit is warring for top spot in his brain with the pretty look on Angel's face when he locked eyes with Bram, hungrier than ever.

Why did it have to be so hot? He didn't want it to be so exciting, least of all when Rohan insistently called it Angel's *dick*. But Angel obviously liked that, and his pleasure is only making Bram's worse.

"Turn him over," Rohan urges, voice low and smoky.

His eyes are so fucking bright, Bram feels Rohan's gaze under his skin as Pearl spins around in his arms, pressing his back to Bram's chest and spreading his legs wide to show off. Pearl's excitement is infectious, his quickening pulse catching Bram's own heart rate up with it.

Rohan sets his hands on either side of Bram's hips, looming over the two of them. That panic squeezes Bram's throat again, pounding beyond his control and transforming into cornered arousal.

"Go on, touch him," Rohan presses.

Bram swallows roughly, forcing his hands to move up Angel's torso, skimming from his belly to his nipples where Bram squeezes the dew drops of flesh. Angel throws his head back onto Bram's shoulder when Bram thumbs over both his nipples, a wheezing moan gracing his ears. Droplets of warmth slip down Angel's groin onto Bram's hips, and Bram doesn't know what to feel as his cock strains against his underwear, much too hot for the fabric.

Why did Rohan have to have a nice body? Why did he have to have a chiseled face? Why did he have to have such a long goddamn dick?

Bram can barely keep his eyes from constantly straying to Rohan's cock with how close they are. When Rohan reaches toward Pearl's hips, pressed against Bram's, Bram's breath catches in his throat as he braces for Rohan to touch *him* instead. Strangely, it's not really a relief at all when Rohan slips two long fingers into Pearl's cunt, avoiding Bram entirely.

Pearl shudders against Bram's chest, and Bram feels the clinging wetness of his underwear sticking to his skin.

"Kiss him already," Rohan says.

Bram has no clue who he's addressing, but Pearl—Pearl? Fuck him—immediately twists around to pull Bram's face toward his and crush their mouths together. Commanding himself to keep moving, Bram chases Pearl's tongue with his own, and rubs the heels of his hands against the buds of Pearl's nipples. It's easier to just keep moving, same way he would in a fight. Just keep moving through, don't let anyone catch him off guard, and don't let them think he doesn't know what he's doing.

At least kissing Pearl is easy, especially with Pearl's panting breaths puffing against his face. When Pearl tugs on the waist of his underwear, Bram braces his hand and picks his hips up, only noticing that it's Rohan stripping him when he sees pale fingers against the black fabric and Rohan's shark-tooth smile.

"Squeeze 'em again," Rohan says, giving a slight nod. It's not fucking fair at all that Rohan talks so calmly during this.

But Bram still cups Pearl's tits, rewarded with a soft groan in Pearl's throat, and Bram's bare cock pressing up against the slick between Pearl's thighs. Pearl's always so blissfully wet for this, like he's always ready for it.

Rohan leans down to brush his lips over Pearl's nipple, and Bram can't stop himself from pushing Pearl's breast up higher, helping Rohan roll his tongue over the perfect button of nerves. Pearl's body jolts against Bram, and his feet slap against Rohan's waist as though magnetized. He gives a soft whine, and when Rohan pulls his mouth away, Bram sees his finger slowly gliding into Pearl's ass, dewy with fluid.

"Which one do you want?" Rohan asks, and Bram almost gasps as he processes just how close their faces are. Rohan meets his gaze, eyes darkening, looking like some kind of predatory bird shadowing Bram and Pearl. "I'm guessing you'd prefer his cunt but I don't want to make assumptions."

The last thing Bram wants to say is *I don't care,* because it doesn't sound right to him, so it probably won't sound right to them, but as soon as he starts trying to formulate a coherent response about how any hole is fine with him, his thoughts immediately jam together into a useless, sticky mess.

"I'll do anything," Bram says, breathless.

Rohan's face pulls into a wicked smile that rockets Bram back to his teenage years when he hadn't yet crossed any of the lines that landed him inextricably on the wrong side of the law. That's the kind of smile that gets Bram into trouble and makes it look like fun.

"Flip him," Rohan says, planting his hand on the wall beside Bram's head. "You take the front, I'll take the back."

Bram's heart is going to burst out of his chest. With a gasp, Pearl picks himself up, whining softly as he meets Bram's gaze with such a spoiled, drunken look in his eyes. There's no way Bram could stop this now, not with Pearl looking like he's getting everything he's ever wanted. Especially not when he kisses Bram again, his nipples brushing Bram's chest, a warm hand firmly gripping Bram's cock.

Bram's hips jump, a muffled groan of pleasure building in his throat as Pearl guides Bram's cock against the mouth of his cunt, Pearl's hands clinging to his face—wait, that's Rohan touching his cock. Bram startles when he realizes, but he knows if he complains now, he's just going to ruin the mood. If he kisses Pearl hard enough, it doesn't really matter. It still feels just as good when someone else is rubbing his cock against Pearl's slit until he slips inside the folds of skin.

It feels incredible, actually, when he doesn't have to think.

Bram and Pearl moan into each other's mouths as Pearl sinks down onto his dick. Bram gives a short pitch of his hips, and Pearl throws his head back, mouth open in relieved pleasure. He looks as beautiful as ever, and then there's Rohan catching Pearl's waist and kissing his shoulder. Pearl turns to nuzzle against his red hair, and then reaches behind him to spread his ass for Rohan.

They're definitely doing this. Every little movement of Pearl's body drives Bram a little closer to madness. He barely recognizes his own hands wrapping around Pearl's hips, digging into Pearl's cheeks to help open him up for Rohan. Rohan's knees slide in against Bram's thighs and another fluttering tangle of panic knots in his throat. It almost looks like Rohan is about to fuck *Bram*, but then Pearl gives a wheezing moan, and he clings tighter to Bram's head as Rohan's cock plunges into Pearl's ass.

Rohan's lids lower over his eyes, and he shows his teeth for a split second, a low, animal groan signaling his pleasure. He looks deep in a haze of lust, and Bram is incredibly grateful that Pearl is safely wedged between them. That would be a hell of a look to weather on his own. Not that Bram would ever be naked and alone with Rohan and his pretty hair and the soft lines of muscle on his freckle-dusted chest and his upsettingly nice ass. His thighs are no joke, taut cords of muscle beneath pale skin that Bram is trying to tear his gaze off of. Rohan isn't built like a brawler, but he obviously does *something* to maintain his physique.

As soon as Rohan starts to fuck Pearl, the movement ricochets through Bram's hips. Pearl looks like he's got stars in his eyes, his hushed panting getting louder and faster. Bram's insides are melting and he grips Pearl's waist, only to feel Rohan's hand underneath his, and it's too late to move. Rohan's other hand is still braced on the wall by Bram's head, his long torso and toothy smile and curtain of red hair blocking everything else from sight. When Pearl buries his face in Bram's neck, legs cinched tight against Bram's waist, the only thing left to see is Rohan.

"You like it, Pearl?" Rohan asks, his voice thick with breath.

Muted sounds of pleasure spills from Pearl's mouth, his fingers digging into Bram's skin like kitten claws. A sudden tightness grips Bram's cock like a fist, and he shudders as he Pearl starts coming, heat gushing from his slit, running over Bram's skin in turn. It *really* looks like Rohan is fucking them both somehow, and Bram's eyes slowly roll back as a wave of sensation steamrolls him from the base of his cock to the crown of his head.

"*Fuck.*" Bram tips his head back, letting his hips roll mindlessly into Pearl, probably into Rohan too, who knows? Who gives a shit.

Bram can't see anything anymore. He's going to come embarrassingly quickly as he shares a cute boy with another guy. He was stupid to think he could keep up with them. This is way beyond his pay grade. Mashing his head against the wall, Bram steadily unwinds. His entire body starts ringing as his balls clench right before he comes inside Pearl with a moan that he can't hold back.

A new voice cracks between them as Pearl opens his mouth and cries out, "*Yes!*"

Bram and Rohan both stare at him, and Rohan's shark-tooth smile quickly transforms into awe. He grips Pearl's hips with both his hands, thrusting faster, the slapping of skin filling Bram's ears like a distant drum beat. Pearl's waist looks tiny with the two of them grabbing his body, their three different skin tones blending in Bram's eyes like paint on a canvas.

How much did he smoke?

"You spent already, vampire?" Rohan's voice is choppy with breath as he meets Bram's gaze and just like that, sparks whirl through Bram's belly. That's a challenge if he's ever heard one.

"F-fuck you," Bram mutters, not exactly the stellar comeback he wanted, but it feels like his mind is splitting open. He's making room for something inside him, a new feeling, or maybe a new way to look at the world. Yeah, maybe that's it. Maybe it's kind of beautiful to fuck the prettiest boy he's ever laid eyes on hand in hand with his rival. Rohan's not so bad anyway. If he's willing to do this just for Pearl, he can't be a bad guy.

That's what Bram is thinking while he stares up at Rohan's face, the lean muscles of his chest taut, staring back at Bram like he's trying to telepathically communicate with him. Bram has never been his close to another guy having sex. He *should* be embarrassed, maybe even ashamed. He could be a lot of things, but at that moment, his dick is waking up again. While he's making eye contact with Rohan, feeling the reverberations of Rohan's hips pumping like a piston into Pearl.

When Rohan leans in closer, it isn't really a surprise, and yet, it is the biggest surprise in the world. Bram only has time to scream within the confines of his skull, *Yes!? No!?* and then Rohan is kissing him on the mouth. Bram shuts his eyes, and everything reduces down to physical sensation.

He's getting kissed. He likes kissing. It feels good, this tongue feels good, the vibrations rippling through his body and his legs and his cock and his back feel good. Everything feels fucking good.

Pearl gives another full-throated moan, his body jostling against Bram's as Rohan moans through their kiss, yet another pleasant vibration right down Bram's throat, and then all the motion stops. Rohan breaks away, panting heavily as he sits back on his knees. Bram hardly remembers to feel strange with Pearl drunkenly pawing at him, wiggling his hips back and forth with a low hum.

Rohan drags his hand down Pearl's spine. "Got what you wanted?"

Pearl gasps, lifting his head as if to answer, but all that comes out is a wheezing sigh, and he goes limp on top of Bram like a wet towel.

"I think that's a yes," Rohan says, smirking at Bram. "And you're not trying to kill me either, so that's a plus."

Bram tightens his arms around Pearl, licking his rapidly drying lips. "I just. Uh. Just."

Rohan tilts his head, curiosity lighting up his eyes again. "Just what?"

Pearl kisses the side of Bram's neck, his lips soft and sloppy. "Mm?"

Bram doesn't know how to finish that sentence. It's almost a relief when he hears his phone ringing from the living room, until he remembers that means he has to get up and go down the stairs and stop doing whatever the fuck it is they're doing up here that feels so damn good.

"Ffffuck, I gotta get that," Bram says.

"Ah, come on," Rohan teases. "Can't take one night off from being a criminal?"

"Lee only calls when it's important." Bram sighs, gently lifting Pearl off his chest even as Pearl reaches for Bram to keep him close. "I'm sorry, I'll be right back."

Pearl makes an annoyed sound and crawls over to Rohan to pull him down to the bed with him. Bram grabs his briefs off the ground, shuffling them back up his legs as Rohan collapses beside Pearl, running his fingers down the center of Pearl's chest.

"Your loss," Rohan says.

Pearl gives a full-body shiver as Rohan circles his belly button.

"God damnit," Bram mumbles, hauling himself back up to his legs.

He does a bold job of pretending he can walk normally, catching himself on the metal rails of the spiral staircase before he takes another glance at the boys. Pearl arches up off the bed like a cat as Rohan flicks his hardened nipples.

"Cute..." Rohan whispers. "You know, I didn't think these were my type, but I'm starting to think they're my type now."

Bram simmers with anger as the obnoxious sound of the ringtone he specifically assigned to Lee draws him down the stairs, his weight barely held up. It takes him way too long to find his phone which he wrestles out of his jeans and then he stalks off into his office, answering with a gruff, "I fucking hope this is good news," as he slams the door shut behind him.

Lee sighs in his ear and Bram feels himself sobering up.

"There was a break-in," Lee says.

"Son of a bitch," Bram whispers, toddling over to his desk so he can sit down. "Alright, what happened? Spiders?"

"That's the weird thing," Lee says. "I can't trace it back to any other other gangs."

"What did they hit?" Bram asks.

"Well, uh. Your office," Lee answers. "At headquarters."

"What?" Bram's brows pinch and he raises his feet up to prop on the edge of his desk. "What do you mean *my* office? There's nothing in there."

"I know," Lee tries to explain. "They broke in tonight, fucked with the security footage again, tore your office apart like they were looking for something, and then left. Nothing is missing, I put everything back together myself. And I've got every ear to the ground right now. If it was the Boars or the Eels, they'd be bragging about infiltrating our office. And if it was the Spiders, well, it wouldn't be. They don't work like this, they're way too clean. If they wanted something in here, they wouldn't leave a mess."

"I don't understand," Bram says, his mind sifting through sludge. "You telling me a fucking rando broke into my office? Someone who knew to screw up security footage, but who didn't bother cleaning up after themselves?"

"I honestly don't know what's going on," Lee tells him. "That's why I needed to ask you...you haven't been, uh, working any side gigs, have you?"

"Of course not, are you kidding me?" Bram's hand tightens on the phone. "I can barely manage my own fucking gang, I'm not double dipping."

"Maybe it was something the former Mr. Stoker was involved in and never told you," Lee suggests. "An old rivalry or grudge?"

"Fuck if I know," Bram mumbles. "This is bad, huh?"

"Well, not as bad as it could be," Lee says. "There's been zero talk of this across any territory lines, and like I said, they didn't take anything. It could be a fluke, but, well, I don't want you using that office until we figure it out. Stay home tomorrow, okay? Don't go out alone. Just let me look into this and get back to you."

"Christ." Bram stares out the floor-to-ceiling window, the neon lights shining back at him. "Someone's trying to back me into a corner."

"We won't let them," Lee tells him. "I won't let them. But I'm sorry we failed you tonight."

"What are you talking about?" Bram leans forward, frowning at the wall. "It's a break-in, Lee, you can't personally prevent all of those."

"I just..." Lee takes a sharp breath on the other end, and Bram can picture him nodding as he recognizes the permission not to take the blame. "Right. I'll figure out what happened, I swear."

"Well, what's done is done," Bram says, rubbing his face. "Just try to get some sleep, alright? You're not as good when you're sleepless."

"Ah, right." Lee's voice diminishes. "I'm sorry to give you bad news. I hope I didn't disturb you too much."

"It's fine," Bram says, hoisting himself back out of his chair. "Keep me updated."

"Yes, sir."

Bram ends the call and sags forward, hands on his desk. Of fucking course. The last thing he needs is some *new* asshole in town who hates him.

At least he's got Pearl in his bed. It's fine that Rohan's there too. He came in handy.

A smirk breaks out over Bram's face and he starts laughing at his own imaginary word play. Snickering, he slips out of his office, making sure to open the door as softly as possible to make up for slamming it earlier, only to catch Rohan's voice drifting down from the loft.

"Me? I'm doing great, thanks for asking."

There's a pause as Bram quietly approaches the staircase.

"He's not so bad..." Rohan's voice drops lower. "I told you, Pearl. If you're happy, then I'm happy. That's all that matters."

Slowly, Bram starts back up the stairs, trying to carry his weight as softly as he can.

"Hey, listen." Rohan's voice loses some of its playfulness, and Bram goes stock still.

"I'm sorry if I...ignored you. These past few weeks. *I know*, I know. Just, I feel stupid knowing we could have been like this, and I put up a wall for no good reason. Feels like I wasted time."

Bram's heart *thuds* awkwardly in his chest, but he can't bring himself to move or stop listening.

"I'm being selfish, aren't I?" Rohan asks. "Maybe you're right. I'm pretty stubborn. Like you."

Rohan laughs, quiet and intimate in a way that gives Bram goosebumps.

"I do like him, Pearl. You kidding me? You've seen his ass more than I have."

More laughter, and even Pearl wheezes along with him.

"Not that he'd let me touch it. Maybe you. Not me."

Bram quickly and quietly creeps back to his office, and then makes a show of closing the door audibly before shouting, "Sorry!"

His pulse beats in his neck as he quickly climbs the stairs again. Pearl straddles Rohan's hips, his phone in hand to type out messages, and Rohan lays sprawled on his back with his hands on Pearl's legs. Even Pearl's lighter skin tone looks much deeper and warmer in color right next to Rohan, though the thin smattering of freckles across Rohan's face, shoulders, and legs all jump to the surface when he's trapped beneath Pearl's dewy, unmarked skin. It's even more apparent how much more muscle mass Rohan has when he's got Pearl's pony legs hitched up so close to the trunks of his thighs.

They look so comfortable together, it almost hurts.

"Trouble?" Rohan asks, looking at Bram.

"Gang business," Bram says immediately. "Nothing to do with you, you made it very clear that you don't want into my business."

"That's hardly fair, I was just very deep inside your business a few minutes ago," Rohan says with a grin.

Pearl gives Bram another wicked smile, and Bram's blood rushes.

"Don't tell me you're still hungry?" Bram asks, sitting down next to Rohan.

Pearl immediately grabs Bram by the shoulders to kiss him, *very* hungrily. Not that Bram minds. Pearl pulls Bram against him, and Bram lets his hands rove across Pearl's body. It's becoming less strange to do this in front of Rohan.

"You guys gonna fuck right there on top of me?" Rohan asks with a whine.

Bram breaks their kiss, and he and Pearl both turn to look at Rohan. Bram can't help but hide behind the dense waves of Pearl's fluffed out hair, and as he peers down at Rohan, he watches those hazel eyes zip back and forth between Pearl and himself with a frantic kind of heat.

"Fuck me," Rohan says.

"*What?*" Bram asks, face heating up.

"Nothing." Rohan perks up, propping himself on his elbows. "Round two? I'm not dead yet."

Bram's pulse is twice as loud as he wraps Pearl up and pulls him down onto the bed between his and Rohan's bodies.

"He told me what he wanted," Bram says. "First night he came here, little freak put on some porn and showed me *exactly* what he was hoping for."

Rohan and Bram lean over Pearl, watching his cheeks turn pink.

"He wants us both in the same hole," Bram says. "Isn't that right?"

"No shit, Pearl you're fucking greedy," Rohan says. "Can you even fit that much?"

Pearl starts nodding over and over.

"Boy's got eyes bigger than his hole." Rohan smirks at Bram. "Worth a shot though."

Bram breaks into a sweat under Rohan's gaze, hoping he doesn't somehow inaudibly convey that he heard them talking about him.

"Worth a shot, yeah."

"Alright," Rohan sinks down beside Pearl, lifting up his closest leg. "Which one of us goes in first?"

Bram mirrors him, lifting Pearl's other leg. "You're longer."

"You're thicker," Rohan counters. "So...same time?"

Bram laughs. "I don't know if I can just yet."

"Trust me, big boy, you'll get there," Rohan says, reaching his hand down to grab Bram's cock.

"Jesus, man." Bram's breath cuts off.

"Touch him," Rohan instructs, husky and pointed.

Pearl's hands immediately latch onto Bram's chest, and Bram's nipples instantly go hard. As soon as Bram thinks about arguing, he feels Pearl's tongue laving over his skin, and his cock starts to pulse with insistence.

"*Mmm.*" Bram goes slack, except for his dick which *someone* is steadily massaging back to life. "*Fuck.*"

Bram breathes the word, his eyes sliding shut as Pearl sucks on his chest, and Rohan works his thumb over Bram's cockhead. The two of them are frighteningly efficient at getting Bram hard, especially after he flops onto his back, and Bram feels a long tongue streaking over his stiffening skin. His knees drift apart, his mind drifting away, more than ready to forget about gangs and allegiances and why this evening was a bad idea.

It feels so fucking good. Bram moans, his hips gently rolling into the movement of the mouth swallowing him whole. Two mouths, fuck him. He loves the slick feeling of two tongues working him over, drawing out a breathless pleasure. He didn't know his chest was this sensitive, but Pearl works him over like it's his job. A little nip of his teeth and Bram spirals into another time and place, another body entirely.

He's never had sex like this before. He could get used to it. He wants to touch them both, so he slips his hands down, one over Pearl's thick fluff of hair, and the other he slips through Rohan's silky curtain of red. His heart is pounding like crazy. Chel wasn't this good with her mouth. Rohan is *very good* with his mouth, not leaving a single inch of Bram's cock dry. He's not afraid to pull the skin back, his tongue pulsing over Bram's slit, his fingers skimming lower. Bram's cock jumps, fluid welling up as Rohan grips Bram's balls and opens his throat.

Pearl switches to his other nipple, and Bram comes with a violent shudder, his stomach fluttering, and his thighs clenching. Sweat breaks out over his entire body, and he swears he can see through the ceiling for a brief moment as he spills down Rohan's throat.

Two mouths. Fuck him.

He can hear Rohan and Pearl both beginning to laugh, and he doesn't give a shit.

When Rohan wakes up in Bram Stoker's bed, Pearl sandwiched between him and the leader of the Vampires, he wonders when the other shoe will drop. One good night does not mean safety.

But it *was* a good night.

As he shuffles aside, Pearl turns to him, sleepy and heavy, his brows arched.

"I'm good," Rohan croaks. "You?"

Pearl nods, leaning his head onto Rohan's arm to kiss his freckled skin. Bram makes a low, deathly sound and stretches his arm out.

"Are we getting up?" He sounds like he's forcing himself awake by sheer will.

"No one's making you," Rohan says. "You can sleep if you want."

Bram swallows, prying his eyes open. "Can't sleep. Things to do."

Bram hauls himself up, staring out at the balcony of the loft like he's in a trance. "Did we. Uh." He sniffs. "Did we."

He twists two fingers together and makes a motion like he's penetrating something.

"Just the once," Rohan tells him. "We lost you after you came in my mouth."

He smiles at Bram, expecting to be met with denial or anger.

Bram's mouth puckers into a frown, and he turns his head away, mumbling, "Sorry about that."

Rohan lets his breath out, freshly annoyed at how fucking cute this vampire is when he gets shy.

"It's alright," Rohan tells him. "We'll just have to make a follow-up appointment so we can properly get acquainted as tunnel buddies."

Pearl gives a wide and gleaming smile against Rohan's arm, his body curling up.

"Jesus. I need a shower," Bram mutters. "You can, uh, help yourself to whatever's in the kitchen."

He avoids Rohan's gaze, but when Pearl tugs on Bram's arm, he leans down to kiss Pearl between the eyes. Rohan watches him slink back down the steps, completely naked. His underwear is still sitting on the edge of the bed where Rohan pulled it off him last night.

Progress? Or so much shame he forgot to dress himself in his hurry to leave?

With a deep sigh, Rohan forces himself up and decides to make himself useful. He pisses and washes his face in the guest bathroom, heading back into the living room to gather up his underwear and pants before taking stock of Bram's refrigerator. Just enough things to scrounge together a halfway decent breakfast.

Pearl watches him cook, standing on the metal rungs of a stool at the kitchen island, his hands planted on the counter, hips swaying back and forth.

"You're energetic," Rohan says.

Pearl grins back at him, gesturing for Rohan's phone which he passes off as the eggs sizzle. Quickly, Pearl jams out a message and shows it to him.

You said you want another date and Bram didn't say no!!!!!!

Rohan feels a horrid pulling in his chest. "It's for *you*. And it's not a date, okay? Relax."

Pearl's gaze burns as Rohan finishes cooking in silence.

By the time Bram comes back out of his bedroom in sweatpants and another muscle shirt, Rohan presents two plates with omelets.

"You need groceries, but I made it work," Rohan says, cutting into his with a fork.

"Did Pearl already eat?" Bram asks, taking the other stool.

Rohan tries not to gloat at the use of *his* nickname.

"All Pearl ever wants to eat is one bite of whatever I'm eating," Rohan explains. "I've never seen him eat more than that. I stopped asking after the fiftieth time."

Bram cocks his head and offers Pearl a small piece of his omelet, which Pearl bites off Bram's fork with a smile.

"Yeah, he didn't eat with me either," Bram says. "Huh."

Pearl glances between them, propping his chin on his hand.

"Your people on fire?" Rohan asks, trying to sound casual between mouthfuls.

"I can neither confirm nor deny," Bram says, taking a huge bite. He raises his fist in front of his mouth as he chews. "Civilians don't need to know."

Rohan shakes his head. "Right, right."

"Very interesting that you're suddenly so curious though," Bram says. "You know something I don't?"

Rohan shrugs. "Wouldn't know if anything I knew was relevant if you won't tell me anything to begin with."

"Then I guess we're in a stalemate," Bram says.

"Guess so." Rohan responds, clipped. "Enjoy your omelet."

"I am," Bram says, then adds under his breath, "Thank you."

As Rohan puffs up to brag, he curses himself in the same breath for caring at all.

"I got a question for you two," Bram says first, raising his fork up to point. "Why haven't you kissed?"

Rohan and Pearl both startle, then turn to Bram with equally confused gazes.

"Don't pull some shit either, I was paying attention," Bram says. "You do it everywhere *but* the mouth. What are you waiting for?"

Rohan and Pearl exchange a surprised glance before Pearl looks away, cheeks reddening.

"I...guess we just didn't think about it," Rohan says, his own face heating up.

Why *haven't* they?

"I should head out anyway," Rohan says. "It's admin day at the club. Pearl wants to stay here today, is that alright?"

"I'll allow it...*if* you two kiss on the mouth before you leave," Bram says, fork still raised in challenge.

Rohan stiffens, then gives a strained laugh. "Damn, so demanding. Are you always like this after sex?"

Bram narrows his eyes. "Are you gonna do it or not?"

Rohan looks over at Pearl, who glances up through his dark lashes, curious and maybe a little shy? Why is he suddenly shy *now*?

"I mean, why *wouldn't* we?" Rohan says, stumbling forward into some kind of agreement. "It's just a kiss."

Pearl gives a slow nod, like he's convincing himself in the moment.

"Then go right ahead," Bram says, slouching back to watch them.

"Fucking, give me a second." Rohan raises his hands up. "I *just* finished eating."

Rohan washes his hands, takes a massive gulp of water, and tries to figure out why the fuck he's so nervous about this. He can fuck Pearl in the ass but apparently one kiss on the mouth is a bridge too far.

As he circles the island, Pearl spins around on his stool to face him. The sight of this slender boy has never been more intimidating. The worst part is Pearl's expression, none of his usual wicked delight, just a wide-eyed, nervous curiosity flickering in his gaze. Rohan approaches him like a loaded gun, unsure where to touch. The face feels too forward, the hips feel too casual, the shoulders far too clinical.

What the fuck is wrong with him?

Rohan raises his arms up, and Pearl reaches toward him, tipping his head back. Pearl's lips part, lids lowering, as cute as he's ever looked with his hair in a willowy fluff. He really does look angelic, but Rohan can feel Bram watching them. This shouldn't be so goddamn stressful. Pearl's hands settle on his chest, little spots of warmth that Rohan wishes could help him breathe easier as he slips an arm around Pearl's back, and takes Pearl's face with his other hand.

He leans in almost all the way, then stops just shy of a kiss so he can slowly brush his lips across Pearl's, testing the waters. Only in that moment does Rohan feel how absolutely desperate he is for Pearl to like it. Quickly, Pearl matches his soft pressure, his fingers tightening against the muscle in Rohan's chest. The two of them press in closer at the same time, and Rohan's entire body pounds like a drum. Neither of them even try to push it any further, no tongue, only the crushingly soft shape of Pearl's mouth against Rohan's.

It feels like his first kiss all over again.

Two seconds later, Rohan and Pearl both break away. Pearl's cheeks are bright pink as he quickly spins to face the kitchen, and Rohan is more than grateful to get the breather.

"Now you can go," Bram says, just the slightest hint of smugness brightening his eyes.

"Nice try, asshole." Rohan wheels on him, grabbing the front of Bram's green shirt. "Now it's your turn."

"Wha—"

Rohan kisses Bram before he misses the chance, crushing their mouths together. Bram flails once, leaning back against the counter, but he doesn't shove Rohan away. He gives a strangled noise, and when Rohan grabs his face, Bram's body relaxes again. Rohan tongues deep into Bram's mouth, taking out the strange, pent-up nervousness on *him* for issuing such a tense challenge. It's even more of a surprise when Bram kisses him back, opening his mouth wider for Rohan, his tongue sliding against Rohan's with caution.

Right when it's starting to feel like it might be worth it just to keep going, Rohan sharply pulls back and gets a full view of Bram's flustered face, panting quietly.

"Call me if you need me," Rohan says.

Pushing away, he grabs the rest of his clothes from the living room floor and shoves his boots on at the door before bustling back out into the hall as quickly as he can. It's not until he's safely in the elevator by himself that Rohan drops to a crouch and drags his hands down his face.

His heart won't stop racing.

Sitting side by side at the kitchen counter, silence opens up like a wound. Bram glances over at Pearl, whose body has been scrunched up taut since he kissed Rohan. His face is still pink as he sticks out his hand, palm up.

Taking his phone out of his pocket, Bram passes it over to Pearl and waits as he types something before sliding it back across the counter.

thanks

Bram gets off the stool and scoops Pearl up into his arms. "You need a bath. You stink."

Pearl's arms snap tight around Bram's neck and he kisses Bram's cheek hard and fast.

"I'm stuck at home today," Bram tells him. "So, do you wanna buy some shit online?"

Pearl perks up, a smile creeping back onto his face. He mouths, *porn!*

Bram starts laughing as he nudges his bathroom door open. "We'll see about that."

He isn't sure why it's the obvious thing to do, but Bram keeps Pearl company while he rinses off in the shower. He sits down on the wet tile and runs his hands over Pearl's legs.

"You wanted that, right?" Bram asks.

Pearl turns to him under the water, his gaze skittering away as he smiles and nods.

"Was *he* pushing you away?" Bram cocks his head, studying Pearl's face.

He meets Bram's gaze again, his smile getting wider as he nods. Pearl drops to a crouch beside Bram, cupping his hands around his mouth and getting in close to Bram's ear. It's almost impossible to hear him over the rushing water, so Bram closes his eyes to concentrate as Pearl starts to whisper as quiet as can be, *"little brother."*

Bram catches his gaze with a smirk. "He say you were like a little brother?"

Pearl nods, and Bram is about to make a comment about Rohan picking the most obvious lie, but the look on Pearl's face is entirely too *sweet.*

"Damn," Bram says, his lips curling into a smile. "You really like him."

Pearl's eyes flash, his breath picking up almost like a gasp. Arms looping around Bram's neck, Pearl kisses Bram, deep and slow. Somehow, Bram has no trouble understanding that this is meant as a *thank you*.

Somehow, Bram isn't jealous.

Rohan's back throbs and his face pulses with pain as he wraps up the last of the monthly accounting. All the numbers are starting to blend by the time he closes his laptop and shoves the legal pad away. He fishes in the top drawer of his desk for two painkillers, which he dry swallows, and a lollipop which he holds onto before heading back out to the hallway and calling, "Spear! You still here?"

A young man leans his head out from two doors down, his short coils sticking out to the side. "What's up?"

"You got a minute?" Rohan asks, holding out the lollipop.

"Now I do," he says, eyes zeroing in on the candy.

Spearmint slips out of his dressing room and plucks the candy from Rohan's fingers, immediately unwrapping a blue lollipop which he sticks into his mouth. Rohan closes the door to his office before he takes a seat on his couch. Spearmint sprawls out on the opposite couch, folding his arms under his head.

"Yeah?" Spearmint prompts.

"How's your boyfriend?" Rohan asks.

Spearmint crosses one stockinged leg over the other with a snort and pulls the lollipop out. "He's got me booked tonight actually. What do you need?"

"Could you ask him a question?" Rohan asks. "I'll give you an extra paid day off this month."

"Oooh, you're desperate," Spearmint sings, eyes glinting beneath the blue contacts. "It's no problem, but you gotta tell me why."

Rohan shakes his head. "You don't need to know why."

Spearmint points at him. "You're acting *weird* lately!"

"I am not acting weird, you're all just gossip hounds," Rohan says with a sigh. "I'm trying to do business and keep us safe. That's all."

"Mm. I don't buy it," Spearmint says. "You look like you haven't slept at all, and you're sighing a lot."

"You're getting worked up over a speck of dust," Rohan assures him. "You're not in any danger, I promise."

Eyes narrowed, Spearmint shakes his head. "I think you're up to something. But *yes*, I'll ask my big spender a question for you. What do you want to know?"

Rohan actively holds in another sigh just to keep Spearmint from fixating on it. "I want to know if any of the gangs in the city are under active investigation."

Spearmint's short black brows shoot up his forehead. "Okay."

"Thank you," Rohan says. "I appreciate your cooperation."

"I'm *such* a good friend," Spearmint says, standing back up to tug his tiny black shorts down. "Anything else?"

"Nah, get out of here," Rohan says. "Wait, actually."

Spearmint cocks his head to the side, hand on his hip, eyes wide.

Rohan shakes his head, banishing thoughts of asking to borrow fishnets for Pearl. "Ah, never mind, sorry."

"If you don't want us to think you're acting weird, stop acting so *weird*," Spearmint says with a smirk. A split second later, his eyes light up. "Holy shit, are you fucking another gang boy?"

"No," Rohan snaps, immediately trying to scrub the defensive tone from his voice. "Gossip gives me migraines, please spare me."

Spearmint's eyes remain narrowed, his lips tugging into a smirk as he heads for the door. "You're so up to something."

"I'm up to *running a business*," Rohan shouts as Spearmint slips out of his office.

As Rohan sits there digesting that accusation, his phone vibrates in his pocket and he checks to see a text from Bram. Immediately, his body *lifts* out of the frustration and exhaustion.

Big Boy [9:27 pm]: *Pearl wants to know if you're coming back tonight.*

Rohan [9:28 pm]: *pearls not the one who pays rent so I don't think he gets to make that request*

Big Boy [9:28 pm]: *come play with us*

Rohan [9:29 pm]: *pearl I know that's you*

Big Boy [9:30 pm]: *no it's not pearl. Come plays with us and kiss and watch porrrrnnnn*

Rohan [9:30 pm]: *you guys are watching porn while I do work all day?*

Big Boy [9:31 pm]: *yes its super sexy and we're taking all of our clothes off and we miss your dick*

Rohan calls Bram's number and puts the phone to his ear. He is answered with the sound of breath puffing into the receiver and Bram's muffled voice going, "What are you doing?"

The phone jostles before Bram says, "Sorry. He took the phone."

"Yeah I solved that mystery," Rohan says. "Do you need me to come get him?"

"I mean…" Bram makes a quiet noise. "You don't have to. But he obviously wants you to come here."

Rohan's chest is collapsing in on itself. "And what about the guy who actually pays for the apartment? What does he want?"

Bram sighs over the line, a few seconds of silence while Pearl no doubt silently pleads from somewhere unseen. "You can come if you want. We're not doing anything."

"No porn?" Rohan asks, teasing.

Bram snorts. "No, we are not watching porn. Pearl's even wearing underwear, it's very tame."

"Wow, that I gotta see," Rohan says. "I just need to wrap some things up and I'll be there."

"We're not going anywhere," Bram says.

Rohan hangs up the phone and rubs his eyes, the exhaustion threatening to leave him entirely as he thinks about another night with Pearl and Bram. When he rises back to his feet, he hears his office door click shut and footsteps tear down the hall.

"STOP SPYING ON ME!" Rohan shouts at whoever was listening in.

"I was just closing your door for you!" *Someone* sings on the other side.

All the fight drains out of Rohan's body and he slinks back to his desk to shut everything down for the night, and slip one more painkiller down his throat. At least he's headed somewhere more comfortable than this office.

He can still feel the ghost of Pearl's lips on his, and the taste of Bram's tongue. The fluttering panic slowly brewing in the depths of his stomach can wait just a little longer.

PEARL

When Rohan knocks on the door, Pearl jumps up to let him inside and immediately pulls up his shirt to show off the black, silky underwear—little shorts that hug his hips and barely cover his ass. "Aren't you proud?"

Bram's gut clenches at the sound of Rohan's voice and he sits upright. "You left your weed here, you know?"

Rohan peels off his shoes—dress shoes—and starts slipping off his black suit jacket. "Good, it's been a long fuckin' day."

He makes a beeline for them and deflates onto Bram's couch with a sigh, head tipped back, eyes closed. Pearl opens up the plastic box and fishes out the pen for him, tapping it against his white dress shirt. Rohan smiles and takes it from him.

"There's leftovers in the fridge if you want any," Bram quietly offers.

"Wow, the service here is incredible," Rohan says with a smirk. He takes an impossibly deep breath of smoke before tossing the pen onto the table. "You weren't kidding about tame."

He looks up at the TV quietly playing a show with doctors in lab coats bustling around.

"Pearl put it on," Bram explains. "We were technically looking at, uh, online shops. Well, *Pearl* was looking at things and I was telling him if it was too much money."

Pearl crawls back into Bram's lap, grabbing his phone and opening one of the saved tabs to show Rohan a picture of a strappy, black lingerie set.

"Okay, that wasn't actually on the list," Bram says. "I thought we closed that tab."

"Listen, Pearl, it's cute, but not for you," Rohan says, taking the phone and crawling closer. He leans his back against Pearl's chest, smushing him against Bram as he holds the phone up so all three of them can see him bring up a different lingerie set, all sheer and fluttery.

Pearl makes a sound of interest and enlarges the image.

"You had that in the chamber," Bram mutters.

"You could say I'm an expert," Rohan says. "A few years on stage, a few years *owning* the stage, I think I know a thing or two about how to dress a guy to his strengths. Pearl looks good in baggy clothes because he's slender. He's got the whole sleepy-little-brother thing going for him."

"Wait, wait, wait," Bram jostles Rohan's shoulder. "You were a dancer first?"

Rohan nods. "'Course I was. Probably would have stayed one if our last owner didn't try to sell us to the Eels. I wasn't about to let the Dandelion fall under their purview so I chased him out. Took it over. Made it better. Doesn't mean I still don't know how a pole works."

Bram goes quiet as all of that sinks in. Rohan's already had his fair share of chasing gangs out of his house. No wonder he had no time for Bram.

Rohan used to be a stripper.

Bram's blood begins to heat up as he wonders what kind of shows Rohan would have put on, what kind of outfits he would have worn. How did he dance for people? Was it *just* dancing? No wonder his ass is so nice...

As soon as Bram opens his mouth to try and squeeze out more details, Rohan immediately says, "I don't dance anymore, I'm retired."

"Wasn't even gonna ask about that so it's fine," Bram responds, breathless, his mouth drying out.

Pearl starts laughing, his body shaking between the two of them.

Rohan passes the phone back to Pearl and closes his eyes. "Turn the TV up."

Bram grabs the remote off the coffee table, turning it up just enough for the music and voices to come through clearly, and takes his phone back from Pearl. Smiling, Pearl wraps his arms around Rohan's chest, and then goes slack against Bram, the top of his hair brushing against Bram's chin. Bram bends his leg against the back of the couch, making a little more room for Rohan, and sets his other foot on the floor, letting the weight of both these boys settle against him.

It's more comfortable than he expected, two bodies sleeping on top of his. Before he knows it, Bram's eyes are sliding shut, lulled by the soft chatter of the television and the heat of two people he never expected to be this close to. Pearl always had a pleasant smell to his skin, but Bram can tell now that Pearl has been wearing *Rohan's* cologne this entire time. The scent fills his nose as Bram falls asleep.

He wakes up to a wheezing giggling and sees Pearl and Rohan typing messages to each other on Rohan's phone.

You should go all out. Get bunk beds up there
Will you sleep in the other bunk?
If you can find one long enough for me
There was one that was twice as big on the bottom as it was on the top! Perfect for long big brothers
You're so considerate

Bram clears his throat, trying to shake the sleep off. "Sorry, I didn't mean to pass out so hard."

"Don't sweat it," Rohan says, picking himself up and running his hand through his long hair. "I did too."

"Did you—" Bram is cut off by the sound of his phone ringing, Lee's tone again. He heaves a sigh. "Goddammit. I have to take this."

Rohan eyes him, but Bram doesn't have to time to pick apart the look on Rohan's face as he gets up and heads for his office. Pearl spills into Rohan's lap, and they both watch him walk away with concern brewing in the air.

Bram shuts the door behind him before he answers. "Please, god, good news."

Lee takes a deep breath and Bram sinks into his desk chair feeling like he weighs twice as much.

"I spoke to an old contact," Lee says. "Someone with ties to the Spiders *and* the Boars."

"And?" Bram asks, bracing for another gut punch.

"They have no idea about the break-in at your office. If this person is to be believed, and I do believe them, the Boars definitely weren't responsible for the break-in at our warehouse either. They've been dealing with their own house for the last few weeks, someone hit their product before they even touched ours."

Bram feels like he's suspended in air. "What the fuck does that mean?"

"It means the Boars haven't actually touched us, and the Spiders are busy battening down the hatches," Lee says. "Boars were willing to take credit for our first incident because it made them look more powerful than they are while they're trying cover up a leak, but that's all it was. Taking credit. If I'm being honest, I had a hard enough time believing that sloppy work was theirs anyway, but I told myself it must have been a new recruit or a hazing situation."

"So what are the Spiders doing?" Bram asks.

"Nothing. There hasn't been a peep out of them for weeks. And we both know the Eels would never bother with scrambling security footage. If they fuck with you, they want you to know."

Bram's stomach drops. "Fuck, are we being *investigated?*"

"We can't rule out the possibility," Lee says.

Bram's vision blurs as he sits there, his heart pounding like a hammer.

"Sonuvabitch. Fuck." Bram fights to keep his voice low.

"Cops might be taking the change of leadership as a chance to get a knife in," Lee says. "I've already sent Foley to check for wires or bugs in the east warehouse. It's the next logical place for a break-in."

"Do we have any favors left at ORPD?" Bram asks.

Lee's silence is like a slap across the face.

"I thought we had an in with the chief?" Bram hisses, desperate.

With a sigh, Lee explains, "The last police chief knew the former Mr. Stoker, but when he passed away, he took all our goodwill with him. The only people we know are too low-level to have any knowledge of operations this...delicate."

"Fuck me, we have to go back over all our buildings," Bram says. "Check for any bugs, any loose ends. Start fucking interviewing all our guys. How fast can we move product at this point? Do we have backup locations?"

"Without drawing attention, it's going to be a few weeks," Lee says. "And if they're already watching us, we have to be *more* careful."

"*Fuck.*" Bram lets himself curse with as much venom as he can get out of his system without raising his voice. "No raids. Call it off. We can't make moves or take swings if the cops have their eye on us."

"I'm sorry, Boss," Lee says at the same time that the door to Bram's office bursts open.

Bram turns all his anger at Rohan as he stalks across the office and slams his hands down on Bram's desk.

"Don't just fucking barge in here!" Bram snaps.

"Boss?" Lee's voice twists in his ear.

"You're not being investigated," Rohan rushes to say.

Bram's back straightens, disbelief rooted through him as he glares at Rohan, who glares back at him with those pretty eyes.

"I'll call you back in five minutes," Bram says into the phone, then hangs up. He tries to muster up every ounce of his intimidation to direct at Rohan like the barrel of a gun. "What the fuck are you talking about?"

Rohan lets his breath out, his shoulders sagging. "I *happen* to have a connection to ORPD. I *happened* to inquire about the city gangs recently. My contact got back to me while you were asleep. I can confirm that the Vampires aren't being targeted by the cops right now, so if someone's giving you trouble, it's not an official order."

Bram exhales slowly, trying to process this wealth of information but he's still choking on something worse.

"You went asking about us?" His voice comes out way too quiet.

Rohan stands up to his full height and pushes his fingers through his hair. "*Yes*, I asked about you. I don't use my goodwill very often, alright?"

Bram's heart is still pounding, his stomach still dropping, but his feet are slowly coming back to solid ground. "You trying to get dirt on me? Keep yourself safe?"

Something hot and piercing flashes through Rohan's eyes, and he rounds Bram's desk to grab him by the front of his shirt—a habit he seems to be developing just for Bram.

"I am *trying* to help you, you dipshit," Rohan seethes. "I can't ask this person for favors whenever I want, it's a pretty delicate resource so *please.*" His voice drops down to a plaintive whisper that cuts straight through Bram's chest. "Let me give you some good news, asshole."

He holds Bram's gaze, his anger cooling like molten metal, all the angles of his face slowly softening into something entirely new.

"I thought you didn't want to get invol—" Bram doesn't get to finish his half-hearted interrogation when Rohan kisses him again.

It may just be to shut him up, but Rohan kisses Bram like he tastes good. Bram's body flushes with heat, melting even faster with an appreciative kiss. He skims his fingers over Rohan's face, his promise to call Lee burning away when he kisses Rohan back, wanting to know how bad this can get.

Rohan crawls onto the chair with Bram, his thighs settling with a pleasing heft astride Bram's hips. Bram slips his fingers into Rohan's long hair, and he forgets that told himself he would never be alone with Rohan like this. Shivering at the needy way Rohan coaxes Bram's tongue into his mouth, Bram traces down the length of Rohan's spine, relishing the long fingers seared to Bram's face.

When Bram grips Rohan's waist, he feels Rohan's hips roll forward, the heated bulge of his cock getting thicker between them. Thinking less and less about whatever boundaries he once set for himself, Bram lets out a low, rumbling moan. He slides his hands down over the taut fabric of Rohan's suit pants, gripping the swell of Rohan's ass to pull them closer so Bram can rub his dick against Rohan's, surprised at how good it feels with just a little friction.

At the sound of a wooden *thunk*, they both violently startle away, turning to see Pearl pulling himself up onto Bram's desk.

"Sorry!" Bram pants.

Pearl sits on his knees, his face bright pink, and his hand cupped over his crotch. He rubs himself through his new underwear, lids low, lips parted.

"I don't think he's angry," Rohan whispers.

Bram lets his breath out, relief replacing the panicked beating of his heart.

Rohan runs his finger down Bram's cheek, gripping Bram's jaw to tip his head back. "Come on. We owe Pearl a meal."

Bram feels his body leaning into Rohan's, drawn toward the promise of more pleasure and that shark-tooth smile, but when he puts his hand on his desk, Bram feels his phone and lets out a breathless sigh.

"I just need to update Lee, i-it'll be two seconds."

Rohan slides out of Bram's chair, rising to his feet to pull Pearl closer. "Then we'll get started without you."

Bram is already pressing Lee's name on his contact list when Rohan kisses Pearl. The flash of Rohan's tongue filling Pearl's mouth is all Bram can see when Lee answers on the first ring.

"Boss?"

Bram's mouth is watering as Pearl gives a hushed gasp. "Uh."

Rohan tugs on the band of Pearl's underwear, and Pearl scrambles across the desk, sitting on the edge so Rohan can peel his underwear off his legs. With a pointed stare, Rohan tosses them into Bram's lap.

"Boss, are you okay?" Lee asks, his voice shifting into a new, frantic pace.

"Yes, yes," Bram rushes to remember what the fuck he was doing while Pearl starts undoing Rohan's pants. His fingers bunch around Pearl's silky underwear. "No cops."

"Sorry?"

Rohan is already hard when Pearl shoves his clothes down, freeing his cock from inside his suit pants. He got that hard just from kissing Bram?

"Fuckin' no cops, *no cops*, we're not being investigated," Bram forces the words up his throat like pebbles, his sweatpants tenting.

"How certain are you?" Lee asks, quick and serious.

Pearl slinks down to lay on the edge of Bram's desk, his bare legs splayed out, pussy already wet as Rohan rubs his cock against Pearl's slit to tease him. Pearl wheezes with delight, his feet arching while Rohan starts pushing into his dripping cunt, inches of hard skin swallowed up by Pearl's endless hunger.

"Very very certain," Bram says, his voice hardening. He wants to touch, to be part of this. "I had a favor I forgot about. It's trustworthy information."

"So that means some outsider is trying to get at us," Lee says.

Rohan's gaze is heavy with lust when he looks at Bram again. In his white button-up and thin black tie, suit pants still clinging to his ass, dick buried to the hilt in the prettiest boy in the world, Rohan looks every bit the boss that Bram used to imagine being before he ever got here. Pearl's hips jump off the desk, his fingers curled around the edge, and Bram has never wanted to bite someone's thighs more than he does at that moment. He barely knows which of the two of them he wants to sink his teeth into more—the slight squish of Pearl's soft body, or the meat of Rohan's muscled thighs and ass.

Bram's hand has a mind of its own as he reaches toward them. Rohan goes still, despite Pearl's desperate, hushed whining, and lets Bram get in close enough to set his finger against Rohan's pulsing cock right where it disappears inside Pearl. Bram is slowly going deaf to everything around him as he nudges his finger past the rim of Pearl's hole, sliding in against Rohan's overheated cock. It's so much easier than he expects it to be, like Pearl's body is automatically stretching to accommodate whatever they put inside him.

"Any leads on who's trying to mess with you?" Lee prompts.

"No fucking clue," Bram whispers, fear skittering down his arms as he reminds himself no one else can see them. All he wants to know is how deeply he can finger Pearl around Rohan's cock. He presses in further, rewarded with a hissing moan from Pearl and Rohan grabbing his shoulder in a vice grip. Rohan's tongue darts out over his lip and he gives a tiny pitch of his hips, squeezing Bram's finger against Pearl's walls.

"Well I'd rather some random outsider than the cops or the Eels on us," Lee admits.

"Yeah, this is definitely an improvement," Bram agrees while he watches Rohan take a heaving breath.

"I gotta go, Lee," Bram says. "Anything else?"

"Ah, no, sorry if I interrupted your evening," Lee says.

"It's fine, we'll talk later," Bram rushes to says, too many years of good manners driven through his brain to let the conversation go without a proper goodbye.

"Yes, sir," Lee says, sounding even more relieved than Bram.

Finally, Bram hangs up the phone and jumps to his feet. "Alright, alright, don't fucking torture me like that."

"I get it now," Rohan says, voice electric while he pulls his dick out, wet with Pearl's slick, his face steeping red. "Feels pretty good in there."

Bram presses in closer, taking his finger out of Pearl to grab the front of his sweatpants. "I'm gonna die if I don't put my dick in something, can we *please* go back upstairs?"

Rohan gives a laugh, and Bram feels it falling over him like snow.

"Yeah, let's get you up there before you cream your pants."

Scooping Pearl up into his arms, Bram makes a beeline for the stairs up to the loft, Rohan hot on his heels, practically herding him back into bed. The freshly laundered sheets fill the air with the scent of detergent as Bram tosses Pearl into bed, appreciating the way Pearl wears his muscle shirt like a dress. He smiles up at Bram, chest fluttering with his panting breaths, and he spreads his legs again.

"You are so fucking greedy," Rohan says, sinking down next to Pearl to pull his face toward Rohan's.

Watching them kiss shouldn't be so hot, but Bram's blood boils as Pearl makes a soft sound and wraps his arms around Rohan's neck. His thighs twitch further apart, and Bram's dick fights against his briefs. He shucks his pants down, kneeling on the bed to admire the way Pearl clings to Rohan, Rohan's long body curled around Pearl's like a snake.

"Let him take his clothes off," Bram says, placing his hand on Pearl's stomach.

Rohan breaks their kiss, and both of them look at Bram like they're drunk, eyes wide, black, and hungry.

"I like the way he looks in your shirt," Rohan says, voice burned down to ash. He nudges the wide hem of the open sleeve of Bram's shirt further over Pearl's chest, exposing his nipple.

Bram tears his own shirt off. "Yeah, okay, I do too."

When Rohan's gaze drags across Bram's body, Bram realizes he's the only one who's naked and his skin simmers.

"Damn, you're both eager," Rohan says.

Bram swallows, his heart struggling in his chest. "You worked me up."

"Oh, so it's *my* fault you're dripping all over yourself?" Rohan asks, his finger slowly teasing at Pearl's nipple.

Pearl writhes on the bed, his hand reaching out to paw at Bram's bare thigh. He grips the muscle, his eyelids fluttering when Rohan tweaks his nipple.

"Both of you," Bram accuses, his cock at full attention. "Driving me fucking crazy."

"Get down here," Rohan says. "Play with him while I take my clothes off."

Bram leans over Pearl, more than ready to lose himself inside this needy boy, but he pauses a moment, face heating up again.

As Rohan starts unbuttoning his white shirt, Bram mutters, "You look good."

Rohan pauses, and Pearl's mouth begins to curl into a smile.

"Sorry?" Rohan asks, and he sounds genuinely confused.

Bram grimaces, shoulders rising, face burning. He shuts his eyes and blurts out, "You look good in the suit. I'm not gonna say it again."

To drive his point home, he lays on top of Pearl and kisses him, tasting where Rohan's tongue had just been. He loves the way Pearl snaps to him, legs and arms seeking out the width of his torso. Neither Pearl nor Rohan are shy about touching him, and Bram never realized how badly he wanted that until the both of them were twined around his body, wanting him.

Pearl presses into Bram, coaxing him backward so Pearl can straddle Bram's stomach and lay his hands on Bram's chest. Bram slides his hands up Pearl's flank, catching Pearl's nipples on his thumbs. Pearl lays his palms on Bram's in turn, rubbing the beads of nerves into hard buttons. It feels like Pearl is changing his body into something new, something more reactive, and Bram doesn't mind at all.

Behind Pearl, Rohan gets on his knees, sliding up closer to take Pearl's waist. Bram is sure these two boys are going to give him a heart attack. It makes him ache to see Rohan lift Pearl's ass up to slide his cock between Pearl's thighs until Bram can see the flushed head underneath Pearl's clit.

"We could probably do it just like this," Rohan says, voice low.

Pearl is already nodding, drunk as ever. He leans his hands on Bram and spreads his knees wider, rubbing against Rohan's cock.

"Slow down," Rohan says with a laugh. "Listen, we should probably get some condoms, huh?"

Immediately, Pearl starts shaking his head frantically, mouthing *no, no no!*

"He, uh, doesn't like condoms," Bram explains. "I tried before but he said it's not an issue."

Rohan's brows pinch and he tilts Pearl's face toward his. "Can't get pregnant?"

Pearl shakes his head again and makes a big X with his hands, putting it over his hips.

With a glare right at Bram, Rohan says, "You better be clean."

"I am!" Bram snaps, sweat prickling down his thighs.

Pearl reaches down to touch Bram's and Rohan's cocks beneath him, trying to hurry them along.

"Okay, okay, okay." Bram takes Pearl's hips, his hands just beneath Rohan's to lift Pearl a little higher.

"Alright, let's see how big you are," Rohan purrs.

Once again, Rohan takes Bram's dick in his hand, guiding him against the mouth of Pearl's cunt, but this time, his own cock presses in beside Bram's, and he grips the two of them tight, squishing the glans together.

"*Fuck*," Bram whispers, answering his own question with a hissing breath. *Yes it feels good to be pressed up against someone else's cock.*

Even Rohan looks a little wild as he shoves them both up against Pearl's cunt, the slick from Pearl's body smearing over their skin. Pearl's mouth peels open, his wheezing moans getting louder and more insistent. He reaches behind him to grab Rohan's waist, trying to keep his thighs as far apart as he can get them, a tremor shivering through his legs. For a second, Bram thinks it's going to be too much.

The moment their cocks slip inside the impossibly tight grip of Pearl's cunt, Bram lets out a choked moan, Pearl's legs jump, and Rohan hunches forward, his eyes going hazy.

"*Ookay, fuck*," Rohan breathes, pushing Pearl forward with him as he leans toward Bram. He sinks down lower, his knees spread wide on the sheets, so Bram bends his legs up to make room for him to get even closer.

Pearl looks like he's rapidly forgetting how to be a person, his eyes completely unfocused, tongue snaking out of his mouth. He leans on his hands over top of Bram and pushes back onto their joined cocks, taking them even deeper without a hint of hesitation. His entire chest is flushed pink, a sheen of sweat making him look iridescent.

When Rohan leans across Pearl, his hair hanging down to one side, he looks right at Bram. Pearl clenches down on them both, his chest stippled with goosebumps, black eyes wide enough to swallow them both up.

"Keep going," Pearl says, as though his own intense pleasure has somehow condensed into a boyish voice.

Rohan jerks his hips immediately, and Pearl lets out a moan as he thrusts in deeper. The sound is pretty and sweet, a youthful voice but strong too—*Pearl's* voice, drenched in syrupy satisfaction.

Bram's thoughts scramble, his focus steadily drilling away as Rohan's cock slides up against his, cased in the sheath of Pearl's cunt. When Pearl's back arches, Rohan tries to adjust his legs, and Bram mindlessly reaches out. He isn't thinking about anything useful, he just needs to do something. He grabs Rohan's ass and feels his own cock surge at the frantic movement traveling up through his body from so many different points of contact, and the deliriously pleasing feel of Rohan's flesh gripped tight in his fingers.

It looks and *feels* like Rohan is fucking them both, and Bram's cock twitches, threatening to come way too soon again.

"*Oh!*" Pearl's voice hitches, and he melts on top of Bram, arms cinching around his shoulders, hips pushing into Rohan's thrusts. "*Don't stop.*"

In the back of Bram's mind, he thinks that maybe he should feel some type of way about how Rohan is always the one on top of Pearl and him. Some old impulse stirs under his skin, whispering that Bram should be the one fucking these two, making them feel good, proving his strength in some way. He's definitely not supposed to be the first one to co—

"*Ahh, fuck,*" Bram digs his fingers into Rohan's ass, his hips jolting at the building of sparks from Rohan's cock sliding against his, the tangy scent of sweat and cum filling the air.

Pearl gasps, and Bram unwinds, coming inside Pearl with volcanic heat, a wave of delirious numbness rolling through his muscles.

"You—*hah*—*need some fucking work,*" Rohan pants, still drilling into Peal.

Bram's eyes roll back as he spills every last drop he has all over Rohan while he fucks the mess deeper inside of Pearl.

For all his talk, Rohan doesn't take much longer. As Bram softens and slips out of Pearl's cunt, Rohan gets even lower, his chest sandwiching Pearl against Bram. Bram's stomach clenches as he expects another kiss, holding his breath while Rohan gets closer and closer. He barely realizes his neck is straining toward it, because he wants it. Rohan's angular face looks even more handsome when he's on the verge of giving in, all his cool confidence draining away.

Bram can't stand to wait for him, grabbing the back of Rohan's head to pull him into a kiss. Pearl gives a delighted yelp as Rohan starts coming, hands snapping to Bram's head. His tongue spears into Bram's mouth as he wrings out the last of his orgasm, warm cum spilling out of Pearl and onto Bram's hips.

Rohan pulls away, panting hard, staring at Bram like he expects something.

Bram stares back, dumbstruck and slack-jawed. "Can't believe that worked."

Rohan's mouth splits into a grin, and he gives a breathy laugh. His next kiss is softer, almost like an apology that he laves into Bram's mouth before swiftly picking his head up and shimmying down to check on Pearl.

"You alive down there?" Rohan asks.

Pearl takes a gasping breath, pawing at Bram's sides, but he seems to lack the strength to pick himself up. "*Hnn, good...*"

His voice is already going scratchy and hoarse, rapidly dwindling back to a muted whisper.

"Hey." Bram wraps his arms around Pearl, rolling onto his side to lay Pearl down on the bed. "You got what you wanted."

Pearl's mouth is fixed in a smile, his eyes barely opened, like a newborn kitten. He touches Bram's face, his fingers warm and soft.

"Can...have more?" he asks like he's half drunk.

Bram and Rohan start laughing.

"I think you need a break," Rohan says, laying behind Bram and peering over his shoulder.

Pearl shakes his head, yet more wheezing rattling out of him as he tries to speak. "*-oo good.*"

Pearl grabs Bram's face to kiss him, his lips sloppy and needy. Even when he's practically drunk, Bram can't stop from returning the kiss, holding Pearl's head up so he doesn't have to work. Rohan's hands press against his back, and Bram shivers as long fingers trail down his hip, another mouth pressing into his shoulder while he kisses Pearl.

It's too easy to keep going. He doesn't really mean to, but when Rohan slips a hand around Bram's chest to feel up his nipple, Bram automatically plunges his tongue into Pearl's mouth, and then Pearl moans, his jellied legs spreading wide again.

"You're *both* greedy," Rohan accuses in a heated whisper at the back of Bram's neck.

Bram doesn't even need to fuck. It feels incredible just to kiss Pearl while Rohan feels him up. He chalks it up to the good news that Rohan gave him, and the ego boost of two beautiful people in his bed. Eventually, Rohan nips Bram's ear.

"Look, look, look at him."

Bram breaks the kiss to ask what Rohan is talking about, but he sees it right away.

Pearl really is shining. His head lolls back onto the bed, eyes closed, lips parted, legs spread. It isn't just sweat. His skin seems to catch the light, rippling across his body like water.

"Holy shit," Bram mumbles.

"It's never been this bright before," Rohan whispers.

"You've seen him do this?" Bram asks.

"Sometimes, yeah," Rohan says. "After I close up the club, sometimes I'll find him passed out on my couch looking like this..."

The two of them go silent as they watch the strange and hypnotic light show just for them.

"Is he okay?" Bram asks quietly.

"Think so," Rohan answers.

Pearl gives a soft moan, rubbing his face against Bram's chest.

"Seems okay at least," Bram says with a laugh.

Rohan reaches around Bram to touch Pearl's cheek. "You know, he really does look like an angel."

Bram lets his breath out in a hushed laugh. "I was gonna say he looks like a pearl."

"Guess we're both right," Rohan says, his voice swinging lower. "We should let him rest. He can barely pick his head up."

"Yeah...let me put him on the pillow at least."

Bram gently picks Pearl back up in his arms, and Rohan pulls down the sheets for Bram to put him in bed properly. Pearl gives another satisfied sigh and deflates into the mattress.

When Bram looks back at Rohan, Rohan's mouth pulls into a smile. "You're still hard."

Bram inches away. "It's hard to stop with him."

With a smirk, Rohan takes one of Pearl's thighs in his hand and parts his legs. "Wanna see something else weird?"

Frowning, entirely too curious, Bram inches down to join Rohan between Pearl's legs.

"We didn't touch his ass tonight, right? Look." Rohan touches a finger to Pearl's ass, drawing out another hushed moan from Pearl's throat. It takes nothing for Rohan to slip his finger all the way to the hilt, and when he pulls his finger back out, the skin is slick from his palm to his nail. "I noticed it the other night. He's fuckin' pre-lubed."

"What the fuck?" Bram touches Rohan's finger, the unmistakable slick feeling of cum slipping over his skin.

"Wanna try?" Rohan asks, holding Pearl's leg aside.

Bram only hesitates a second before he presses his own finger against Pearl's ass. It's slick and warm, beating with his rabbit pulse as Bram slowly pushes past his rim. Rohan reaches down to join him, gliding his middle finger in beside Bram's.

Pearl gives an ineffectual, sleepy wheeze of pleasure, his thighs twitching.

"So fucking cute," Bram mutters.

"He's beautiful," Rohan says, his face right next to Bram's.

A slight tilt of Bram's head and his mouth is touching Rohan's freckled cheek. "He's really too good for us."

"I know," Rohan responds, turning toward Bram, his eyes full of embers as they slip their fingers out of Pearl, their faces close enough to kiss. "You want more?"

Bram's breath instantly shortens, heart beating faster, their fingers still tangled together, sticky with fluid. "Feels weird without Pearl."

Rohan pushes closer, his forehead touching Bram's. "He wants us to get along, remember?"

Bram can see Rohan's hard too, fine red hairs wicked around the base of his thickened cock. "You don't think he'd be jealous? That he wasn't part of everything?"

Bram already knows the answer, but he still needs to give the excuse to soothe the panic lighting up his brain as Rohan pushes a hand to his chest, forcing Bram back to the sheets.

"Stop talking," Rohan instructs, draping himself on top of Bram to kiss him again.

Bram instantly gives in, grabbing at Rohan's back to keep him close. Their legs seem to effortlessly tangle together, and Bram feels like he's been punched in the gut. It *thrills* him—wrapped up with someone else like he's having his first make-out session in his childhood bedroom, hot and desperate, half-clueless but determined to make it work. His breath shudders and his cock throbs as all his jumpiness turns to an electric current.

Rohan pulls away to say in a breath, "Tell me you have lube."

Bram's thighs clench, his stomach dropping like a roller coaster. "Sorry, no."

"Figures," Rohan sighs. "Guess we'll do it the old fashioned way."

Bram knows he's starting to have a reaction to that husky tone of voice Rohan uses when he's turned on.

"The fuck does that mean?" Bram asks in a hush.

Rohan pulls Bram toward him, getting them both on their sides so he can reach between them and hold their cocks together in his hand. Bram shudders at the certainty of Rohan's grip, his balls tightening in an instant.

"*Fuck me*," Bram breathes, mesmerized by the sight of their flushed cocks pressed into the tunnel of Rohan's fist.

"I would, but you don't *have lube*," Rohan whispers, his thumb pulling at their slits.

Fluid wells up under his touch, and Bram's chest shudders with a gasp.

"I didn't say you could fuck *me*," Bram hisses back, looping his arm around Rohan's neck.

"What if Pearl asks you to do it?" Rohan asks, his fingers getting wetter as Bram's cock weeps onto his hand. "Would you let me fuck you if it was for him?"

Bram tries to sound firm. The increasingly slick glide of Rohan's hand against his dick, pulsing alongside Rohan's just like they were inside of Pearl, steadily takes his confidence apart.

"F-Fucking...hasn't happened so it doesn't matter."

Bram presses his chest against Rohan's, his nipples lighting up as they drag against Rohan's skin.

"What if Pearl says I have to fuck you, what then?" Bram asks.

With the first good pump of Rohan's hand over both their dicks, Bram immediately groans in the back of his throat like an animal.

"Guess you'll have to fuck your second boy then," Rohan answers him in a whisper, his hand squeezing tighter around their skin. "What then, vampire?"

Bram wants to come so badly it hurts. He wants Rohan to come, and he wants to feel it on his skin. He wants Rohan to moan into him the way Pearl does when they fuck. *He wants to make Rohan come until he's limp and useless like Pearl.*

Of course, before he can make it happen, Bram starts panting like a dog. He pushes his hips into Rohan's hand, noises spilling out of him, slowly getting louder as Rohan fucks his tongue into Bram's mouth. There's no hope for him with these boys. He wants them both so badly, nothing else seems to matter.

Bram comes on Rohan's hand and stomach, and he immediately cinches his fingers around Rohan's cock to finish him off with the extra mess of his own slick. Rohan's breath *gasps* out of him, and he bites Bram's bottom lip before a streak of warm fluid paints Bram's chest.

They lay there panting at each other for a long moment of silence, until Bram feels thin arms slipping around his neck. Pearl shuffles up against his back, laying his head on top of Bram's cheek. When he speaks, it sounds like he's forcing his voice up through several layers of fabric.

"So handsome..."

Rohan kisses Pearl first, and the sound of it makes Bram shiver. Rohan kisses Bram after, and Bram knows he's well and truly fucked.

In the morning, Bram insists on making breakfast himself. His own cooking tastes twice as good when Rohan gives him a surprised expression on the first bite, and then cleans his plate.

"Alright, alright, you're not useless," Rohan says.

"Thank you," Bram says. "Listen, I have to go to the office. Both of you are welcome to stay if you want."

"I have to work too," Rohan says, turning to Pearl. "We can't all be spoiled princes."

Pearl grins at him, and leans onto the arm of Rohan's chair to lick a spot of salsa off his mouth.

"Well, uh, I guess we can just...talk later..." As soon as he says it, Bram clocks his own awkwardness and shrinks in on himself.

Rohan starts laughing. "Do you want my number or what?"

Face burning, Bram pulls his phone out, answering quietly, "Yeah."

They swap numbers while Pearl watches, eyes practically luminescent.

"I need a shower," Bram says.

"Yeah, me too," Rohan says, rubbing his eyes.

Pearl raises his hand, and neither of them seem to have any problem understanding his intent. Bram doesn't mean to take an hour-long shower, but things go a lot slower with three of them pressed in under the water.

By the time Bram meets up with Lee, he can still feel the faint echo of pleasure ringing beneath his skin along with the memory of their moans reverberating off the tile. It's all too easy to let things spiral out of control with those two, especially when Pearl puts his mouth to work.

Lee sits across from Bram in the empty office and holds out a pack of cigarettes.

"Nah, thank you," Bram waves the offer away and Lee gives the hint of a smile before putting them away. "I can't think of a goddamn soul who could be doing this."

Lee crosses one lean leg over the other and puts his glasses on. "I've been digging all night and I have a list of connections and scenarios to go over."

"This is gonna take a while, isn't it?" Bram asks.

Lee flips open his tablet, bringing up hand-scrawled notes. "I've already ordered coffee."

"Thank christ," Bram sighs. "Let's get to it."

It's nearly seven in the evening by the time Bram is finished going over every possible loose end from the Vampires, the Eels, and anyone else who could be trying to fuck them over. Bram's head is pounding as he parks in the garage and heads into the elevator. His entire body is already counting the seconds until he can lay down in bed. Maybe Pearl will curl up with him.

With a sigh, Bram acknowledges that he wants Rohan to come back as well. He wants them both in his bed, one boy pressed to his chest, one draped over his back. The image doesn't feel complete without Pearl *and* Rohan.

Bram drags himself to the door of his apartment, shuffling inside and kicking his shoes off, trying to make some kind of peace with the fact that all he can think about is Rohan's dick sliding up against his own inside of Pearl, even just in their hands. He is waiting for the sound of Pearl's bare feet thumping over hardwood, but no one comes to greet him as he pulls his jacket off. Rounding the corner into the hallway that bridges his bedroom and the kitchen, Bram stops dead in his tracks.

Chel is sitting at the counter, her black bag on the chair beside her, hair a vibrant new shade of rosy pink, trailing down her back in thick waves. She stares at him like he's late for an appointment and she knew he would be, round eyes piercing through him.

Chelsea "Chel" Richardson: heiress and daughter of a wealthy politician, and Bram Stoker's ex-girlfriend.

"What the *fuck* are you doing here?" Bram asks, anger tearing through his sternum.

"Visiting my boyfriend?" Her voice is full of forced confusion. "You haven't texted or called in over a month."

Bram keeps his distance from her, eyes narrowed. "You made a copy of my fucking key without telling me."

She shrugs. "It's normal to make copies."

"Not without my permission, Chel, what is wrong with you?" Bram snaps.

"What's wrong with *you?*" Chel fires back, bracelets jingling as she gestures at him. "Did you delete my number or something? I've been trying to reach you."

"I didn't just delete it, Chel, I blocked your number because *you broke up with me.*" Bram enunciates every last word, barely able to keep himself from shouting.

Chel's brows pinch together. "I did not break up with you."

Bram's face twitches, and his voice explodes out of him, "*You fucked my lieutenant in my own bed!* What the hell were you doing if not breaking up with me?"

"I was *trying* to make you *jealous!*" Chel roars back, matching his enunciation. "You were so busy all the time, we never did anything fun anymore! As soon as you got promoted, all you did was work."

"Congratu-fucking-lations, Chel, your plan worked," Bram says, his anger quickly burning out into exhaustion. "I put a man in the fucking hospital for you, and now we're done. Get the fuck out of my house. You can keep the copied key, I'll be changing the locks the second you're out the door."

Chel swallows, staring at Bram with wide-eyed, childish fixation. She crosses her arms over her chest.

"You found someone else, didn't you?" she asks, eyes narrowed. "I saw the underwear in your office."

"Yes," Bram tells her, finally calming down at the memory of his *very* good night. "I've been doing a lot better since you screwed me over, so thanks for that. Now get. The fuck. Out."

He points at the door, and the second his arm extends into a straight line, two hands snap down around it, twisting Bram's arm behind his back with a painful tightness. Whoever it is spins Bram to the right, and slams his face into the wall.

A voice Bram has never heard before breathes in his ear. "You stole something from me. I'd like it back."

Pain zips down his face, one of his eyes forced shut against the wall, but Bram can still see Chel sitting at the kitchen counter, her hand in front of her mouth, holding her breath. This guy must have been hiding in the bedroom, waiting for Bram to do something stupid.

"Do you know who this is?" Bram shouts at her, understanding coalescing in a moment.

His attacker's grip is iron-tight.

"Where is Shining Star?" the man asks, his voice like the rumble of an ancient engine.

"I don't know what the fuck you're talking about." Bram grits his teeth as the man forces his arm even closer toward a dislocation.

"I can smell him here," the man states. "I can smell him on your skin. You have my Shining Star somewhere, no doubt defiling him. Return him to me now, and I will not disembowel you."

"You said you weren't gonna kill him!" Chel shouts.

"Thank you for your aid, human," the attacker says. "Leave now, or I make no promises about your safety."

Human? Bram's mind screeches to a halt.

"Uhm..." Chel sits there, doing fearful calculations as she clutches her bag to her chest.

Something sharp slides underneath Bram's shirt, no doubt the edge of a knife pressed to the soft skin of his belly.

"I'll ask again," his attacker drags the sharp object across Bram's stomach. "Where have you hidden my Shining Star?"

He must be talking about Pearl. Bram realizes in the pit of his stomach that he's been ignoring the most obvious lead. Pearl must have belonged to a different gang—a fucking bizarre and dangerous one—and was hiding from *them* this whole time.

The sound of Pearl's footsteps *thunk thunk thunking* across the hardwood is the last thing Bram wants to hear. Pearl seems to appear out of thin air beside them, his naked skin melting into view like he's been poured out of the atmosphere to stand in front of them, pulling on Bram's attacker to try and separate them. It's nearly identical to when Bram had Rohan up against the wall of his office, only this time, Bram has no intention of playing nice.

"There you are," the man says. "This human has had you imprisoned so I have come to rescue you."

Pearl starts shaking his head wildly, beating his fists against the guy's massive arm. Something that looks disturbingly similar to a tail made of human flesh slithers around Pearl's naked waist and lifts him off the ground.

"What the *fuck* are you?" Bram asks, his voice thick with fear and anger as he watches Pearl flailing out of the corner of his vision, obviously struggling.

Behind them, Chel is inching her way toward the foyer. Bram shouts at her, "Call Lee!"

"Don't kill each other," she mutters under her breath as she slips down the hall and out of his sight.

When he hears the sound of the front door opening behind him, Bram is about to curse Chel out, but *Rohan's* voice bursts into the room.

"Pearl I got your tex—*what the fuck?*"

"GET PEARL!" Bram shouts, trying to hook his leg around the ankle of this guy.

Before Bram can try and tip him off balance, a fist connects with the back of Bram's head. His vision breaks, black and white flashing into strange colors as he slumps down the wall.

"Whoa!"

He can hear Rohan's voice from behind him, and Bram tries to shake himself out of the shock, scrambling back to his feet to see the biggest fucking man he's ever laid eyes on swinging a knife at Rohan, forcing Rohan back toward the front door just to avoid getting cut. The man's skin is a similar sandy, pale brown as Pearl's, only his body is mottled with large patches of pale pink, almost like the spots of color on a cow's hide. As Chel tries to slip unseen out of the apartment behind them, Rohan jumps backwards directly into her, and both her and Rohan go sprawling across the tiled floor of the outer hallway with a yelp.

"*Chel!*" Bram roars as her arms shoot out and she slams the front door shut behind them.

Pearl silently screams, his face pinched in fury, his mouth torn open as he tries, in vain, to free himself from the tail wrapped firmly around his stomach. Ignoring the roiling nausea in his gut, Bram sprints forward and throws himself onto the guy's back, kneeing him as hard as he can in the ribs. The guy only grunts. Bram tries to thread his arm under the stranger's thick neck to try and choke him, and Bram hears a slightly strained *huff.*

With a sudden *crunch,* the stranger kicks open Bram's front door, breaking it off on the top hinge and forcing it out the wrong direction.

"You are complicit!" their attacker declares, going straight for Rohan. The flash of his knife is like lightning in the distance. Bram braces himself for searing pain, pulling back on the stranger's arm with all his strength to keep the knife from connecting with anyone.

Rohan darts in, slamming into the guy's chest like a quarterback. The stranger lets out a growl, wrenching his arm against Bram's desperate grip. When he can't get his knife hand free, he shoves Rohan away with an open palm, and Rohan goes staggering back into an end table, knocking the decorative vase to the tile with a *crash.*

Bram's grips falters, and he drops off the guy's back just as the knife slices into his thigh, pain zipping down his skin. Burning heat simmers throughout his body as Bram grabs Pearl and tries to pull him back into the apartment. The stranger *with the fucking tail* tries to yank Pearl back to him, dragging Bram a few feet closer.

"Stubborn," the guy growls, his meaty hand clapping around Bram's neck.

Bram stares at the guy's deep, endless black eyes, unwilling to let go of Pearl, who is busy chewing on the thick tail now trying to gag him.

"Remember this, Shining Star. Humans are greedy," the stranger diagnoses, his fingers tightening on Bram's throat. "And full of tricks."

Bram is breathing through a pinhole as the stranger rips open his coat and touches his side as though he expects to find a wound there. Bram's gaze snaps to the man's naked hips, his eyes bugging out as he sees the impossible shape of his body.

Whirling around with Bram and Pearl still held in his grip, the *thing* with a tail and two massive cocks stares Rohan down. "What have you done to me?"

???: name unknown. Species unknown. Intent: to kidnap Pearl.

Panting, Rohan's mouth falls open when he sees it as well. "Fuck me, *two dicks?*"

Bram tries to kick the guy's flank, his socked foot landing with an ineffectual *thump.*

"Do you truly think you are enough for my Shining Star?" the stranger asks, bearing down on Rohan. "Not even three humans are enough to feed him. Give up. He belongs to me."

"Fuck you," Rohan says, his voice thinned down with breathless fear. "He chose us man, I don't know what to tell you."

With a sigh, the stranger drags Pearl and Bram with him, and his fist shoots out to sock Rohan in the stomach. Rohan makes him a horrible sound, slumping onto the floor and clutching his middle.

Anger flickers across the strange creature's face as he watches Rohan sputtering on the ground. He rips Pearl out of Bram's arms, collecting Pearl's struggling body like a feral cat.

"My sweet, why have you allowed yourself to be caged by these pathetic things?"

Pearl looks like he's hissing at this guy. When the tail unwinds from his mouth, Pearl starts silently shouting at him, lips moving a mile a minute, his wheezing breath seething out like steam. The stranger pays no heed to the obvious fury directed at him, and forces Pearl into a kiss.

Pearl's eyes go wide, his torso writhing, legs kicking wildly. Bram has never hated anyone more than he hates this monster with its tail and—*fuck him,* there are two smooth, fleshy horns now protruding from the stranger's hairless skull, the same mottled pink and brown as the rest of his skin.

Bram watches in shock as two petite, membranous wings burst out of Pearl's back, and a thin whip of a tail extends from the base of his spine like a snake. His thrashing feet elongate into an animalistic shape, closer to a rabbit or a cat than a human. Thick claws press out of the skin of his toes which Pearl immediately digs into the side of the monster's torso to break their kiss.

Pearl's chest is at *least* twice as full with two round breasts that swiftly turn rosy red with the rest of his skin as he blushes fiercely. Bram has never seen Pearl as angry as he looks in that moment, his face gone completely scarlet.

"*You fucking dick!*" Pearl shouts, lunging forward to rake his nails across the other guy's face. "*I'll kill you!*"

His captor's lip curls as Pearl connects with his skin. He tries to grab Pearl and pluck him away, but Rohan latches onto his arm and drives his knee up into the guy's two dicks. Instantly, the hand loosens around Bram's throat as the stranger falls to his knee with a gasp, and Bram shoves forward, quickly undoing the black belt from his suit pants.

Wrenching the leather around the monster's throat, Bram places his knee on the guy's back and *yanks,* waiting to hear the sound of a body with no breath choking for air.

"Get away from him," Bram coughs out, his own throat still burning from the near-crushing.

Rohan stumbles back, snatching Pearl around the waist and hauling him out of the way before that tail can snake around him once more.

As the *thing* begins to get desperate, that tail slams hard into Bram's side, nearly knocking him off his feet.

"How do we get him out of here?" Rohan asks.

"We need his chalk!" Pearl shouts, wriggling out of Rohan's arms and dropping to the floor.

Before he can spring toward the monster, the room goes black. Bram's eyes widen, his skin prickling with a rush of heat. Very quickly, the strain of the belt against his hand doesn't feel so important, and Bram drops it to give his aching palms a break.

He blinks, trying to clear this strange fog from his eyes. Where the hell are they? He was just with Pearl and Rohan and they were...

They had a date, that's right. He was so ready to come home to his apartment and have sex with Pearl and Rohan again. He's never wanted anyone the way he wants both of these boys. They've been rattling around his head like candy day in and day out, and Bram knows in the depths of his stomach that he would do anything for either of them.

He remembers where he is. Rohan invited him and Pearl to the club, just the two of them. Bram turns toward a blue stage light illuminating a narrow hall, and he walks toward it, a helpless moth.

"Pearl?" he calls.

A small hand slots into his own and Bram smiles at Pearl, opening his arms for him.

"Come on. I want to carry you."

Pearl blinks up at him, his black eyes wide and glassy and *god he's so fucking cute.* Rohan was right about that little brother look.

"You don't mind?" Pearl asks. He's got two little wings poking out from his back, and a tail coiled like rope around his naked hips. "Even though I'm all weird?"

Bram's breath leaves him in a rush. "You're so fucking pretty, angel. Let me hold you."

Pearl blushes and leaps into Bram's arms, pressing his perfectly round breasts against Bram's chest, his breath huffing out of him. "I'm embarrassed about my boobs, but it always feels so good when you play with them."

"I love your chest," Bram blurts out, his face burning at the confession. "No matter the size."

"I know you do," Pearl says, kissing Bram's cheek. As Bram carries him into the empty floor of the Dandelion, Pearl whispers in his ear. "Sometimes I make them bigger just for you."

"You're so fucking perfect," Bram mutters, approaching the lit-up stage. A lone folding chair faces the raised platform with a long metal pole jutting out from the center. Bram sits down, already getting hard at the thought of what's to come.

"You like Rohan's body too," Pearl whispers, rubbing his chest against Bram's, his tail slithering over Bram's thigh.

"He's beautiful," Bram says, his tongue heavy. It doesn't even occur to him to lie about it anymore.

"You like it when Rohan and I kiss," Pearl says.

"Yeah." Bram nods, running his hands over Pearl's hips, touching the base of that flexible tail. "I want to touch this."

"It feels good," Pearl tells him. "I could put it inside you if you wanted."

Bram's body flushes—a wild thought indeed.

"But you'd rather see something else, wouldn't you?" Pearl asks.

Bram is panting as the curtains part, revealing Rohan posing in nothing but a pair of skin-tight black stockings and a band of black fabric masquerading as shorts. Bram's cock thickens inside his suit pants as Rohan stalks forward, his long legs and his lean torso rooting Bram to the spot.

"He wants you so bad," Pearl whispers. "But he keeps going back and forth on how."

Rohan wears a pair of shiny black heels, his long red hair in a high ponytail that Bram's fingers are already twitching to touch. Some mild music barely scratches at Bram's consciousness, but all his senses are focused on Rohan's body as he drops to sit on the edge of the stage and lifts his leg to rest his heel against Bram's shoulder.

"Thought you didn't dance anymore," Bram says.

"I don't dance for money," Rohan says, the apples of his high cheeks gone red. "But someone's gotta teach the new boys how a pole works."

Bram starts shaking his head. "I want to touch you so bad."

Pearl melts out of Bram's arms *just* at the right time. It's too tempting, Bram has to get up and grip Rohan's legs and press his face to the fine mesh of the stockings. Bram's breath shudders against a perfectly sculpted thigh, the smell of skin and cologne mingling in his nose.

"I should have asked for this years ago," Bram sighs, pressing a kiss to Rohan's inner thigh. "Need to thank Pearl later."

Rohan watches him, his mouth hanging open as he stiffens beneath his tiny shorts. "Sometimes it makes me angry how hot you are."

Bram presses his mouth to the growing shape of Rohan's erection, mouthing at him like he's starving. "It's hot when you're angry."

Rohan slips his hand into Bram's short hair, panting softly. "I like telling you what to do."

Bram moans against Rohan's cock, slipping his fingers into the waist of his shorts. "It's always easier when you do."

He peels the shorts from Rohan's thighs, salivating at his naked dick pressing against the mesh stockings, just a little bit of cum creating a wet spot at the tip. Rohan leans backward, his ponytail pooling on the stage, his shorts dangling from his ankle.

"It's not the only thing I want," Rohan groans the words, pleased and annoyed at his own admission.

Bram sinks down to nuzzle Rohan's cock with his face, deeply breathing in the musk of his body. What else does Rohan want? Pearl said he was *going back and forth on how*, but Bram can only wonder what that really means. It doesn't really matter to him now. Bram is dripping into his briefs as he kisses Rohan's cock through the mesh, not a hint of embarrassment left in him. He only hopes Pearl is enjoying the show as much as Bram is.

"You make me fucking *crazy*," Rohan says, rolling his hips against Bram's face. "I'm not supposed to do this anymore. I'm not supposed to fuck guys like you."

Heart pounding, Bram hooks a single finger in the waistband of the stockings, slowly peeling them down over Rohan's skin so he can lick the thickened base of his cock. He knows what Rohan is saying, that Bram is no good for anyone, least of all someone who clearly wants out of any gang associations. Bram knows it's true, that Rohan *and* Pearl would be better off without Bram anywhere near them, *but...*

"Can't stay away from you," Rohan moans, his thighs spreading further as Bram pulls his cock out from his stockings, licking the drop of cum from his slit.

"*Mmm, where's Pearl?*" Rohan moans. "He wanted to see this."

Bram stops, a hollowness in his chest. "I thought he was here...where is he?"

~~Pearl doesn't want to be with them.~~

They both look around the club, but no one else is there. A shadow rises in their eyes and when Bram looks back at Rohan, he is struck like lightning all over again at how badly he wants to kiss every inch of Rohan's body.

"God, you look so fucking good with your hair up," Bram sighs, dropping his head to kiss Rohan's cock, savoring the burst of salt on his tongue.

They're in bed, in his loft, alone for the night. They decided they wanted a break, just the two of them. Pearl was always ~~getting in the way.~~ They needed a chance to let off some steam.

"Don't just tease me all night," Rohan huffs, his face gone pink.

They're both naked, no pesky clothes in the way, and Bram *knows* he's being too timid. He wraps his hand around Rohan's cock, determined to show that he isn't scared of this. Pearl wouldn't hesitate, why should he? Bram wants it, the taut, pulsing skin in his hand, the fluid dripping over his fingers. A beautiful cock in his mouth.

He catches Rohan's aroused expression, that shark-smile gone heavy with lust, his hair loosening from its perfect tie after all their fooling around. Bram's heart skips a beat when he feels Rohan's cock twitch in his hand.

"Do it," Rohan says, dazed like he's been smoking.

Bram opens his mouth to take him, startling at the taste coating his tongue as he eases Rohan's pretty cock past his lips. It's so much longer than he was ready for, but not so thick he can't fill his mouth. He can suck on the head of Rohan's cock just fine, shivering as bitter salt takes over his senses. Pearl must be losing it, wherever he's watching from.

"*Ooh, god.*" Rohan's breath shakes. "Don't make me come yet. Where's Pearl?"

Something prickles down Bram's spine as the thrill of sucking Rohan's dick gives way to concern. Bram pulls back, staring right at the slit in Rohan's cock.

"He'd want to see this," Bram says.

Rohan pants heavily, picking himself up on his elbows. "Is he mad at us?"

"I don't...think so," Bram says. His gaze is glued to Rohan's cock, needy and flushed and begging for Bram's mouth. ~~He doesn't need Pearl.~~ Bram swallows, and there's cum laced through his saliva. If he fucked Rohan like this, he could watch Rohan come all over himself. Would he still look like a shark with Bram's cock buried in his ass?

"Can I eat you out?" Bram asks, his voice thick and sticky as the desire punches through him. "Maybe we can skip the lube if I just get you wet enough."

Rohan lets out another desperate moan as Bram thumbs over his slit. "Fuck, *fuck*, I want it so bad, what the hell's wrong with me? Did we smoke too much?"

Bram licks his lips as he watches Rohan's body squirm on the sheets of his bed. "Why are you both so damn hot?"

Rohan looks up at him in disbelief. "You gotta wait 'til Pearl's here to say that shit. He wants to see us get along."

Bram smirks. "He wants two dicks in him."

Rohan starts laughing. "He wants *our* dicks in him."

"Where is he?" Bram asks, glancing around the loft.

They both see him there, where he's always been, on hands and knees on the floor beside the bed, watching intently. His eyes instantly brighten when he sees them looking at him, and he licks his lips. He looks like a cat about to pounce—a cat with little wings and a strange, serpentine tail—and the thought of it makes Bram want to grab him and wrestle him to the bed.

"It's okay," Pearl says, voice full of breath like he's running out of air. "I'll just watch."

Bram reaches toward him. "We want you here."

Pearl starts to move forward, then seems to catch himself. "No, I...I think I just want to stay here?"

Rohan groans. "Pearl, come on. I wanted you to—"

Pearl's eyes go wide, some of the color draining from his face.

"Pearl?" Bram asks.

When Pearl speaks again, it's as though his voice has been stripped of all texture. "I want to have sex with Bram and Rohan."

"No, you don't." A gruff voice responds behind Pearl.

When Bram tries to focus on the source of it, his gaze can only settle on Pearl. Something shimmers in the air around him, like heat waves in the middle of the summer.

"I like when Bram and Rohan touch me," Pearl says again in that strange monotone. "They take care of me."

"Stop." The fourth voice is none-too-pleased, and suddenly Pearl's head tilts backwards. "These men are strangers."

"I want to play with them," Pearl says, looking like a doll on strings.

Bram's blood roars, and he grips Rohan's waist, squeezing as he struggles to see what he can't see. Rohan reaches down and grips the back of Bram's head in fear, pulling at his hair just enough for prickles of pain to zip across Bram's scalp.

That two-dicked, horned monster is knelt behind Pearl, his mottled skin bared, completely naked. He has Pearl by the throat, one of his cocks buried in Pearl, the other one stiffly wedged against Pearl's belly.

"Be good and I'll give you both," the giant creature coos in a deep, rumbling voice. He jerks his hips forward, and Pearl's body jumps with the movement, no reaction on his face to the thrust.

Anger explodes through Bram. He and Rohan come back to life at the same moment, lunging forward to extricate Pearl from this stranger. All of his injuries light up like fireworks beneath Bram's skin as he grabs the stranger by his fleshy horns and slams his head back against the metal railing of the loft without a single thought.

"Wait!" Pearl's voice sings out, and Bram glances over to see him wriggle out of Rohan's arms and dive for the monster's dazed body.

"Get away from him!" Bram snarls.

"I need his chalk!" Pearl yells. "Hit him again and go downstairs!"

Bram watches Pearl grab a pouch slung around the guy's wide hips and rip it off his body. As soon as he starts for the stairs with Rohan's hand in his, Bram hauls the guy's giant head back up to give him a second ring against the railing.

With a grunt, the guy goes slack, groaning like the burbling of a volcano.

"Bram! Come down here!" Pearl's voice is like a beacon.

Bram stares at the guy who laid his hands on Pearl, and that old, volatile anger fills his fingers, his chest, his gums. He wants to make this monster regret what he's done. He wants to make it painfully, *lethally* clear that no one gets to touch *his* boys.

"Bram! Let him go!" Rohan pleads with him from below, and the plaintive sound releases Bram's fingers like a lock springing open.

He sprints away and runs down the stairs as fast as he can while the *thing* behind him stirs again.

"My Shining Star, what have they done to you? T-To me?" His voice comes out strained as he hauls himself back to his feet.

As soon as Bram's foot touches the floor, Rohan grabs him and pulls him away while Pearl draws a circle in black chalk around the entirety of the tight spiral staircase, right on the hardwood.

"*I will kill them both!*" the creature's voice booms through the apartment like thunder, and Bram and Rohan both grab at each other as the guy steps onto the first stair, catching himself on the railing like his balance isn't quite there.

"My sweet—" He takes another step, his tail flicking through the air as Pearl jerks his hand to the right, completing the chalk circle.

A burst of incomprehensible blackness shoots up from the outline, engulfing the metal staircase completely. It only lasts a few seconds, but staring at the wall of perfect, wretched, smooth, light-absorbing black instantly gives Bram a headache. He hears a voice in the back of his head for a brief moment whispering words he can't understand, and then the black void vanishes, taking *most* of the monster with it.

A small chunk of mottled pink and brown tail lands on the floor in front of them, blood oozing from the severed end.

"Oh, *fuck.*" Rohan turns away, grabbing his stomach.

Bram slings an arm around his back, and looks over at Pearl. "Is he gone?"

Pearl stands there panting with a thick piece of black chalk in his hand. The chalk drops to the floor, and Pearl wraps his arms around his full chest, his face scrunching up into a mask of distress. His skin has gone ashy, but his eyes are full of emotion again.

"Pearl?"

Bram and Rohan's strained voices layer over each other, concern growing between them. It looks like Pearl might burst into tears, his face swiftly turning bright red, the color leeching across his newly rounded chest and the caps of his shoulders. Bram and Rohan both take a step toward him, and Pearl's thin tail coils tight against his body like a spring.

"*Serves you right, asshole!*" he snarls.

Bram and Rohan look at each other, and back to him.

"Pearl, are you okay?" Rohan asks.

His black eyes pop open, bigger than ever as he frantically glances between Bram and Rohan. "He hurt you both...damnit, I'm so sorry! He hurt you and *he made me ugly again!*" His voice twists in his throat, face still ripped into a furious mask.

Bram's breath leaves him in a relieved sigh. "Jesus, Pearl, we don't give a shit about that. Are you *okay?*"

Pearl holds his own body like he's about to fly apart. His small wings go flat against his back and he whispers, "I'm really sorry."

Rohan takes a moment to kneel down, grimacing through the pain, and puts a hand on Pearl's shoulder. "I'll be honest with you, Pearl, I thought you were just a trans guy with some weird medical condition but it's fine! We'll figure it out. You could have warned us someone was going to try to kidnap you though."

"Uhm, about that." Pearl's tiny little wings twitch, and his head suddenly whips toward the hallway. "Someone's coming up to check your floor and your door is broken! Please don't let them see me!"

He scrambles behind Bram's body, clinging to his naked hips.

"Shit." Bram braces himself on the loft staircase, his mind still in panic mode. "Everybody cover up and meet me outside the building stairs in the hallway. I'll be right behind you. Don't waste time."

Rohan grabs Pearl, and the three of them bolt into Bram's bedroom to jam whatever clothes they can find onto their bodies. Bram grabs a blanket off his bed to wrap around Pearl's wings and tail, and hands the cocoon off to Rohan.

"Go," Bram says, ushering Pearl and Rohan out of the apartment. "I'll be right there."

Rohan looks like he wants to argue, but Bram whispers, "You don't want to deal with the chunk of tail, do you?"

"Right." Rohan takes Pearl in his bundle and rushes into the hall.

Fighting through the aches now howling across his body, Bram forces himself to shove his shoes back on and run, limping, into his kitchen to grab a plastic bag which he shoves the severed tail tip into, as well as the pouch full of black chalk that Pearl grabbed off that thing. As he crosses the hallway outside his apartment, he wonders if Chel is still hiding somewhere, or if she took off running without looking back. A problem for later.

By the time Bram pushes open the door to the stairwell for Rohan and Pearl, he can hear the elevator about to stop on his floor. Rohan stares at him as Bram quietly shuts the door to keep it from echoing. Bram puts his finger to his lips and points down, leading them to the next floor so he can call the elevator without being seen by whoever it is investigating his apartment.

Tucking the blanket safely around Pearl's naked body, Bram whispers, "Am I right to guess that the security footage is probably a little fucked up right now?"

Pearl turns toward him, a miserable look in his eyes. "Yeah."

"Good," Bram says. "We can pretend someone broke into my apartment and get the locks changed without management getting on my ass."

He keeps his hand on Pearl's back as they ride the elevator into the garage. Rohan stands there in a pair of fuzzy pajama pants too short to reach his feet, a muscle tank that doesn't quite meet the edge of his pants, his dress shoes and his silky blue jacket. A woman steps into the elevator with them midway down, and her face lights up when she sees the bundle in Rohan's arms, only a head of fluff visible.

"Aw, someone's shy," she says, eyes wide.

Rohan gives an impressively earnest-sounding laugh, and meets her gaze with a smile while Bram hides behind Rohan's back, angling the bloody plastic bag against his thigh to keep it from sight.

"You know how they get," Rohan says, voice loud enough to cover the exhaustion. "Ran himself raw and then passed right out."

"Aw." She coos at the shapeless lump. "I bet you're glad he's tired!"

"Sure am!" Rohan says, his face a mask of perfectly generic kindness. "I think we're all ready to sleep for the next eighteen hours."

She gives him a conspiratorial little smirk and whispers, "Enjoy these days while you can."

Blissfully, she exits at the ground-level lobby, and the three of them plunge into the parking garage by themselves.

"Fucking kill me," Pearl whispers from inside the blanket.

"No dice," Bram tells him as the doors slide open.

As soon as they exit the elevator, Bram's gaze lands on a black car haphazardly parked between the nearest visitor parking space and the yellow striped loading zone.

"Nice work," Bram says.

Rohan gives a tight smile, fishing in his jacket pocket with one hand for his keys. "Shut up. I was in a rush."

"Let's get the fuck out of here before they notice," Bram says, circling to the passenger side as the car beeps, the locks undoing with a *chunk*.

As soon as they're inside, Rohan and Bram both let out groans of pain. Rohan starts the car, and grips the steering wheel with both hands, his arms locked around Pearl's body, but he doesn't move from there. His breath only comes at half the volume, his lip twitching in pain. Bram sits there, not wanting to force Rohan while he's hurt, but wanting them all as far from this place as he can get them. He glances through the back window, making sure no one else is walking through the lot.

When he looks back, Rohan is in exactly the same position, his eyes staring out the windshield at the cement wall, a thousand miles away.

"Rohan," Bram prompts. "You good?"

"Yeah. What? Yeah I'm good," Rohan says, swallowing. "I'm fine, I'm fine, it's nothing. It's just actually, no, no I'm not fine. Can you drive? It's fine, I just—"

His breath is shortening up and Bram reaches out to touch his bicep. "Yes, I can drive."

"Okay." Rohan nods.

Bram forces himself out of the passenger seat and painfully lumbers over to the driver's side door, opening it up for Rohan.

"Come on."

"Yeah, yeah, yeah," Rohan nods, gripping Pearl to his chest as he swings his legs out of the car one at a time.

"You want me to take Pearl?" Bram asks.

"Yeah—*no*, no, I want him." Rohan corrects, shaking his head.

Bram holds his arms out to steady Rohan as he gets back to his feet with a grimace. It takes Rohan a few seconds to catch his breath and Bram shadows him the entire time it takes Rohan to get into the passenger seat.

When they're both seated again, Bram looks over at Rohan's sickly face, his lips gone pale. Pearl slips his hands around Rohan's cheeks, the blanket stuck on his wings.

"Rohan?"

Rohan blinks like he's trying to get something out of his eyes, and hugs Pearl tight to his chest. "Let's go to my place."

"Sure," Bram nods. "Just give me the address."

Rohan shoves his phone into the magnetic grip and opens up the map, selecting the button for *home*. Bram doesn't ask questions, just drives them out of there as a suffocating silence descends. Pearl kisses Rohan's cheek, nuzzling against him.

"Thank you for helping me," he murmurs.

Rohan's leg bounces up and down on the floor of the car as he says, "No one gets to do that to my boys."

Bram reaches across the gear shift and, as lightly as he can, lays his hand on Rohan's shaking knee.

"It's fine," Rohan says, leaning his head back.

"Yeah, we're fine," Bram says.

Pearl kisses him again, lining Rohan's face inch by inch until Rohan's arms finally start to unclench.

"Sorry," Rohan mutters after a while. Bram is taking pains not to go a single mile over the speed limit as they roll through the outer suburbs. "Just had a moment."

Bram looks Rohan over as they drive. "I'm guessing this wasn't your first time in a fight."

A ghost of a smile crosses Rohan's lips. "I wish it was."

"I'm sorry I couldn't get a handle on him faster," Bram mutters.

"Oh shut up," Rohan replies, his smile clinging to life at the corners of his mouth. "You were good. You didn't look scared at all."

"Well..." Bram rolls his shoulders, the growing soreness all across his body getting worse with every minute. "Definitely not my first fight either."

"Yeah, I fuckin' bet," Rohan says, eyes sliding closed. He laughs. "I'm sure you've been in way too many. It only took one little incident for me to decide I never wanted to be in one again."

"You shouldn't have to be near dangerous people," Bram says. "Neither of you. It's not right."

When Rohan lets his breath out, it sounds like he's finally getting a proper lungful of air. "So fuckin' chivalrous, aren't you?"

All the oxygen seems to vanish from the air as all of them go quiet. Every time Bram adjusts his foot on the gas or the brakes, his thigh rings with pain from the knife wound, and suddenly, asking a bunch of questions doesn't feel so important. He just needs to get them out of danger, somewhere safe and comfortable. He can't even bring himself to get angry about Chel letting that guy into his apartment. Every time he glances over at Pearl cuddled up against Rohan, the only thing he cares about is *them*.

They're five minutes away from their destination, and Bram begins to recognize the streets of Beechwood.

"You okay?" Bram asks, nudging Rohan's leg.

Rohan makes a soft sound and opens his eyes again. "Yeah, I'm alright."

"Handled yourself pretty well back there," Bram says. "The fuck did you do to that guy anyway? You bring a knife or something?"

Rohan starts laughing. "It was my fucking meds."

"What?" Bram's brain screeches to a halt, and he starts to laugh in a manic sort of way. "Sorry?"

Rohan starts laughing harder. "I didn't know what to do, so I brought my injection with me and I stabbed him with it. Probably left the damn pen in your hallway."

An uncontrollable laugh bursts out of Bram, and he pulls the car over just to clutch his body in pain. "You used your—*ah, ahh god*—fucking medication as a weapon?"

"I know," Rohan reaches out to grab him, laughing with him. "I know—*ow*—it was stupid."

They wheeze-laugh for a minute, clutching each other's arms and wincing every other breath.

"Don't let me get in another fight," Rohan gasps. "I won't get a refill until next month."

Bram throws the car into park, unbuckles his seatbelt, and reaches for Rohan's face. His ribs scream, his thigh wound lighting up, the trunk of his neck sending pain radiating down into his chest and up into his skull, but he kisses Rohan anyway. Rohan grabs him in return, sighing through the kiss, his fingers sinking into Bram's hair.

Bram pulls away, grimacing. "Fuck, *ow*."

"Yeah me too," Rohan grits his teeth.

"Don't be stupid," Pearl scolds, his voice hoarse like he's got a bad cough. "You're both hurt."

Bram pulls a pouting Pearl closer and kisses him too. A soft squeak startles out of Pearl's throat before he grabs the front of Bram's shirt, pressing into him to return the kiss and nuzzle Bram's face.

"Don't think you're out of the woods," Bram warns him. "You gotta tell us what the fuck is going on."

Pearl nods, sinking back into the blanket bundle. "I will."

Rohan pulls Pearl back against his chest. "We're almost there anyway."

Bram starts shaking his head, relief beginning to undo some of the panic in his chest. "Didn't you know lived out here in the burbs."

"It's technically my granddad's house," Rohan explains. "He left it to me after he passed."

Bram wants to keep asking him questions, but he clams up as they drive by the very same stop sign where he first met Pearl. The map is leading him to a house on the same damn block.

"Pearl, be honest," Bram says as he pulls into the driveway of a perfectly boring house with a perfectly boring little square of lawn out front. "When I met you, were you looking for Rohan?"

Pearl pulls the blanket over his head. "Not exactly..."

"What does that mean?" Rohan asks.

Bram snorts, killing the engine. "We're about to have a long fucking conversation, aren't we? You got any painkillers in there?"

"I'll do you one better, I got medicinal weed," Rohan says, cracking the door open.

Bram lets himself finally smile, and follows Rohan to the front door of the most blessedly boring house he's ever seen. An overgrown flower box hangs in front of the window, the lawn shows tracks from a mower, and the garage door has a slight dent in the bottom of it. Bram hasn't set foot inside a place like this since he was a kid.

Rohan opens the front door and all three of them spill into a warm, beige living room with a worn-out couch facing a deeply out-of-place, modern television. With a sigh, Rohan reaches over the back of the couch to set Pearl down, and pulls his shiny blue jacket off to hang it on a wooden peg on the wall. There's a line of jackets taking up most of the space, but he moves one aside to clear a peg for Bram.

"I gotta warn the club I'm not coming back," Rohan says, leaning down with effort to unzip his boots.

Bram checks his phone and sees a missed call from his building manager. "That'll be my landlord telling me someone broke into my house."

Pearl hangs over the couch, frowning. "Uhm. Can I borrow a shirt?"

"I'll get one," Rohan says, pulling his phone out of his pocket with a grimace. "Just stay there."

He shuffles down the hall, an arm held to his stomach, and the phone up to his ear. Bram leans against the back of the couch and starts peeling his shoes off in a bout of fresh pain.

Rohan's voice drifts down the hall. "Hey, Taka, it's Rohan. How busy is it in there?"

"I'm sorry," Pearl says again, his hand circling Bram's wrist.

Bram slips his arm around Pearl's back and presses his face to the fluff of his hair, breathing in deep the scent of his skin. "I know. We'll figure it out."

Bram and Rohan sit side by side on Rohan's old couch, several ice packs wound in t-shirts and rags packed in around them—and some frozen food items to supplement. Rohan wears a pair of heavily washed, gray sweatpants and nothing else, his long hair draped over the back of the couch, still damp from the shower. Bram sits beside him in his maroon briefs and a borrowed, fuzzy pink bathrobe, the smell of rubbing alcohol wafting from the cut on his thigh. Pearl perches on the coffee table across from them, holding his bent legs to his chest, his long feet poised in front of him. He drowns in a large, black t-shirt with two brand new scissor cuts down the back to make room for his wings. The shirt displays a joke advertisement for fishing lures that reads: *it's easy to lure 'em in when you've got a big dick.*

The air smells of weed, a lavender candle, and a frozen pizza slowly baking in the oven.

"Alright, Pearl," Bram says, exhaling a lungful of air. "You're up. Who was that guy?"

"*What* was that guy?" Rohan adds.

Pearl pouts at the floor, taking a steadying breath as he chooses his words. The seconds tick by, one after the other, and Pearl knows he's taking too long, so he tips his head back to groan, "*Ahh, I fucking hate him.*"

"Is that your ex-boyfriend?" Rohan guesses.

Chewing on the inside of his lip, Pearl growls for a second before answering. "Technically he's my owner."

"*What?*" Bram and Rohan both demand, lurching forward and immediately whimpering in pain.

Pearl sighs heavily, his voice full of scratchy static. "Sorry. Humans don't have a good word for it..."

Bram winces as he tries to lay back against the couch. "You're gonna have to run that part by me again."

"I'm not human!" Pearl shouts, his wings springing out from his back to stretch to their full span. It's only about a foot on each side. His tail coils defensively around his own body, the claws at the ends of his feet flexing. "I'm sorry! I lied! I was pretending to be a human boy! It's easier."

"I don't want to sound rude when I ask this," Rohan starts, hand raised.

Pearl turns his head away and mutters, "You're not gonna get a disease or anything."

Rohan pouts back at him, pity in his gaze. "I wasn't going to ask, but thanks. No, Pearl, I was gonna ask if you've *always* been like this or if there's some kind of condition, or...?"

Pearl's shoulders jump up, and his face goes red-hot. "I was born like this. I'm." Another deep breath and he starts to play with his tail. "I was *born* a succubus. That guy who attacked you, he's the incubus who's training me. I'm still...technically a...fledgling cub."

"What does—what does that mean?" Bram asks, waving his hand. "How old are you?"

"I wasn't even born in this reality," Pearl deadpans. "I'm a cub because my body is small. I'm a fledgling because I'm still in training. I'm *still in training* because my stupid owner *refuses* to let me graduate! He's kept me held back for a billion cycles! It's got nothing to do with age, plenty of cubs choose never to graduate so they can always look cute and small. But I chose to go into training because I wanted to *be an incubus!*"

His voice fills with venom as he picks up steam, old wounds fissuring open inside him.

"When a fledgling reaches the end of their training, it's up to us how to style our bodies. We get to decide what traits we want to emphasize, and which to diminish! He *knew* I was going to clip my wings and flatten my chest, but he decided he liked me better like this and he's been delaying my graduation since then! He just keeps fucking me whenever I bring it up and saying he'll schedule it later. The last time I asked him, he took my voice because he said I needed to *save my energy.* Bullshit!"

Pearl is sure his entire face is pink as he sits there panting, eyes peeled open.

"So I ran away," Pearl says. "I paid someone to get me to the human world. At least when I'm here, I can shape-shift into my human form and people think I'm a boy. Or, *I could,* before that asshole reset me. I don't have any energy left to shift."

His gaze flicks over his audience of two, and he immediately shies at the looks on their faces. Concern, fear, worry—nothing but affection for *him.*

"Is he gonna come back for you?" Bram asks.

"How did he find you in the first place?" Rohan adds.

"That chalk I used to send him away," Pearl starts. "It's a really valuable resource back home. He's going to get in a shit ton of trouble for losing his supply. Also." Pearl's face cracks into a grin that he tries and fails to suppress. "Human chemicals hit us *very* hard. That injection is probably going to make him puke his guts up for a week. He put you guys into that trance because he was getting desperate. He'll be out of commission for a long time."

"I hope he feels like death," Bram says, face gone dark.

Pearl covers his mouth as he laughs. "You look so mean."

"I'm trying *not* to lose my temper," Bram responds. "Not every problem needs a fist in the face."

Rohan tilts his head to look at Bram. "To be fair, this guy *does* deserve everything we did to him."

Pearl squeezes himself tighter, a softer smile taking hold of his face.

"You guys aren't bothered? By how weird I look? No humans have ever seen me like this."

They both turn to him, eyes warm, a little hazy around the edges from the THC coursing through their blood.

"Mm, still pretty cute," Bram murmurs at the same time as Rohan says, "Little demon slut," his mouth in a smirk.

"What?" Bram turns to Rohan with a frown.

"What'd you say?" Rohan asks.

Pearl starts laughing harder, satisfied with *both* compliments. "My owner, he's pretty stupid. I think he probably went looking for me with other stolen goods because he thought someone stole me from him."

Bram coughs up a laugh. "Christ, *that's* who's been breaking into our fucking warehouses."

"Sorry," Pearl whispers, scrunching up tighter. "I didn't mean to cause problems for you."

"I know," Bram says, and cracks a smile. "He didn't actually take anything. Couldn't even take *you* back."

Pearl lets himself smile at Bram, enjoying the smug look on Bram's face. "Thanks for everything you did. I'm sorry he hit you so many times."

Bram gestures weakly with his hand, sighing a bit. "I've had worse."

Rohan snorts. "Oh, is that why you guys call yourself the Vampires? You fight a lot of incubus?"

Bram gives a hissing, pained laugh. "Okay, no, the real reason we're called the Vampires is way fucking lamer than that."

"I always thought it was because you guys do so much night work that you all get pale as shit," Rohan says, slapping Bram's thigh.

Bram sucks in a breath at the pain ringing out from the knife wound. "Can't keep anything secret around here."

Rohan grins, turning his increasingly hazy gaze onto Pearl. "So, all those times I found you shining in my office?"

Pearl's cheeks burn. He can feel his throat starting to dry up again with all this talking, but for the first time in his life, Pearl *wants* to tell these boys everything there is to tell.

"I was feeding," Pearl admits, guilt nipping at the back of his neck. "I don't eat food like you, I live off desire."

"So that's why you didn't want to stay with me out here," Rohan says, nodding as he makes sense of it. "You wanted a free meal off my customers."

"Sorry," Pearl squeaks out, his voice cracking.

Bram peels one eye back open. "*Just* desire?"

"Well." Pearl tilts his head. "Cum is technically more filling."

Rohan snorts. "You *are* a little demon slut."

Pearl burns, the embarrassment of spilling his own secrets fighting with the pleasure of Rohan and Bram both giving him those appraising looks. Already, there is new desire building in the atmosphere of this little house, easing the aches lining Pearl's torso.

Pearl rests his chin on his knees, his body starting to unclench. "Where I come from, incubus all have short, one word names. All the succubus have long, multi-word names. I know you didn't mean to, but you both gave me names that an incubus would have had. You have no idea how sick I was of hearing *Shining Silver Starlight* a hundred times a day. I like your names a lot better."

"What's your ex's name?" Bram asks.

Pearl spits it out like it's worthless. "*Ram.*"

Rohan immediately bursts out laughing. "Seriously—*ah!*"

"God, don't," Bram sighs. "You know I wasn't born *Bram Stoker*, right? It's just an alias."

"I know," Rohan squeezes the words out between pained breaths, his face twinging every other second. "It's just so funny. Men and their tough guy names. *Oww, fuck.*"

When Pearl's legs start to ache from being bent up for too long, he sets his feet on the floor and wraps his arms around his chest. "You don't have anything I could flatten my chest with, do you? I need to feed before I can reshape myself."

Bram's gaze hones in on Pearl and his chest. "Isn't that...bad for you? Like your chest? Your ribs. You just got squeezed by that guy, right? M-maybe you shouldn't."

Pearl quirks an eyebrow as Rohan finally stops laughing. "Don't mind him, Pearl. He's a boob guy, he doesn't want you to cover them up. If you really want something, I can order it for you but he's got a point about your ribs. I don't want to make any bruises worse."

Pearl's face reddens again. "You don't...mind if I'm like this?"

Bram swallows as he stares. "'Course not. Do whatever you want."

Pearl's eyes narrow, and his lips curl back into a delighted grin. He jumps up and sits down on the couch beside Bram, tenting his legs over Bram's lap and dropping his arms to his sides to push his chest out.

"Oh *no*...whatever will I do? My *big boobs* are in the way." Pearl pouts up at him. "And I'm *soo* embarrassed."

Bram takes a deep breath, his gaze heated on Pearl's body, until he visibly jolts with pain, his mouth twisting into a grimace. "It's mean to do that when I'm hurt."

Pearl meets his gaze with a sudden ferocity. "You can touch them if you promise never to call me a succubus."

"I promise," Bram whispers, his hands twitching. "I shouldn't right now anyway. We're all injured."

"I'll do it," Rohan says, reaching to wrap his arm around Pearl's body and cup one of his boobs. "Hey, that's pretty fun."

Pearl's back straightens, his shoulders jumping up. "*H-Hey!*"

"*What*, you offered," Rohan reminds him, his voice dropping into that low husky tone.

Pearl can feel it when Bram's nerves light up at the sight of Rohan's hands fondling Pearl's chest. He can tell when Bram's cock swells just from the look on Pearl's face, his open mouth and his pink cheeks. Bram's desire echoes back to Pearl, but unlike all the other meals he's had of human lust, he *wants* this one as much as they want him.

"Not fair," Pearl's voice is full of breath as Rohan thumbs over his nipple. He's felt this a hundred times, but it's never been this *real*. "I never liked it when Ram did this."

"Yeah we're all learning a lot about ourselves," Rohan says, peeking over Pearl's shoulder to look at his fingers pinching the buds of Pearl's nipples through the t-shirt, his shark-smile returning while he revels in every twitch of Pearl's body.

Pearl *huffs*, his legs squirming, his tail coiling around Bram's arm as the sure knowledge of Rohan's swelling desire slips down Pearl's throat. "Rohan, I'm *really* hungry."

"What does that mean?" Bram asks, pulse throbbing. He slips his hand up Pearl's thigh, nudging his legs further apart.

Pearl's wings flatten as he presses into Rohan's chest, his eyes fluttering shut as he feels Rohan's hardening dick pushing against the small of his back. "*I'm gonna come if you keep touching me!*"

Rohan's hands go still, and Pearl pants hard, his body still taut.

"Sorry, I don't want cum on my couch," Rohan says. "Let's go to the bedroom."

"*Really?*" Pearl demands. "I thought you were both injured!"

"You said you were hungry, right?" Rohan asks. "That means we gotta feed you."

"Yeah, yeah, we have to feed you," Bram says. "It'd be irresponsible not to."

Pearl tries to catch his breath, glancing between Rohan and Bram, all of them hard, desire pulsing between the three of them, hot and fresh and dense. Pearl's body instantly covers in goosebumps.

"You guys are so fucking horny," Pearl mutters, his cheeks burning, hips rapidly throbbing.

"Come on, let's go," Rohan says.

They pick themselves up from the couch with some effort, Rohan and Bram clinging to each other to get back to their feet. Rohan takes another generous hit of his weed, and offers it to Bram for a more modest breath to help dull the pain of the bruises lining their bodies.

Rohan leads them down a carpeted hallway. "Don't make fun of the pictures. I never got around to changing the decor after my granddad passed."

Neither Pearl nor Bram try to tease, but they do look at the smiling photos of a gangly light-skinned boy with a tuft of red hair and a face full of freckles smiling in a soccer jersey. Beside him, a thick-set man with pale skin and a shock of red hair smiles proudly beside a thin, elegant woman with slightly warmer skin and stick-straight black hair, a small smile pulling at her lips.

They duck into a bedroom full of even more out-of-place furniture, dark wood and metal that clashes with the rest of the warm, natural beige of the house. Rohan sits down on the edge of the dark blue bedding and pats the covers beside him.

Pearl hesitates. "It's *really* messy when I'm hungry."

Bram braces himself before he bends down and scoops Pearl up by the hips, tossing him onto the bed. Pearl scrambles up, his tail slithering over the covers.

"I don't see why that's a deterrent," Bram tells him.

Pearl glances between them, perching on the balls of his long feet. "Okay, okay. I just wasn't expecting you to be so...fine with this. There's a reason we don't show up on recording devices! Humans get weirded out by our real bodies."

Rohan reaches out to gather Pearl's tail in his hand. "Does this feel good?"

Pearl shivers at the light touch on his thin skin. "It can."

"You ever jerk off with it?" Rohan asks, eyes bright.

"Everyone with a tail jerks off with it," Pearl responds, matter-of-fact. "If they say they don't, they're lying."

Rohan smirks as Bram pulls himself onto the bed, stretching out over the covers in his borrowed pink bath robe.

"So, that's a yes," Bram says.

"Obviously." Pearl flicks his snake-like tail into a loop. "It's very handy."

Bram and Rohan both stare at the softly looping appendage, muscle flexing beneath the flesh, and the faintest pale pink mottling that colors the skin.

"I bet that's..." Bram starts, his mouth going dry.

"Really hot," Rohan finishes.

Pearl takes a deep breath, rich desire filling his chest like smoke. "You guys are way too easy, you know that? Not all incubus are as nice as me."

"We're injured," Bram says.

"You *have* to be nice," Rohan says.

Pearl smiles at them both, his body already filling up with their lust, strengthening his shaky limbs. "There's no way you can keep your hands to yourself if I do."

"That's our problem," Bram tells him, inching back toward the headboard.

Rohan pulls himself up beside Bram. "Yeah, show us how a professional incubus jerks off. We need to learn."

The boys sink down onto the pillows, their shoulders touching, obvious arousal slithering through their bodies. Slowly, Pearl rises up to stand on the bed between them, calling up memories of the dancers from Rohan's club posed on stage.

"If I do this, you both need to tell me about your crazy exes," Pearl says, hands on hips.

Bram reaches out to touch Pearl's ankle. "Fine, fine."

Rohan gives an intoxicated smile. "Seems fair."

"Come on, *angel*," Bram coaxes.

Pearl curls his tail around his hip and drops to his knees, heat filling his face. It takes him a moment to thread his wings back through the holes in his t-shirt, but he tosses the shirt aside, baring his chest for them with only a little bit of nervousness tightening his muscles.

"Promise this doesn't change anything?" Pearl asks.

He's starting to like the way Bram's gaze magnetizes to his nipples, Bram's adam's apple bobbing as he swallows, practically licking his lips.

"Still Pearl," Bram mutters.

"Still got a cute dick," Rohan says, his eyebrow quirking, gaze slipping between Pearl's thighs to his pulsing hips.

Biting his lip, Pearl shifts his thighs further apart, and both boys immediately touch his legs, their fingers drawing goosebumps across his skin.

"Don't hurt yourselves," Pearl warns, leaning back on his hands, his feet arched underneath his body, knees resting against Bram and Rohan's hips.

Pearl AKA Angel. Age: unknown. A fledgling incubus-in-training turned incubus-on-the-run. Currently in hiding from his former owner, Ram, styling himself as a human for safety (and pleasure). Shared partner of Bram Stoker, leader of the Southside Vampires, and Rohan, owner of the Dandelion Club.

Pearl slips his tail around his thigh and places the thin tip against his belly, breathing in the taste of Bram and Rohan's lust. He can pick apart the desires manifesting in their scents as he flicks his tail over the small knob of his dick—it was Rohan who made him realize he could call it whatever he wanted. Electricity zips through Pearl's skin at the contact while Bram and Rohan both slip their fingers in toward the center of his body.

"*Knew* you couldn't keep your hands to yourself," Pearl huffs.

"Just want a better look," Bram says.

"No," Pearl says, sliding his tail over his cock with a groan before he pulls at the mouth of his cunt. "You want to touch."

Bram lets his breath out in a rush. "Yeah, okay, I want to touch."

"I know *exactly* what you want," Pearl sighs, slipping his tail inside himself. His vision goes fuzzy as he plunges deeper, rubbing against his dick as he slowly fucks himself. Fluid immediately wells up along his slit, dripping down the curve of his tail.

"Holy shit," Bram mutters, grabbing Rohan's arm.

"I know," Rohan breathes back, grabbing Bram's hand and dragging it closer to Pearl.

Pearl knows how badly they want to touch his tail even before their fingers brush over his skin. Pleasure rushes through his body, the pleasure of fulfilling their desires, their desire for *him*. Pearl's head tips back, and he starts thrusting his tail harder into himself. His movements are getting frantic as sensation swells through his nerves, but he can't stop himself.

The first press of Bram and Rohan's fingers inside Pearl's cunt steals his breath. He immediately spills onto their hands, his hips rolling with the increasingly wild rhythm of his tail. It's not just him they want. The scent of their lust for each other is like candy melting in Pearl's mouth, the richest food he's ever tasted. It fills his lungs and his belly as Pearl slips his tail out of his cunt and Bram and Rohan's fingers immediately twine together inside him. Pearl pushes his tail into his ass instead, letting the boys fuck him with their fingers, quickly spiraling into a drunken haze with all three of them touching each other.

It's even stronger when they all want each other. His owner never taught Pearl about that.

When one of the boys rubs their slicked thumb over Pearl's cock, Pearl immediately comes with a gasp, his hips pushing outward, feet flexing, knees spreading as far apart as he can get them. Power returns to his body in thick waves, solidifying him back into a real being, erasing the memory of his ex's hands all over him.

"You weren't kidding," Bram says in awe with fluid gushing over his hand.

"You are so hard right now," Rohan's voice is all breath.

"So are you."

Pearl leans forward, his mouth open and gasping. "Can you guys just touch each other already? I feel like I'm getting edged."

Bram looks at Rohan, but Rohan doesn't need any more permission than that. He pulls his fingers out of Pearl and shoves his hand down Bram's underwear, his tongue darting across his lips.

"*Fuck,* easy," Bram cautions.

Rohan pulls himself closer to Bram, panting and laughing in Bram's ear. "Keep touching Pearl."

"Who's going to touch you?" Bram asks.

"You can owe me," Rohan says, pushing Bram's underwear out of the way.

Pearl *shudders,* blissful. It's never been better than this. Desire so thick, it erases the pain. Even when their lips curl from their injuries getting aggravated, neither Bram nor Rohan dares ask to stop. Not when their hands rove across each other's bodies, and certainly not when Pearl wraps his mouth around their cocks to swallow them, one after the other, until they're both empty, and Pearl is pleasantly full. Pearl likes it when Bram pets his face while Pearl sucks his dick, both Bram's hands gently cupped around his head, moaning quietly in awe. Pearl likes the way Rohan gives a breathless kind of laugh when Pearl takes Rohan into his throat, his hips jumping and his hand closing around Pearl's neck.

He *loves* it when Bram kisses Rohan while Pearl swallows Rohan's cum.

With a sigh of relief, Pearl flattens his wings against his back and slowly reabsorbs them into his body. His arms feel dense and solid once more, and he rolls his shoulders to test the range. One shift down, he'll deal with the rest of his body later.

"You're welcome," Pearl says, grinning at Bram's exhausted expression. "I could have flattened my chest first, but I wanted you to get the chance to enjoy them a little longer."

Pearl pushes his boobs up, trying not to blush at this newfound appreciation, and Bram lets out a strained moan. "You *are* an angel."

Rohan starts laughing, his gaze fixed on Pearl's chest as well. "I always knew I liked guys with nice tits." He pointedly turns to Bram and smiles. "Didn't know you were such a thigh guy."

Bram's eyes widen. "I thought...I hallucinated that."

Pearl crawls up between them. "Oh, the trance? It's one of the neat little tricks that my owner was *supposed* to teach me and never did. That's how I knew he was panicking."

He gives a wicked grin as he remembers Ram stumbling down the stairs, pumped full of human chemicals.

"Trance?" Rohan echoes.

Pearl gives a guilty pout. "A full fledged incubus can basically hypnotize you? He shows you what you want to see. The setting isn't real but you are. What you do with your body is real. If they're desperate, an incubus can even try to influence you, but it's *really* difficult to force desire onto someone who doesn't have it, or to invent if it wasn't there. Ram was trying to rewrite my desire for you, and your desire for me."

"Well *that* didn't work," Rohan says.

Bram goes stiff. "So...which one of us was...responsible..."

Pearl cocks his head and smiles. "You wanted the pantyhose. And Rohan on stage."

"Yeah, okay." Bram mutters, cheeks turning red. "Shouldn't have asked."

Rohan's mouth slowly lifts, eyes shining. "If it's any consolation, you're much cuter than the last guy I danced for."

Bram's eyes slide shut, steadily filling his lungs with air as some kind of strange peace settles over him. "It was good. That was good. It was fake but it was good."

"Wasn't fake when you sucked my dick," Rohan says, preening visibly.

Bram reaches without looking, searching out Rohan's hand to pluck off the bed and press to his mouth. Rohan's eyes widen as Bram kisses his palm, and Pearl shivers at the rich scent in the air.

"Really want to fuck you," Bram whispers into Rohan's long fingers, face burning. "*Really* want to fuck you, Rohan."

Neither of them look at each other. Rohan's gaze drifts to the ceiling, and he shifts his legs over the bed. "Not letting you touch me until you're healed."

"You're the one who *just* put his hand on my dick," Bram snaps.

Rohan bursts into pained laughter as the oven in the kitchen lets out a high-pitched *beeep!*

"I'll get your pizza!" Pearl jumps up from the bed. "Oh, and your ice!"

As soon as Pearl sprints out of the room, Rohan reaches beneath him to grab the covers. "Let's get these off the bed, they're fucking soaked."

Inch by painful inch, Bram helps him kick the soiled covers off the bed, settling on the sheets below as Pearl rattles around the kitchen.

"Are you okay?" Rohan asks. "I don't like the way your chest is bruising."

"You don't look much better," Bram tells him in a whisper, his fingers brushing over Rohan's rapidly bruising stomach.

"I'm worried you broke a rib," Rohan states dully, glancing down at the brown bruise steeping under Bram's tan skin. "I'll be fine, it wasn't as bad as you."

Bram sighs, the pain crackling through his chest with every breath. His throat is still raw, stinging with every word he says. "My lieutenant has a background in nursing, I'll ask him to look at it tomorrow."

"Do it now," Rohan says, voice gone quiet. "It's that Lee guy, right?"

Bram's brows cinch as he nods. "Yeah, Lee. He's a good guy, but I don't want you to feel like—"

"Jesus, just do it," Rohan says with a laugh. "You strike me as the kind of guy who plays down all his wounds and then re-injures himself a week later when he's trying to prove how fine he is."

Bram sighs again, his mouth creeping into a frown. "Do you know my social security number too?"

Rohan laughs harder and grips his stomach in pain. "Stop making me laugh, you fuck."

It takes Pearl a few trips to deliver pizza, ice packs, and pillows to help situate the boys so they can eat in bed a little easier. He brings their phones as well, and Bram makes a call to Lee to quietly ask to get checked over after a fight. They can all hear Lee's voice rising on the other end of the phone as he says, *"You can't keep trying to solve problems on your own! Use us!"*

Bram immediately stiffens, his shoulders tensing toward his ears. "The guy came to me, I swear to god! I would have called, but it happened too fast. He was after us specifically, it wasn't a gang issue. I even have witnesses who will tell you the same."

Lee's voice goes quiet again, "Oh. Alright. Sorry, boss."

Bram rolls his eyes. "No, it's fine. You were right to assume that. I'm trying to do better, okay? Listen, I gotta talk to you about Chel when you get here—it's *not* what you think, trust me."

Once he gives Lee the address and hangs up, Bram sinks into the pillows.

"*Soo*," Rohan starts, obvious curiosity in his eyes. "Why was your ex-girlfriend in your apartment?"

Bram grabs one of his ice packs and lays it on his forehead. "She made a copy of my key without telling me and used it to let Pearl's ex in. I'm guessing she thought he was going to scare me, maybe rough me up a little bit, and I'd, I don't know, be moved to try to protect her or something."

"Was she always like this or did she go nuts *after* you started dating?" Rohan asks.

Bram heaves a sigh. "Fuck, I don't know. It didn't feel this insane when we got together but that was a while ago, and well. We met because she wanted to fuck the guy who would piss her dad off the most. I didn't know she was so...vengeful..."

Rohan glances at Pearl, his eyes wide.

"I'm glad you threw her out," Pearl says.

Bram gives a quiet, defeated laugh. "I probably should have done it a while ago. Maybe when she ruined the birthday cake I got her just because I showed up late to dinner."

"Yeah, that would have been a good time," Rohan says, patting Bram's shoulder.

Bram jostles Rohan's arm. "What about you. Got any crazy exes we need to know about?"

"Ahh, mine's stupid," Rohan says, waving his hand. "Literally everyone told me to stay away from him. I was just in a bad place so I didn't listen.

It was right after my granddad died. I was panicking about bills and the rest of my family was breathing down my neck to give them the house instead and I just... I knew he was an asshole. But apparently I have a bit of weakness for tough guys who like to pretend they're not gay."

Bram stiffens, and Rohan scrubs a hand over his hair. "Yeah, sorry about that, but you are kinda my type. And not just because of your tits."

With a soft laugh, Bram asks, "Is all the magic going to vanish if I tell you I'm attracted to you both?"

Rohan shakes his head, avoiding both Bram's and Pearl's gazes as he responds, "Trust me, I'm way more into stability these days than guys who try to strangle you because you *correctly* pointed out that sucking dick is one of the gayest things you can do."

"Jesus." Bram's brows furrow. "Strangled you?"

Rohan shrugs. "He wanted me to quit the club so he wouldn't have to share me. I told him I liked my job but that I was proud of him for coming out of the closet. It didn't go well. Wound up in the hospital for a few days, but you know? Mike trying to kill me didn't make me nearly as mad as when he showed up with his brother at the club and I found out he was two degrees from the runner of the Eels. They tried to convince the former owner to sell the Dandelion to the Eels so they could make it a female strip club and get all the boys working the streets for them instead."

"I think I'm more angry about him trying to kill you," Bram tells him.

"Don't be," Rohan says, though a smile pulls at his mouth. "I haven't seen him in years, and I obviously won that fight. No more gangs allowed at the Dandelion, and no more assholes threatening anyone who flirts with me."

Despite his attempt at smugness, there is clear exhaustion in his voice that's not *just* from the long day they've all had.

Pearl lays his hand on Rohan's chest, gently skimming his fingers over the lines of lean muscle. Rohan fits his hand around Pearl's knee, smiling up at him with such a fondness, Pearl can feel it affecting *Bram*. "I don't need to date. I just want to keep all my boys at the club safe."

Pearl smiles at him, glancing over at Bram who stares openly at Rohan like he's trying to see through his head to his thoughts.

"Can I ask you a question?" Bram starts, drawing Rohan's gaze back to him. "Not as Bram Stoker, but as...as *me*. The guy who just fought off an incubus with you and...rescued your little brother."

Rohan starts smirking. "As my tunnel buddy, yeah."

Bram snorts, nodding to himself. "Right, yeah. As your *friend*, I'm just curious. Is the Dandelion *just* a strip club?"

Rohan looks down at his own hands, examining his fingernails for a few seconds. "Almost everyone has a side hustle. No one can just work one job and pay their bills anymore. Hypothetically, if one of my dancers had a private gig, I'd rather they do it at the club where we have bouncers who get paid to keep them safe, than go to a stranger's house and hope everything goes well."

Bram inhales deeply, like Rohan's quiet words are feeding him the way their desires feed Pearl.

Bram's brows pinch together. "That contact you mentioned before...the one who may or may not have a connection with ORPD..."

Rohan snorts. "I'm sworn to secrecy about any and all VIP clients who may or may not have upcoming elections to worry about and *definitely* don't need anyone talking about what they do on their weekends, or the protections they've given my *legal* club."

Bram shakes his head, letting his breath out in a quiet sigh. "I fuckin' knew it."

"Try not to gloat too much," Rohan tells him.

"What about you?" Bram asks quietly. "Do you have a, uh, side hustle?"

"Used to," Rohan whispers, nodding his head. "That's actually how I wound up here." He gestures around the room, and then seems to catch himself. "Well, my first bedroom was the one across the hall. That's where I finished high school after my parents threw me out. They didn't like getting a call from my prestigious private school informing them that I had been expelled for taking money in exchange for—" he raises his hands in the air to quote himself, "sexual favors."

Rohan shrugs. "My granddad took me in and I never looked back. He always told me this place would be open to me. I didn't know at the time that he meant he was going to leave the whole damn house to me, but I'm not complaining. It's just hard to, uh, redecorate, you know? Sorry, what were we talking about?"

He blinks like he's coming out of another trance, eyes darting between Pearl and Bram.

Bram can't stop himself from laughing, opening his mouth to respond and immediately going red in the face again. It's his turn to be honest. "My dad threw me out when he found out I was running with a gang. He needed help paying bills after my mom went to prison and, well. Dad didn't want me around my little brother if I was just at risk of winding up in the same place as my mom."

"I'm guessing you didn't have a cool and tolerant aunt waiting to take you in," Rohan says with a dry smile.

Bram tries not to smile, and does anyway. "No. No, I had a new job and, for all I was concerned, a new family. But that didn't mean I wasn't finding new and creative ways to make mistakes throughout my entire twenties."

Rohan makes the effort to turn onto his side, facing Bram even as his exhaustion deepens. "How many *Chels* have there been?"

Bram's lips thin down. "No comment."

Pearl starts to snicker and leans forward on his hands to nuzzle his face against Rohan's shoulder. "Can I stay with you tonight?"

"You're *both* obviously staying here tonight, are you kidding me? I'm not letting Bram drive home if he has a broken rib," Rohan states. "I'm gonna tie you both to the damn bed and force you to rest until we know what's going on."

Bram's smile tugs wider and Pearl kisses Rohan's shoulder.

"Thank you," Pearl says. "You two rest. I'll watch for your lieutenant."

They both nod, eyes already shut, draped in ice packs. Pearl watches over them, soaking up the lovely desire that permeates the entire house.

Lee is shockingly easy to bring up to speed, but it helps when he sees Pearl's tail and feet for himself, and the severed tip of Ram's tail in a bloody plastic bag. He promises to incinerate the entire thing with a graveness to him that makes Pearl laugh.

Back in the living room, Lee sits straight-backed on the coffee table. With his glasses on and his tie neatly tucked into his breast pocket, Lee diagnoses Bram with a few bruised ribs, and Rohan with no major injuries.

"Maybe you should stay here for a little while," Lee cautions Bram. "Get yourself back in order before going back to a place that someone else knows about."

"Don't worry, I'm not letting him drive until the bruising goes down," Rohan says from beside him on the couch.

"I appreciate your cooperation, Mr. Rohan," Lee says.

"Haven't agreed yet," Bram says, holding up a hand. "But thank you for the recommendation."

Lee uses his wrist to push his glasses up his nose, and pulls his gloves off with a latex *snap*. "Boss, you just solved the biggest problem in the city. The boys will be a little disappointed that there's no fight to be won, but I'm sure business going back to normal will help smooth things over. There's no reason for you not to take a vacation while you can."

"A *vacation*, god. What must that be like?" Rohan asks.

"I don't know," Pearl says, perched on the arm of the couch with his feet in Rohan's lap. "I've never had one."

Bram suddenly goes still, visions pouring through his head of taking Pearl and Rohan somewhere warm and sunny. *Bathing suits. Does Pearl tan? Bathing suits. Rohan and Pearl napping together in a hammock. Bathing suits. Hotel room sex.*

"I'll think about it," Bram says.

"If that's all, Boss, I'll leave you to it." Lee rises up to his feet to start packing away his nursing kit. "Lots of ice, mix rest and gentle activity, painkillers as needed. You'll both be fine in a few weeks."

"One more thing," Bram says, and his voice swings low. "Chel."

"Ah." Lee sets the kit aside and sits down once more. "She saw the incubus."

"She did this," Bram says. "Let him into my house. For all I know, she gave him hints to our warehouses. I'd appreciate it if someone could check in on her, make sure she's not hurt, and then *gently* suggest that if she expects to formally extricate herself from the Vampires without incurring punishment, I have some medical bills leftover from my former lieutenant that she can take on."

Lee nods once. "Understood, sir."

"Thank you," Bram tells him, letting out a relieved sigh. "Make sure she chooses the smart option."

Lee stands up again, straightens his tie and collects his kit. "I'll personally see to it to, Boss."

As he heads for the door, Pearl follows after to lock up behind him. The moment the door clicks shut, all three of them relax. The trouble finally seems to be solidly behind them.

"Careful, you actually looked like a scary boss for a second there," Rohan says with a smirk.

"Sorry," Bram says immediately, and Rohan laughs under his breath.

"You think too much," Rohan tells him.

Bram turns to him, looking over the side of Rohan's angular face, the way his body meshes with the couch cushions. "Would you ever let yourself take a vacation?"

Rohan starts to smile, drumming his fingers on the couch. "I haven't taken any days off since I took over the club. I think the boys would throw me a party if I told them I wasn't going to work on a Saturday."

Pearl plops down between them. "Bram wants to go somewhere warm so he can see us in bathing suits. Rohan doesn't care where we go, he just wants to get spoiled."

The boys go quiet, heat creeping into their faces as Pearl lays their desires bare.

"I don't know if I could afford it," Rohan starts, but Bram leans across the couch and grabs Rohan's thigh.

"I can afford it. Just take the time off."

Rohan's cheeks flush red and he angles his face away from Bram. "If you insist."

"I insist," Bram says, his hand squeezing tighter. "Let me take care of you both for a little while. It's the least I can do…"

Rohan makes a quiet, grumbling sound, so Pearl leans in and whispers, "He *wants* to."

"Fine, fine," Rohan says, folding his arms. "After you're healed up. We can consider it payback for you staying here."

Bram starts laughing. "I'd rather it just be a gift, Rohan."

"Oh." Rohan clenches tighter, self-consciousness gripping him with teeth. "Well. I'll have to give you a gift in return."

"I mean you don't have to—"

"Well, I'm gonna."

"Alright, fine."

"Good, it's settled."

Pearl basks in their voices, a smile stuck to his face. He can feel Rohan scheming beside him, and Bram mentally making space for the reality of traveling with people he wants to please. Impulses and desires take shape in Pearl's mind, swirling through the air.

"Yes, fine, I'll wear a bikini," Pearl says. "But you're buying it."

"That's, w-whu, yeah, of course," Bram stutters. "Wear whatever you like."

Rohan starts snickering, and Pearl politely does not mention Rohan's vision of stealthily packing away a pair of pantyhose in his luggage.

Pearl has never had such a good meal without even lifting a finger.

▶▶▷

A month of good behavior while Bram heals up is harder than any of them expected, but to Pearl's surprise, *he* is the one who seems most bothered by the new routine. Bram is shockingly gracious when he winds up taking longest to heal. He doesn't stay in Rohan's house a minute longer than he needs to, only sticking around a single extra, exhausted night before returning to his apartment to deal with the aftermath. Rohan instantly throws himself back to working every single day, and Pearl bounces between their homes as they wait for their bruises to heal.

When Pearl is with Bram, he tells Pearl that he's probably safer staying with Rohan since Ram's never been to that house. When Pearl is with Rohan, he tells Pearl that Bram probably needs the company more than Rohan does while he heals.

All too soon, Pearl is trying to get them to spend nights together, and they *both* resist the invitation every time.

Pearl's voice is going by the end of the first week of Bram and Rohan only interacting for brief, thirty-minute chunks while they're dropping Pearl off at the other's house.

"Stay with us!" Pearl demands, grabbing Rohan's arm in the foyer of Bram's apartment.

"Bram's still healing," Rohan tells him. "I don't want to be an asshole."

"We *want* you to stay," Pearl says, pulling him into the kitchen.

"Yeah, well, it feels rude to start something he can't finish," Rohan whispers.

"It's fine," Bram says, shuffling over with his hands in his pockets. "We don't need to keep Rohan. He's probably got work anyway, right?"

"Yeah, I-I can't stay the whole night." Rohan gives his excuse even while Pearl is inhaling the unmistakable scent of two men who *wish* they could have sex at that exact moment.

"Then don't stay the whole night," Pearl says, eyes wide, his voice broken up by scratches and pops. "Just hang out with us for a little while!"

Rohan sighs, glancing over at Bram who gives an awkward shrug.

"I mean, you're always welcome to stay," Bram tells him. "But don't let me fuck up your work night."

Rohan looks back at Pearl, who raises his hands up and claps them together. "Please stay! Just for a little while!"

"Fuck, alright," Rohan says. "I'm not opening tonight so I can stick around for a bit."

It's a little like trying to remove a splinter from deep under the skin to get Rohan and Bram comfortable sitting on the same couch again, but

Pearl does not let up until they are all seated together, and Pearl can touch them both at the same time.

"You guys said we were going to take a vacation," Pearl reminds them, sitting with his back to the TV so he can glare at them both. "And for some reason, we haven't talked about it once since then."

Bram touches the back of his neck as Rohan looks away.

"It just didn't come up," Bram mutters.

"I've been working, he's been healing." Rohan waves his hand through the air.

"So do it now!" Pearl shakes them both by the shoulders. "What are we waiting for? I want to see a new place! The human world is *huge* and I want to see more of it, and I want you both to be in the same room for more than five minutes."

His face burns when he hears how whiny he sounds. *Little brother* indeed.

"Sorry, angel." Rohan cups Pearl's knee with a tiny smile. "I just didn't want to make things more complicated."

"I didn't want to pressure you to take time off from work," Bram admits in a hush, his gaze flicking toward Rohan and immediately jumping away. "If it was stressing you out. I just figured you weren't able to do it after all, so I didn't press."

Rohan's eyes flash and he stares at Bram. "You were waiting for me to give you dates."

Bram shrugs voice dropping to a pitiful mumble. "No big deal, if you can't do it, you can't do it—"

"He can do it," Pearl says, fixing Rohan with a sharp stare. "He's just dragging his feet because he doesn't want to impose."

Rohan's shoulders tic up a degree higher, pinned by Pearl's gaze.

"It's not imposing," Bram says, turning to face Rohan head on. "At least let me say thank you for letting me crash at your place."

Rohan's jaw stutters as he looks at Bram like a caged animal.

Pearl grabs Rohan's shoulders, straddling his hips just to shake him with both hands. "Just say yes, you're driving me crazy!"

"Ah, god, fine, fine!" Rohan plucks Pearl's hands away and grabs him around the middle, wrestling Pearl to the couch. "You're such a pest!"

Pearl can't stop himself from grinning with Rohan so close to him, especially when he can feel the strengthening desire building like steam between them all.

"You guys really are like brothers sometimes," Bram says, smiling fondly as Pearl struggles ineffectually against Rohan's arms.

Pearl flushes, surprised to find that it isn't just him who likes hearing that spoken aloud. Rohan flips Pearl onto his stomach, propping himself up on the arm rest.

"Alright, alright, if I'm taking the time off, I do *not* want to be making decisions about where we're going."

He pulls his phone out, and Bram does the same, staring hard at the screen as a fierce bit of pleasure fills his chest—and Pearl's.

Finally.

As soon as the ball gets rolling, it's so simple to plan everything out. Bram takes care of most of the decisions, and suddenly they are booked to fly out together in three weeks, right when Bram's doctor estimated he'd be ready for *heavy lifting* again.

"Pearl, is your voice going away again?" Bram asks. "I thought your ex gave it back to you."

Pearl startles, giving a little shrug. "It just gets quieter when I'm hungry."

"Oh." Bram and Rohan both go still.

"Sorry, I haven't been able to—" Bram starts, but Pearl shakes his head.

"It's okay!" Pearl rushes over to him, kissing Bram on the cheek. "Your job is to get better."

"You should have said something," Rohan says, picking himself up. "I can feed you if you need it, I'm all healed now."

Pearl smiles at him. "Soon we'll have a whole week where we can all feed each other as much as we want."

As soon as he says it, the air seems to swell around them, and Pearl takes a deep breath, slumping against Bram's arm with a pleased sigh.

"I can't wait," Pearl murmurs.

"Yeah, it'll be nice," Bram says, glancing over at Rohan again, hesitant like he expects to be glared at.

Rohan turns around and lays his head in Pearl's lap, throwing his legs over the arm rest. "I'll follow your lead on the whole *vacation* thing."

Pearl can feel their shifting desires like a gathering storm.

He starts with Bram, once Rohan has left for the night.

"So." Pearl sits beside Bram on the couch, snagging Bram's arm with his tail. "You want to fuck Rohan?"

"Jesus." Bram's breath leaves him in a rush, and he leans his hand on Pearl's knee. "Give me a little warning before we launch into these things."

Pearl smiles sweetly, pulling Bram's face toward his. "I'd kill to see it."

Bram's face is steeping with another blush. "Yeah, well...so would I, but I don't think he's that...he seems more interested in the opposite."

Lids low over his eyes, Pearl runs his thumb over Bram's lips, drinking in the growing lust. "Rohan wants a lot of things."

Bram's gaze brightens, his heart racing beneath where Pearl is pressed up against him. "Yeah?"

"The way he likes me is different than how he likes you," Pearl whispers. "You bring something out in him that I don't."

The sudden rush of arousal through Bram's body is enough to make Pearl dizzy.

"No shit?" Bram asks, matching his whisper.

Pearl leans close enough to kiss, speaking against Bram's lips. "If you play it right, he'll let you fuck him."

Bram starts nodding, his breathlessness like a match striking against Pearl's skin, igniting in giddiness. "Tell me what I have to do."

"You need training," Pearl says. "So you don't come immediately when you stick it in."

Bram makes a sound like he's been punched in the gut, his breath sucking into his lungs. Silently, he nods.

"Good." Pearl grins at him. "We'll start today."

He brings it up with Rohan next. Pearl crawls into Rohan's lap where he sits in bed, his phone in his hand, freshly showered after work.

"Can't believe we're actually going on a trip," Rohan says, looking over their itinerary one more time.

"All thanks to Bram," Pearl says.

"Never thought I'd be grateful to know a guy who can get convincing fake ID cards," Rohan says with a laugh.

Pearl plucks the phone from Rohan's hand and wraps his arms around Rohan's neck. "What are you looking forward to the most?"

Rohan leans his head back against the wall, giving a dry laugh. "I don't know, Pearl. I think the last time I went on a trip like this, it was for school."

"It'll be so nice to relax," Pearl says, running his hand through Rohan's hair. "You won't have to think about anything except having a good time."

Rohan's hands settle on Pearl's waist, and to Pearl's most pleasant surprise, desire slips in through Rohan's breath. "What do *you* want to do?"

Pearl smiles and starts counting off on his fingers. "I want go to an amusement park, I want to try some cotton candy, I want to see you both eat really good food, and I want to see *you* get pampered."

Rohan gives a startled laugh. "Me?"

Pearl grins at him. "Bram wants it too, you know?"

Rohan's gaze slides off of Pearl, his voice lowering to a wary tone. "Of course he does...seems like the kind of guy who likes buying elaborate gifts."

"You make it sound like a bad thing!" Pearl laughs. "Imagine how good he'd feel if you let him take care of you."

Pearl can feel Rohan's body shifting gears beneath him even while Rohan pouts. "The two of you are already ruining my appetite."

Pearl cocks his head to the side.

Rohan's frown deepens, grumbling, "I haven't been this horny in *years*. It's distracting."

Undeterred, Pearl rubs his fingers over Rohan's scalp, enjoying the sigh he gives. "You were *starving* before. And now you can eat whenever you want. Isn't that a good thing?"

Rohan simmers in his indecision, his eyelids slowly lowering as Pearl scratches his head. He bites the inside of his lip once, and then his lets his breath out in a soft groan.

"You're making it worse," he mumbles, almost petulantly.

Pearl kisses his jaw, his tail slithering behind his back, curling between Rohan's thighs. "I'm hungry too."

Rohan starts laughing, hitching Pearl up into his arms. "Guess we have to."

"I know!" Pearl grabs the front of Rohan's t-shirt. "Let me put my tail in you!"

Rohan's eyes go wide. "I don't know about that."

"Aw, come on," Pearl begs, wrapping his tail around Rohan's thigh to squeeze him gently. "It'll be fun! And besides, you've seen how thick Bram is."

The air is getting denser around them as Rohan avoids Pearl's gaze.

"It feels *soo* good," Pearl whispers against Rohan's cheek, coiling his tail higher around Rohan's thigh. "Just having him inside me is enough to make me come. He stretches me out and then all it takes is—"

"Alright, *alright.*" Rohan starts laughing, but his face is stained with blush. "I didn't know we were recording ASMR porn."

Pearl perks up. "Is that something we can do? Can we send it to Bram?"

Laughing harder, Rohan leans his forehead against Pearl's, his hands cupping Pearl's ass. "I'm open to discussing it."

Pearl grins.

Rohan [8:52 pm]: *important business message incoming*

Bram has never tried to edge himself on purpose, but when he gets a voice recording from Rohan's phone of the sound of heavy breathing and moaning and laughing, he gives it his best effort. Training, or whatever. He listens to it over and over again, absorbed in the breathlessly casual way that Pearl and Rohan interact, an easy joy in the way they tease each other while fucking. But it's the end of the recording that gets Bram's blood pounding.

"*Hey.*" Rohan's voice comes out a hiss of steam as he gives a strained laugh. "Watch that tail, huh?"

"Oh?" Pearl's boyish voice is full of wicked delight. "I barely touched you."

Rohan gives a stuttering gasp that bursts into a yelp of a moan that makes Bram's cock surge in his hand as he jerks off on the edge of his bed.

"*Okay that's all, bye,*" Rohan says before the recording ends, his voice shredded to pieces.

The potential haunts all three of them right up until they are herding each other through a busy airport. Rohan wears a massive pair of sunglasses to hide the fact that he took an edible right before Bram picked them up to get to the airport. All of them wear thick black masks to cover their faces as they move through the long hallways full of people dragging luggage behind them. Neither Rohan nor Bram wanted to risk a single person recognizing either of them out of their places of business, *on a joint vacation* accompanied by a boy of dubiously youthful features. Pearl's brand new fake ID puts him at eighteen years and one month old.

For the entire takeoff and landing, and every single second of turbulence, Rohan squeezes Bram's arm so hard there might be bruises, while Pearl keeps trying to sit in their laps, confused as to why any of them are wearing seat belts.

It takes an hour to retrieve all their luggage, and then the rental car company tells them the car Bram reserved was recently in an accident, and all they had left was a teal minivan.

"Fucking incredible," Rohan mutters as the boxy van rolls up to them at the curb. "Should we just drive it into the ocean? Do them a favor?"

Bram takes the keys from the employee and rattles them at Rohan. "Come on, it's time for your court-mandated relaxation."

"I'm relaxed!" Rohan snaps, his face immediately going red behind the mask.

"In, in, in." Pearl pushes on his back, forcing Rohan into the car.

By the time they make it all the way to the hotel, park the car, check in, get their keys, realize they have to drive to their suite at a secondary location, get the car back, and finally roll into the auxiliary parking lot outside the VIP suites, it's dark outside, and they have been traveling for most of the day.

"This place is fucking fancy," Rohan says, flicking on the lights.

"Turns out I had a useful favor to call in," Bram tells him, hauling two suitcases behind him.

"Whoa, is that the ocean?" Pearl glues himself to the glass door leading to the patio. "One time, Ram and I worked a couple out by a lake, but it wasn't like this!"

Bram and Rohan both stop to look at him, then glance at each other. Immediately, Rohan breaks eye contact and joins Pearl at the door, his arms looping around Pearl's chest.

"Yes, this is one of our finest oceans," Rohan starts telling him.

Bram takes their things further into the suite, past the living room to the two separate bedrooms.

"Hey, which bed do you guys want?" he calls.

"Wait, we have more than one room?" Pearl asks, his bare feet thumping closer. He's already in the middle of pulling his clothes off and he pauses to get his shirt the rest of the way off. "I thought we were going to share."

"Well, I-I just figured it was easier to, uh..." Bram rubs the back of his neck. "I don't know, more space is nice."

Rohan slinks up behind them, leaning his shoulder up against the wall as Pearl shimmies out of his pants.

"Ooh," Pearl nods as he sticks his head into the second bedroom. "One is for sleeping and one is for sex?"

Rohan starts snickering, and Bram gives a shrug. "Whatever we want."

Pearl stands in the hallway, buck naked once more, and straightens his back, rolling his shoulders as his tail unfurls from the base of his spine. "You guys should order food, you're both hungry."

"He takes charge real easy," Rohan whispers at Bram's back.

Bram's entire body instantly covers in goosebumps as he remembers they're finally alone again.

"He's right," Bram says, grabbing the edge of his sweatshirt and pulling it over his head. His black mask gets tangled up in the fabric, but he doesn't stop to fix it, just wads his sweatshirt up and throws it into the first bedroom. "What do you want to eat?"

Rohan starts unzipping his jacket. "I'll eat anything once."

Bram doubles back and starts opening drawers until he finds the menu for room service and holds it out to Rohan. "Pick two entrées, get whatever you want."

Rohan's brow quirks as he takes the hard-backed booklet. He scans over the pages, asking quietly, "What kind of food do you usually eat?"

"I like most things," Bram says back, voice flat. "I'm asking what *you* like."

"Mm, but it would be easier if we got something both of us liked," Rohan suggests, gaze still fixed on the menu.

"Rohan," Bram sighs his name, drawing Rohan's gaze back to Bram's, his hazel eyes gone wide. Bram can instantly feel the tension drawn across Rohan's shoulders, and Bram tries to offer up a comforting smile, though he's sure it's fit to his mouth wrong.

"I'm kinda trying to wine and dine you," Bram whispers, his chest heated with nervous fear. "Work with me?"

Rohan's fingers curl around the edge of the menu. "I don't really do this anymore."

"Do what?" Bram asks, his chest surely caving in.

Rohan eyes Bram with a frantic energy. "Last guy I dated put me in the hospital. So I stopped dating."

Bram's smile falters, a swift realization punching him in the gut—Rohan is saying *they are not dating.*

"Uhh." Bram stares at Rohan, slack-jawed and clueless. He should have known that. He never asked. Of course they're not dating. *Fucking around* and *dating* are two very different things, and Bram's chest aches as the shape of things clarifies in his mind. If Bram can't even own up to sleeping with guys in front of anyone else, Rohan is obviously not going to date Bram.

"Can I buy you dinner as a friend, then?"

Rohan's brows pinch, and he gives a little laugh. "Sure, but I'll owe you."

Bram rolls his eyes. "Fine, fine, you'll owe me. Just get us some food, alright? I'm going to take a shower, don't get too wild out here while I'm gone."

Rohan laughs again, hushed under his breath as Bram heads into the bedroom to dig through his clothes.

"You hear that, Pearl? Don't get wild."

"Too late!"

The entire time Bram is in the shower, he can't get the thought out of his head that Rohan would obviously never date another gang member again—especially not the fucking *boss* of a gang. Rohan saw firsthand exactly the kind of violence that Bram is capable of. He's had a month to digest that fight with Pearl's ex. Rohan has probably figured out by now that Bram is just a brawler with a big title. He's not a smart match. It's convenient for Pearl who needs protection and fake papers, but Rohan expressly wanted out of that world. And here Bram is, trying to force him right back into it with free dinner.

For the last month, Bram has been resisting the urge to order a watch dog to keep an eye on Rohan's house. The Eels must know Rohan lives at the edges of their territory. Just because it's been a few years doesn't mean they won't try something when they think he's not paying attention. Bram knows the playbook all too well.

Dragging his hands down his face, Bram tries to let go of this stupid idea. He knows he's no different than any other asshole who would try to force their ways on another person. Having it confirmed face-to-face that Rohan only sees him as a friend still stings though.

Bram tries to make his peace with it, scrubbing shampoo into his hair. He's determined not to ruin this vacation for any of them. So what if Rohan doesn't want to date him? Bram gives himself a pep talk as he sorts through all his nicer clothes for the usual *I'm too tired to give a shit* outfit. Being friends with Rohan and Pearl has opened his entire world up. He's better off having met them than he was before. That's enough to be grateful for. And they do still get to fuck—having better sex than Bram's ever had with anyone else is frankly worth the trip alone.

Bram is about to join the boys back in the living room when he hears his own thought come back to him like a horrible echo.

Rohan thinks you're trying to pay him for the sex.

In the most beautiful place he's ever stayed, Rohan is more anxious than ever. Every five minutes, he feels his hand reaching for his phone, the urge to call Spear or Taka to get an update on the club itching like a mosquito bite.

The food helps. Pearl strutting around the hotel room naked helps. Watching TV on the couch and wondering which one of them is going to start touching the other does *not* help. Pearl keeps pulling them closer and closer until he is seated on both their thighs like a lap dog. When Bram loops his arm around the back of the couch to make room, Rohan is hyper-aware of his hand curled up and conspicuously distant from Rohan's shoulders—but their thighs are pressed together beneath Pearl's ass.

Biting his lip, Pearl leans his head back onto the couch cushion. "I'm hungry."

As soon as Rohan looks at Bram, and sees Bram looking right at him, his nerves jump to the surface. Suddenly, it feels like everything is Rohan's decision, and he has no goddamn clue *why*.

"Well," Rohan starts, face heating up. "What do you want to eat?"

Smirking, Pearl answers, "Two hot dogs."

Despite himself, Rohan starts laughing. Even Bram can't keep the laughter from his breath.

"Uh, do you want them...on the same bun?" Bram asks, his expression crumpling into uncertainty.

Rohan laughs harder, his own giddiness getting the best of him.

Pearl grabs both their thighs in his hands. "One in each, like the first time we ate together."

It shouldn't be *more* difficult to look at Bram when Rohan is getting hard, but Bram's gaze is so much heavier than it used to be. It's been a month since the three of them fucked, so Rohan chalks up all his flinching nerves to that. Never mind the fact that Rohan and Bram have texted every single day since Bram left Rohan's house. Never mind that he knows more about these two boys than ever before. Never mind that Rohan is already hard when Pearl corrals them into what he has decided is the *sex bedroom*—he can't stop thinking about how good it's going to feel.

They don't need to ask who's doing what. They fall into the same places on instinct, only this time, there's no hesitance in the way they move. When Bram pulls Pearl up into his arms, kissing Pearl as he spreads Pearl's thighs over his cock, he's not hiding at all. Pearl gives a delighted moan when Bram presses his cock against the mouth of Pearl's cunt.

"You feel *so good*," Pearl sighs, his eyes sliding closed as he sinks down onto the thick length of his cock.

Rohan can't tell if Pearl is *trying* to rile him up or not, but either way, it's working. It always works. As Rohan grips Pearl's ass, sliding up as close as he can to bring all three of them together, he is determined not to let on how much worse this is for him. It'll be fine, as long as they can do this like they did before.

That's what Rohan recites inside his head as he moans under his breath from the slick heat of Pearl's ass squeezing his dick. He isn't ready for Bram's fingers automatically seeking out *Rohan's* ass, pulling him forward and stealing his breath as he bottoms out inside Pearl much faster. Rohan's gaze lands back on Bram, his heated eyes staring into Rohan like he can read Rohan's thoughts.

"Go on," Bram murmurs, his voice so soft but that's all it takes. Rohan feels that low tone in his blood like gasoline.

Rohan throws himself into it, determined to prove that everything is as it should be. By this point, he's fucked Pearl enough times that it should be easy to keep things going. He doesn't even need to deal with the extra delirious friction of Bram's cock shoved up against his, making him a different kind of crazy. Fucking Pearl is *fun*. It gives him a rush of satisfaction to hear Pearl moaning, his voice coalescing into a full sound once more as he babbles their names, clinging to Bram's chest. His thin tail snaking around Rohan's hips is filled with adrenaline-fueled delight.

When he looks at Bram's molten gaze, Rohan feels like he's about to drown. He gets stuck in it while he's fucking Pearl and it feels amazing with Bram's hands gripping his ass. Rohan feels the need to come boiling harder the longer he looks at Bram's awestruck, drunken expression. It's always Bram who goes off first, and Rohan keeps waiting for the inevitable shift of his features, the change in his grip, the drop in his voice when he starts to lose it.

Panting softly, Bram whispers to Rohan, "Want to see you come."

Rohan's breath catches, lightning searing through his body. His nipples instantly go hard, and he grabs Bram's face to kiss him, nearly losing his balance as he shifts his weight so he can keep thrusting into Pearl and swallow Bram's tongue.

Bram's hand slips into the cleft of Rohan's ass, his overheated finger pressing against Rohan's hole. The need to get something inside his ass hits Rohan so swiftly and so sharply, he is helpless to the wave of sensation crashing into him. Rohan breaks their kiss just to moan against Bram's face as he comes inside Pearl, barely recognizing his own voice as his hips twitch into the orgasm. His cock goes numb as he wrings out every drop he can with Bram rubbing his hole. It's not enough.

When his cock is too soft to keep going, Bram picks up where Rohan left off. He presses forward, pushing them all in the other direction across the bed.

"Take him," Bram breathes, passing Pearl off for Rohan to hold.

That's how they wind up with Rohan on his back, holding Pearl's tits for Bram to admire while he finishes fucking Pearl.

Rohan's stomach clenches, wondering what Pearl feels. It must be good to make him chant louder and louder, "*yes, yes, yes, yes!*" while his body tightens, his legs jostling with every thrust of Bram's hips.

"So fucking *pretty*," Bram groans, pointedly making eye contact with each of them before his eyes flutter shut.

Rohan is too stunned to say anything, least of all how good Bram looks—the solid trunk of his body, muscles straining across his arms, the soft fat of his chest bouncing every time his hips connect with Pearl's.

With cum dripping down Rohan's hips, he feels himself listing toward old habits.

While Pearl takes a bath, Bram steps outside to smoke a cigarette on the small stone patio. Rohan slinks out after him, lured by the fond smell of bad decisions.

"It's weird," Bram says, gesturing at the three-by-three square of empty stone connecting the back door of their suite to the stretch of sand. "You'd think if they're going to go the extra mile of giving you a patio, they'd put furniture out here for you to sit on."

Rohan laughs, drawn to stand beside Bram. He itches for contact, annoyed at his own weakness as he leans his arm against Bram's shoulder.

He *wants* Bram to touch him, but he's glad when there is no hand placed on his waist.

"Wanna go stand in the water?" Rohan asks.

"Yeah, sure," Bram nods.

They roll up the legs of their sweatpants and walk down the wide swath of sand until they find a wooden staircase leading to the shoreline. The air is humid and sticky, and the cool touch of the water instantly sends goosebumps rippling up Rohan's skin. Looping his arm around Bram's shoulder, Rohan holds his hand out.

"Let me get a hit off that," Rohan says.

Laughing, Bram holds out the cigarette. "You sure?"

"Very," Rohan says, taking it from him. "If I can't have weed, I gotta smoke something."

"We can probably get you weed out here," Bram whispers.

Rohan takes a drag, resting his chin on Bram's head as he blows smoke into the air. Bram smells like hotel shampoo, but Rohan doesn't really mind. His hair is thick and his scalp is warm so Rohan presses his face to it, letting his arms wrap around Bram's shoulders. Bram takes the cigarette back from him, and touches Rohan's wrist with one finger.

"Things are easy with Pearl," Rohan says.

"Yeah," Bram responds quietly.

"He just fell into my lap, ya know?" Rohan laughs. "I didn't have to think. He was just there and he needed help, and then before I knew it, he was like the little brother I never had."

When Bram exhales cigarette smoke, Rohan likes the scent twice as much.

"It's funny," Bram says. "I already have one, so I guess I wasn't looking for another. But you two really do feel like a pair of idiotic brothers."

"Shut up," Rohan says, laughing through it. The goosebumps are worse when Bram traces the shape of Rohan's hand, each individual finger. "It doesn't feel like we're dating. Really does feel like he's family."

"You don't usually fuck your family," Bram responds, and Rohan can tell even in the dark that he's smirking as he speaks.

"Well, if you're married to 'em, you do," Rohan says.

"You feel married to Pearl?"

"Nah, but do you know what I'm trying to say?" Rohan asks.

Bram is silent for a moment, taking another drag as the surf steadily rolls past their ankles.

"Yeah, I think I do," Bram says. "You're comfortable with him."

"Yeah." Rohan takes another deep breath, shamelessly inhaling the smell of Bram's skin. "Like I don't need to think about anything. When he's happy, I'm happy. I like when he's around. Gives me cute aggression. Wanna squeeze him until he pops."

"Yeah." Bram nods, a hushed laugh. "He wants you happy too, you know?"

A hot, prickling sensation creeps down Rohan's neck. "Yeah."

"I'm pretty sure that's why he picked me up," Bram says.

"Hm?" Rohan asks, his cheek resting on Bram's head, suddenly very glad that they can't see each other's eyes.

Laughing, Bram drops his arms to his sides. "He can read our desires, right? He knows what we want before we even do." Rohan goes very quiet as Bram lifts the cigarette, and then decides against it. "I think he knew I wanted something that I wasn't going to get on my own."

Rohan's face is full of heat. He recognizes that rising in his stomach, the weightless feeling spreading through his limbs.

"Eating ass?" Rohan asks.

Bram starts laughing, trying to bite it back down. Rohan is ready for all this tension to snap and for things to go back to normal, but Bram shifts his weight from one foot to the other, and he says with disarming confidence, "You're right, though."

Rohan's heart skips a beat. "*Really?*" He purrs, hoping to tease him.

Bram's voice is as quiet as the surf. "Think I'd pretty much do anything either of you asked me to."

There's a fire growing under Rohan's skin, and he can't stop himself from chasing it. "You're the one who's new to this club. What do *you* want, Bram?"

"Already told you," Bram says, turning his body toward Rohan's. He tucks his face in close to Rohan's neck, and it's so much worse when he *doesn't* touch Rohan. "I want to fuck you."

Heat sweeps through Rohan's body. He could kiss Bram so easily. He knows how good it would feel. His lips ache for the pressure, the tongue in his mouth, the hands on his body.

Rohan may as well be speaking through a pinhole as he whispers, "You keep working on that."

"I will," Bram tells him, no hesitation.

It would be so good to kiss Bram right there, but Rohan knows how that would look. He knows what that invites.

"We should head back before your drop your cigarette in the ocean," Rohan says.

He hears the soft hush of Bram's laugh as he pulls away. "Yeah, let's go."

The silence on the walk does not ease any of the charged energy crawling over Rohan's skin. He hurries toward the light of their rooms, the safety of Pearl equalizing their presences into one thing. Being alone with Bram suddenly feels like waiting for the jump scare in a horror movie— breath held, nerves jumping, gripping the seat, grinning through the fear.

They rinse their feet off on the stone porch under the spigot attached to the wall and Bram crushes his cigarette before opening the door for them. Rohan steps into the living room first, a chill sweeping down his bare arms at the blast of cool air.

"Do you think there's any extra blankets in the—"

Before he finishes asking, Bram grabs Rohan's arm, spinning him back around. In the span of a breath, Rohan turns toward Bram, something snakes out behind his ankle to pull him off balance, and Rohan immediately stumbles back to clumsily sit on the armrest of the couch, his hands flying out to grab Bram's wrist. Before he has a second to catch his breath, Bram is on him.

Rohan's eyes fly open as Bram kisses the gasp off his lips. His tongue chases the soft moan from Rohan's throat. The adrenaline from nearly tripping quickly transmutes into painful arousal as Rohan grabs Bram's face to kiss him back. Suddenly, he's ten years younger, making another mistake in the shadowed corner of a noisy club. This time, there is no thumping music, no alcohol or drugs loosening his limbs, no strangers pressed in around them.

Rohan pushes his hand through Bram's hair, breathing hard, automatically pushing up against a willing, warm body. It's just the two of them in a quiet hotel room, Bram's hips pressing in between Rohan's thighs, his hands roaming over Rohan's back until he squeezes the swell of Rohan's ass.

Rohan's blood surges, his skin prickling with the urge to pull his clothes back off so he can feel Bram's skin against his. Static fills his thoughts. His back arches, his right thigh lifting to squeeze into Bram's side, his fingers bunching up Bram's shirt. *He wants to fuck again, he wants Bram, he wants to forget who he is—*

Bram breaks their kiss with a harsh breath, settling his hands on Rohan's hips.

"Sorry," he mumbles, voice barely audible. "Couldn't stop myself."

Rohan pushes on Bram's chest, desperate for the fresh air to clear his head of all the steam. It's not fair that Bram can look so shy after doing that. Those damn doe eyes of his just make Rohan want to keep going.

"So *this* is the guy who picked up a stranger on the side of the road to fuck in his car," Rohan says, still panting quietly.

Bram takes a step back, but his mouth twitches toward a smirk. "I'm going to get ready for bed. You can take the clean room for yourself, I don't mind using the messy one."

Pearl's feet *thump thump thump* into the room and he throws his arms around Bram's neck, hiking his legs up Bram's sides to cling to his back. With a smile, Bram takes Pearl's legs and carries him toward the bedrooms, but not before Pearl fixes Rohan with a smile so smug and so satisfied, it almost seems like Pearl was the one who just feverishly made out with Bram.

With a sigh, Rohan trails after them, staking his claim in the unused bedroom. Eventually, Pearl crawls into bed with him, pressing in close against Rohan's back and pulling his hair aside from his ear to whisper, "Feels good, doesn't it?"

Rohan petulantly stays silent, even while goosebumps sweep down his skin.

"When he wants you more than anything," Pearl whispers.

"You're relentless," Rohan hisses back. "Go to bed."

Pearl giggles in his ear. "Goodnight."

The next day, Rohan and Bram both wake up determined to cater to Pearl's every whim.

Pearl breathes in their nerves like spun sugar. His throat crackles and pops with every sound, so he keeps his words sparse, but Rohan and Bram have no trouble talking when the three of them are together. Pearl forces them to the nearby boardwalk where Bram gets very into the carnival games, and Rohan joins Pearl on every ride they have to offer.

"Need an umbrella?" Bram asks as Rohan reapplies sunscreen in the shadow of a drink stand.

"No," Rohan snaps, knelt down in front of Pearl with his mask off so Pearl can cover every inch of Rohan's face.

"Maybe *you're* the vampire," Bram whispers, stealing a glob off Pearl's hand. "Pick your hair up."

As Rohan gathers his long hair up into his hands, Pearl takes a deep, selfish breath. With Bram's fingers pressing into Rohan's neck, slipping under the straps of his shirt, desire pulses through their bodies, filling Pearl up with warmth.

On Pearl's instruction, Bram wins three stuffed animals, which Pearl dutifully assigns to each of them: a horse for Rohan, a pit bull for Bram, and a rabbit for Pearl. When the person running the booth hands over the speckled stuffed rabbit, they smile at Pearl before pointedly looking at Rohan and Bram to say, "I hope your family has a wonderful day."

Rohan lets out a too-loud laugh, grabbing Bram's arm and Pearl's shoulder. "Thanks so much! You too!"

He drags them away, his face beet-red above the black mask as he declares that he's had enough boardwalk for one day.

"I think your sunscreen wore off," Bram whispers in his ear.

Pearl can practically feel the goosebumps rolling down Rohan's skin as he slaps Bram's bicep.

Sitting in Rohan's lap in the car, Pearl feeds all three of them pieces of cotton candy. The sugar melting on his tongue is only half as good as the emotions melting into Pearl's skin.

As the afternoon dissolves into evening, Bram announces that he's found the closest dispensary if Rohan wants weed.

"Oh thank christ," Rohan says, downing his glass of water. "Let's go."

Bram stops to look at Pearl where he's perched at the table, arranging their three stuffed animals like a bouquet of flowers. "Sorry, angel, even with your fake ID, they won't let you inside the place. It's twenty-one plus."

Pearl shakes his head, smiling and waving them both toward the door.

"You good?" Rohan asks, pointing at his throat.

Pearl gives him a nod and holds up the menu for room service, brows raised.

Rohan puts his hand on his hip. "You probably already know what we want, huh?"

Pearl's smile turns to a grin.

The drive to the dispensary is more peaceful than either of them expected. Rohan puts the radio on, and Bram is quietly grateful that he doesn't mind the music Rohan chooses.

A car with an out-of-state plate cuts them off trying to get into the parking lot, and Rohan is more relieved than he realized when Bram laughs it off instead of tensing up.

"Someone needs weed even more than you do," Bram says.

Rohan laughs with him. "Now that's the desperation of a person who *doesn't* have a medical card."

Bram looks him over. "Is it just for migraines?"

Rohan shrugs, stretching his neck out. "Mike left me with a few parting gifts."

Bram doesn't ask more, and Rohan is shocked to find that his silence isn't uncomfortable.

"What about Chel?" Rohan asks in a whisper as they join a long line of eager customers. "What did she leave you with?"

Bram shifts his weight, staying close to Rohan just to keep his voice low, but he's pleased to discover that the topic doesn't really bother him as much as he thought it might. "I still get jumpy if my apartment is too quiet. I have to leave the bedroom door open so I can see inside it. Make sure nothing's going on that I don't want to see."

"How long were you two together?" Rohan asks.

Bram shrugs. "A few years."

"*Years?*" Rohan's eyes widen. "Jesus, no wonder it fucked you up. I only knew Mike for a few months."

As the line shuffles along, pushing everyone closer together, Bram presses up against Rohan's back to keep their conversation private. "I wonder how long Pearl was stuck with Ram."

"Too fucking long," Rohan deadpans.

They both agree to that.

Bram takes a backseat when they get to the register, letting Rohan sweet-talk the cashier with a pot-leaf name tag into a few free samples.

Bram likes the way Rohan so easily paves the way with conversation.

Rohan likes knowing that Bram is right behind him, quiet and steady, even if he *does* quickly shove a wad of bills at the cashier before Rohan can even get his wallet out.

"I'll owe you," Rohan whispers almost like a threat, eyes bright.

Bram smiles behind his mask. "We can discuss it later."

Rohan texts Pearl from the car. "He wants to watch a movie. I told him no porn."

"I mean, it is a vacation," Bram says.

"Well, alright then." Rohan continues texting. "Porn's back on the menu."

Pearl does *not* make them watch porn, but rather an action-horror movie that neither Rohan nor Bram would have chosen on their own, and yet, all three of them are glued to the screen. Rohan and Bram pass a joint back and forth as Pearl lounges over their laps, his body tingling with unmet desire.

When the movie is over, Pearl gets up and stretches. It takes him a few seconds to work up his voice to tell them, "Going to take a bath."

Bram's brow furrows. "You're so quiet even after we fed you."

Pearl glances between them, nerves prickling down his back and straight down his tail. Pushing his hands together, he searches for the most efficient way to explain it.

"Is it Ram?" Rohan asks.

Pearl nods, tipping his head back to frown at the ceiling. He taps his throat, looking at the two of them before he pulls up the words, *"He's my owner."*

The way they both instantly react to such a simple thing pleases Pearl in the very bottom of his stomach.

"He owns your voice?" Rohan asks, his face drawing itself even sharper.

Pearl rubs the back of his neck, guilt rising. He should really tell them these things sooner.

"Sorry," Pearl whispers. "Didn't want to ruin vacation."

"Can we get it back?" Bram asks, his doleful eyes fixed on Pearl. "That's all I want to know."

A smile spreads over Pearl's face and he leans in to kiss both of them on the cheek, whispering, "Maybe. Not sure. It's okay. Don't need it."

Pearl looks at them, drinking in the *new* desire settling into them both.

"We'll talk about it when we get home," Bram tells him.

Pearl nods, then points down the hall. "Bath."

"You're getting addicted to that tub, I can tell," Rohan says, waving the joint at him.

Pearl smiles and nods, splaying his fingers out to say, "Jets!"

Bram starts laughing. "Take as many baths as you want."

"Enjoy your evening, Prince Pearl." Rohan gives a mock-bow, and Pearl straightens his back, returning the bow with his tail coiled neatly at his hip.

As he walks away from the living room, he can feel the atmosphere begin to crackle.

"We're gonna help him, right?" Rohan whispers.

"Obviously, yeah," Bram hushes back to him.

"Wanna watch another movie?" Rohan asks a little louder, a smile in his voice.

Bram picks up the remote. "It's got a sequel."

"Let her rip." Rohan says.

With Pearl no longer draped over their bodies, they sit thigh-to-thigh, warmth gathering between their legs. Rohan almost regrets wearing sweatpants with Bram sitting there in gym shorts, his tanned knee pressed to ugly gray fabric.

"You know, I brought all these nice clothes for some reason," Bram says. "Not sure why. It's much nicer not to give a shit."

Rohan laughs, until he remembers the stockings shoved into the bottom of his suitcase, and his face heats up. "Better to be over-prepared than under-prepared."

"Yeah," Bram says, rubbing the heel of his hand against his muscled thigh. "Hey."

Rohan's stomach clenches at the earnest tone of his voice. "Yeah?"

Bram looks at his own knees, mentally sorting through his words. "Listen, uh."

Rohan can't tell if he's about to laugh or throw up as a markedly worse action movie about hunting down were-people plays out on the television.

"I just wanted to say. Uh." Bram swallows. "Look, I get it. I know you don't want to date. I know you don't want to be involved with someone like me. That's fine. I get it. I don't want you to think I'm trying to be someone I'm not. Even if you *were* looking for that kind of thing, I'm pretty much the opposite of what you'd want anyway." Bram holds up his finger to count off his own sins. "Gang ties. History of violence. Impulsive. Shit taste in women."

Despite himself, Rohan laughs while his face fills with heat.

Bram keeps his gaze locked on his lap. "I just. I-I get it. I don't know if you'll believe me, but I really just want you and Pearl in my life."

Rohan covers his mouth as he listens, his elbow anchored to the armrest, trying to hide the strange expression blooming on his face.

"I was thinking about what you said," Bram goes on, gesturing with his hand at nothing. "About how easy it is with Pearl. You're right about that. He's easy to be around. He knows what we want without having to ask, and he's got no shame about telling us what *he* wants. Fuck, I mean he's better at making himself heard than I am when he doesn't have a damn voice."

Rohan nods, queasy from the emotion brewing in his stomach. "Yeah."

When Bram turns his head to look at him, Rohan wants to crawl off the couch and out of sight. He can tell without even seeing for himself how heavy Bram's gaze is on the side of Rohan's face.

"I meant what I said." Bram's voice is low. "I don't lie to either of you. I'll be happy as long as I get to see you."

Rohan can't bring himself to move, his body locked in place with his thigh pressed against Bram's, his hand covering his mouth and the blush spreading over his cheeks. His heart will not stop pounding. This isn't the end, he knows. There's always a—

"*But.*" Bram leans toward him, just a little, just enough for Rohan's stomach to suck inward with a slight breath. "If you *were* looking for that kind of thing, I'd give just about anything for the chance to take you on a date. I'm not asking. Just saying. I wouldn't be ashamed to tell people I had you in my bed."

His voice sends sparks flying up through Rohan's lungs.

"*Well.*" Rohan clears his throat, speaking through his fingers as he shifts his hips over the couch. That goddamn weed is tearing through his blood and the way Bram speaks is making him hard.

"Even though I'm *not* looking to date anyone," Rohan says, gaze fixed on the corner of the cabinet that holds the TV. "And you are a gang boy with a checkered past and deeply questionable taste in men *and* women." Bram's lips curl into a smirk in the corner of Rohan's vision, and Rohan can't stop his lips twitching toward a smile beneath his fingers. "Even though all of that is true." Rohan swallows compulsively as his pulse beats louder. "It's still kinda nice to hear...that someone still thinks I'm, you know, that you wouldn't just want to fuck, but..."

He waves his hand in the air, unable to put to words what he can see the shape of in his mind with perfect clarity.

"You don't mind me saying it?" Bram asks.

Rohan shrugs. "Wouldn't want you to start lying."

"Even though we're not dating," Bram says.

"I'm not gonna date Bram Stoker," Rohan tells him. "Doesn't mean he can't say nice things about me."

Bram shifts toward Rohan, placing his hand on the back of the couch. "Can I tell you how gorgeous you are?"

Rohan's hips fill with heat as he curls toward the armrest. "It's a free country, you can do whatever you want."

Bram's fingers slip into Rohan's hair, sending a violent wave of goosebumps crashing down Rohan's back as Bram uncovers his neck. Panic flutters in Rohan's chest at the warm breath on his skin.

"You're so fuckin' handsome," Bram says, his lips pressing against the slope of Rohan's neck.

Rohan's mind tries to produce some kind of smarmy quip, anything to reassert his presence, to take control of the situation again, but Bram's warm hand circling his thigh scatters all his thoughts like fish.

"I do like it," Bram whispers, his fingers slinking up through Rohan's hair. "When you or Pearl just take control of things. Takes the uncertainty away."

Rohan's cock thickens in his sweatpants, his mind too hazy to remind him that dominance is usually what keeps him safe, composed, in control.

"It's just sometimes," Bram breathes the words against Rohan's neck, his fingers skimming over the shape of Rohan's growing erection. "You bring something out in me."

There should be alarm bells blaring in Rohan's head. There might be, and he just can't hear them over the sound of his own pounding blood. Rohan braces his hands on the armrest, sliding his thighs further apart even while he leans away from Bram. He needs air, tipping his head back as Bram kisses his throat. He needs to tell Bram this is a bad idea, but he's too busy moaning softly as Bram slips his hand down Rohan's old sweatpants to grip the hard length of his dick. He needs—Bram gropes the front of Rohan's tank top, searching out the tip of Rohan's nipple to rub his thumb into and Rohan presses his hips down and back into Bram's, his breath catching when he feels how hard Bram is.

Bram licks the column of Rohan's throat, his fingers tightening up over Rohan's cock as he pants, "Wanna fuck you until you come all over yourself."

Lightning shocks Rohan's system, a flash of anticipation so strong—*too strong*. Even as Rohan's dick pulses in Bram's hand, Rohan is driven back to his feet and off the couch, suddenly standing three feet away from Bram, his body stiffly locked into a tensed arrow.

"Uh." Bram sounds too stunned to be upset.

"*Just a second*," Rohan snaps, his feet carrying him from the room at light speed. Before he knows it, he is sitting on the edge of the bed he slept in last night with his head in his hands, eyes wide, heart pounding.

He has no idea how much time has passed when Pearl slips into the room with him, but as soon as Pearl is in front of him, Rohan grips him by the shoulders.

"I can't do this! What the fuck was I thinking?" He spews the words like venom. *"There's a reason I don't bottom anymore!"*

Pearl responds by kissing him on the mouth, probably to shut him up, but Rohan finally remembers to take a breath, softening his hold on Pearl's shoulders.

"Sorry," he whispers, pressing his forehead to Pearl's. "I don't know if I can do this, it's probably easier if we just keep—"

Pearl shoves his hand against Rohan's chest, and Rohan feels the bundle of fabric wadded up in his palm. He doesn't need to look to know what it is. Pearl fixes him with a firm gaze and Rohan shrinks in on himself.

"Will you at least stay with us? It's easier if you're there."

With a laugh, Pearl lets Rohan go and steps away. He holds his hand up with two fingers raised.

"Okay, okay, I'll be quick," Rohan says, reaching for the waist of his pants.

With a smile, Pearl slips out of the room.

Bram is sitting on the couch, frozen in fear, hands plastered to his face. When Pearl marches up to him, Bram mutters, "I fucked up. Ooh boy, I fucked up."

Pearl pulls one of his hands away, wrapping his fingers around the back of Bram's neck to pull their faces together. Bram latches onto him, gripping his waist, breathing easier with Pearl so close.

"I don't know why I thought I'd just be able to—"

Before he can finish, Pearl takes his hand and presses a small container into it. Glancing down, Bram flushes at the sight of the brand new bottle of lube he bought just for this trip on the very vain hope that they could escalate things. Now, it doesn't feel quite so out of reach when Pearl smirks at him and pulls Bram off the couch. With a rush of blood to Bram's hips, Pearl once again leads him toward exactly what he wants.

Pearl sees it all. He *feels* it all.

Bram can hardly breathe when Pearl pushes open the bedroom door where Rohan is holed up. As soon as Bram catches a glimpse of black pantyhose stretched over long legs, his stomach clenches.

Rohan sits at the foot of the haphazardly made bed, facing the long glass windows that offer a view of the ocean. One muscled leg is crossed over the other, but he's bouncing his foot up and down as he sits there, his neat ponytail dangling over his bare back. Rohan is entirely naked, save for the pantyhose, and Bram stares at the meat of his ass filling out the sheer material—until Pearl shoves him further into the room.

Rohan turns his head to look behind him at Bram, the tops of his cheeks gone red. "You seemed to like it so I thought I'd do you a favor."

Bram takes a deep breath, gripping the bottle in his right hand as he slowly creeps past the length of the bed, approaching Rohan like a spooked horse. "That mean you like me?"

"Don't push it, vampire." Rohan's gaze scans over Bram's face, the obvious lust in Bram's eyes, the slow but steady way he moves his body, his empty hand casually rubbing his own hip as he rounds the corner of the bed, standing only a few feet away.

With his heart in his throat, Rohan parts his legs. "C'mere."

Bram closes the gap immediately, swooping in to kneel in front of Rohan, and drops the bottle so he can run both his hands up Rohan's thighs. Both of them stutter as they inhale, desire welling up through their skin. Bram grips the back of Rohan's knee and lifts, running his face against the nylon. Rohan gives a tight gasp at the heat of Bram's breath drawing closer to his hips.

"You smell so fuckin' good," Bram mutters, inhaling the sharp tang of skin cutting through citrusy soap.

Rohan's cock pounds beneath the tight mesh, dizziness threatening to take hold. "I haven't done this in a while."

Bram's eyes slide shut as he cups Rohan's ass with both hands and nuzzles his face to the bulge trapped beneath the translucent black fabric, his mouth watering as Rohan's dick thickens against his cheek and lips.

Rohan tips back onto his elbows, trying to keep the panic at bay as his cock practically goes numb from the soft touch. "How much did we smoke?"

Bram drags his tongue over the head of Rohan's cock through the nylon, swallowing the taste of salt. "Want to lick every inch of you."

"Oh god." Rohan's thoughts are boiling away, replaced by urges.

Bram nips at the pantyhose right around the tightening skin of Rohan's balls, and they both startle at the sound Rohan makes—a sudden, instinctual yelp wrenched out from Rohan's belly as he tries to jerk his hips back, but Bram grips him tight.

Rohan goes still, glancing down his torso at Bram who stares back at him, his brown eyes wide and focused, hands flexed around Rohan's ass.

"Something you want down here?" Bram asks under his breath, his lips still touching the fine nylon. His cock aches, untouched in his shorts, and even though he's sure it'll be worth it to wait, that sound speaks to his blood.

Panting, Rohan doesn't know which voice in his head to ignore—the one screaming not to let go of his control, or the one begging for thoughtless pleasure. Bram watches him like a hawk, his thick arms wrapped tight around Rohan's thighs. Even with their height gap, Bram could probably lift Rohan if he wanted. They could get into all sorts of trouble. They could do anything.

This is what Bram wants. Rohan recalls what Pearl and Bram have been trying to tell him for the last few weeks. Bram wants to do the work, and he wants to do it well.

Bram can swear he sees the moment that Rohan stops fighting whatever it is that's been keeping him back. His bright eyes sink into a haze, not the shark-tooth smile that he likes to tease Bram with, but a single-minded lust that nearly bowls Bram over. The heat of Rohan's body sinks into Bram's fingertips as Rohan says in a low voice, "Take 'em off.'

Bram does not hesitate, peeling the pantyhose from Rohan's ass, hiking his long legs up to get them all the way off and onto the floor. Bram sets his hand on the covers, poised to pull himself up on top of Rohan, but Rohan stops him with a tilt of his head. Bram's heart pounds, his dick pulsing hard as Rohan takes Bram's hand and guides his fingers to the root of Rohan's cock, the sound of Rohan's breathing gone choppy and strained. Rohan guides Bram's fingers up against the soft skin of his balls, and Bram sees Rohan's eyelids flutter over his unfocused gaze.

Bram's lips part as Rohan presses harder, pushing Bram in closer to his hip until the loose folds of skin envelop the pad of Bram's finger, sucking him into a small, tight pocket of heat. Rohan's belly stutters with a gasp when Bram tucks that soft skin back up into his body, creating a heated tunnel for Bram to slowly finger. Bram can't stop from pressing his dick into the side of the mattress as he leans in closer. He sits there, stunned breathless, fucking the empty canal of Rohan's balls as heat rushes through Bram's limbs. As softly as he can, Bram rubs against the little ring at the entrance of the hole, his mouth watering at the bulge in Rohan's skin next to his cock where Bram's finger is now sheathed.

"*Hhn, oh fuck.*" Rohan swiftly loses control of his voice. Every time he inhales, his entire body shudders, but he holds Bram's wrist right where it is, not letting him go. "Get the fucking lube," he pants.

Bram blinks out of his hypnotic reverie and glances around for the bottle, nearly flinging it across the room in his frantic excitement to get inside Rohan even deeper. He can't think straight with his finger pressed into Rohan's hole, the scent of cum and sweat filling his nose.

"Give it to me." Rohan swats at the bottle and Bram passes it to him so he can open without having to stop Bram from fucking the tight tunnel of Rohan's skin. Rohan pours lube onto Bram's free hand, his breath getting increasingly ragged, his cock thick on his belly, pulling at the skin wrapped around Bram's finger.

Bram pushes Rohan's thigh back to give himself more space, leaving sticky fingerprints across Rohan's skin. His tongue is heavy in his mouth as Bram draws a slick finger over the rim of Rohan's asshole.

"Don't fucking *tease me.*" Rohan's voice comes out a miserable whine, but Bram shakes his head.

"I want to take my time," he says back, a new calm coming over him as he pulls his finger back out, and lets Rohan's balls go. "We're on vacation, aren't we?"

"Jesus fuck." Rohan grabs Bram's wrist again. "Don't give me time to *think!*"

Rohan's eyes are wild, and Bram holds his frenzied gaze, his pulse throbbing through every part of his body.

Rohan is actively fighting the urge to crawl away from Bram and this slow bleed of pleasure filling him up. It's almost too overwhelming when Bram looks directly at him like this. It's not just the lust, it's not just the need to fuck—Bram wants Rohan to be *his.* It's obvious in the way he moves, the way he talks, the way he touches Rohan's body like he's scared this will be the last time.

"I want you to think about me," Bram tells him, soft and low, a velvet voice to match his lips when he kisses the inside of Rohan's thigh, once, twice, moving in toward the center of Rohan's body. As Bram licks Rohan's rim, feeling the muscles twitch against his tongue, Rohan spreads his legs, his mouth falling open.

"*Ooh you—fuck.*" Rohan grabs his thighs, pulling them back as his face turns scarlet. "Gonna get you—*hah—get you back for this.*"

Bram ignores his threats, spearing his tongue into Rohan's ass, reveling in the soft fluttering of muscle around him, and the catch in Rohan's breath. Rohan tries to hold back for all of five writhing seconds before he grabs the back of Bram's head and pulls him even closer. As Bram hauls Rohan's hips to the edge of the bed, and Rohan loses himself to the pounding of his own heart and the wet *shlick* of Bram's tongue wetting his insides, Pearl could swear his body is *lifting* even without full-grown wings.

Pearl has never felt more alive. His skin tingles, his insides vibrating. Sitting on the floor by the side of the bed, Pearl watches his two favorite people finally give in to their deepest desires. All because of *him*.

Rohan moans when Bram slips two fingers into his ass, and Pearl digs his fingers into the bedding. Bram rises up to his knees, pulling his gym shorts down with one hand and Pearl bites the covers, sending the slightest bit of suggestion down Rohan's throat so he picks his head up. As soon as Rohan sees Bram attempting to undress, he lurches forward, forcing Bram to pull his fingers out just so Rohan can sit up and wrench Bram's clothes down himself. Rohan grabs Bram's dick to hold it up to his mouth, running his tongue over the slit to catch a bead of cum.

"You're just as fucking greedy as Pearl," Bram says, voice full of breath, his cockhead tingling.

Rohan's gaze flicks up to his. "So are you."

The corner of Bram's mouth pulls into a smirk. He brushes his knuckles over Rohan's cheek and, much to Rohan's annoyance, the tenderness feels just as good as the reckless lust. "You're not gonna bolt again, are you?"

Rohan glares at those pretty brown eyes, his body feeling weightless as he imagines how good it will feel when Bram is moaning in his ear. "Depends how long it takes you to get your dick inside me."

"Hm, might be more fun to just tease you all night. See how mad you get." Bram eases his knee onto the bed beside Rohan's thigh, his stomach clenching with anticipation.

Rohan swallows, his thighs buzzing as he slides backward to make room for them both. "One of us is getting fucked tonight or I'm taking the next flight home. Not too late to change your mind if you want me to do the honors."

Bram pulls his shirt off and crawls after Rohan, herding him toward the headboard. "We can save that for another night."

Rohan swallows, taking in the heft of Bram's bare chest, the wide set of his shoulders, thick muscle padded with soft fat. "Why'd you have to be so goddamn handsome?" Rohan asks.

Bram's face blooms with heat, his lips pulling into a small smile that Rohan knows is going to be seared into his mind for the next six months.

Pearl holds tight to the covers, letting just the smallest hint of impatience wash over their skin. They both shift toward the other, their breath filling their chests, sparks flying off embers. Finally, Bram grabs Rohan's thigh and dives his hand back into Rohan's cleft.

"H-hold on!" Rohan grabs Bram's arm but he can't hold Bram back from burying his middle and ring fingers into Rohan's ass. "*Hoh god!*"

"Have to make sure you're good for it," Bram murmurs, his cock throbbing where it hangs. He fucks his fingers harder into Rohan's hole as Rohan clenches down on his knuckles. "I've been told I'm kind of thick so I don't want it to hurt."

"*Fuck!*" Rohan's voice leaps out of him, his legs tensing. "Wait, wait—*ahh!*"

His torso jumps at the third finger slipped inside. Rohan's hands shoot out to grab Bram's shoulders, slapping his palm down on Bram's bicep several times as sensation drills through him. Bram drinks up the sight of Rohan's overwhelm, staring at Rohan's cock straining between them, already dripping wet.

"You want another?" Bram asks, not waiting for an answer as he bunches his fingers together to stretch Rohan's hole even wider.

Rohan curls forward, panic in his eyes as he jerks his hips away from the electric pleasure overwhelming his entire body. "Too much, oh fuck, *oh fuck!*"

He blindly reaches for Bram's hair, yanking hard while his hips shudder with the rhythm of Bram's hand fucking his ass. Pain zips down Bram's scalp, bringing a strange smile to his lips as he watches the deep tan of his fingers filling Rohan's hole. It's never been more rewarding to draw this out and really watch someone fall apart. Rohan still looks like he's trying to escape, even while he hips thrust with Bram's hand, his eyes slowly losing focus.

As tempting as it is to make Rohan come just from his fingers, Bram pulls his hand back, deciding in a flash how he wants to do this. With a shivering gasp, Rohan goes still again, save for his heaving chest as he pants for air. As soon as Bram has the thought that he'd like to fuck Rohan on his back so he can see when Rohan comes, Rohan's gaze fixes on Bram as if he can see the image in Bram's mind.

Cheeks red, Rohan braces his hands like he's going to pull away, and Bram snaps down on top of him.

Rohan twists around like a snake in Bram's grasp, so Bram clamps his arms tight around Rohan's chest. All of a sudden, they're wrestling, no different really than when Rohan has wrestled Pearl to the couch, or how Bram used to wrangle his little brother into submission when they would fight over the single video game console in the house. A wild smile lights up Bram's face as he pins Rohan face first to the bed, his wrists held at the small of his back, his hard cock pressed to Rohan's ass.

Bram leans down, panting softly as he whispers in Rohan's ear. "I win."

"Fuck you," Rohan says immediately, though even Rohan can hear how desperate he sounds.

Rohan bites his lip to keep from gasping when Bram nudges his thighs apart with the bulb of his knee. Rohan doesn't want to make it easy. He wants to make Bram work for this. He wants, *he wants, he wants Bram to fuck him until he can't think.*

Every time Rohan pulls against Bram's grip, Bram's blood rushes to his hips. Anyone else, and Bram wouldn't be able to let himself do this. Only here can Bram grip Rohan's wrists in one hand and set his throbbing dick against the wet heat of Rohan's rim without fearing what someone else will think of him. He can spread Rohan open and shove his cock into the slicked walls of Rohan's ass while Rohan squirms beneath him.

"*Ahh!*"

They both moan at the way Rohan squeezes Bram's tip, but Pearl is the only one aware enough to see it happen. Rubbing his tail between his thighs, Pearl does not blink as Bram fucks his cock in deeper, inch by inch, lengthening each thrust, holding Rohan in place by the wrists.

Rohan's voices rises into a warbling, broken gasp and he pushes his knees further apart, lifting his ass up to meet Bram's hips. Bram looks hypnotized as he stares at the length of Rohan's back, his long hair strewn over the covers, the spread of his ass around Bram's cock. He wants Rohan speechless. He wants to be the one that finally gets Rohan to let go and give in. He wants, *he wants, he wants to fuck Rohan until he can't breathe.*

Pearl is intoxicated by the way Bram groans when he bottoms out, the deep bellowing moan that Rohan gives as he presses his face into the covers. Pearl has never concentrated this hard in his life, and he has never been more enthralled by the wild thrill of desires getting met.

Ever since he went out hunting to find someone who gave off the same rich and lovely scent as Rohan, Pearl has been holding his breath for this moment. It's almost too much for him.

"*Fu-uck!*" Rohan's voice stutters.

"*So fucking good,*" Bram mindlessly babbles, frantically pulling Rohan onto his side so he can wrap his arms around Rohan's chest and bury his face in Rohan's shoulder.

Rohan digs his fingers into Bram's thigh and bends his own leg back, unable to stop his endless, mindless noise. Bram is relentless, so much worse than Pearl prepared him for—fucking Rohan like he's got endless energy. His dick is thick enough to steal Rohan's breath every time it fills his ass.

"*Oo-oh, oh no.*" Rohan's voice abruptly cuts off, his body tensing inward.

Bram perks up at the sudden shift, watching in awe as Rohan starts to peak, a burst of cum lining the rumpled covers in front of them. With pride swelling in his belly for the first time in weeks, Bram pulls Rohan's back against his chest, trying to brace his feet so he can fuck Rohan even harder. Every little twitch of Rohan's hips, his arms scrabbling for purchase, his legs splayed out and swaying with the movement, echoes back through Bram until he can't take it.

Pearl whines quietly as Rohan comes onto his own stomach, his body stuck in a taut arc over top of Bram, long enough to cover Bram end-to-end. Bram's dark tan skin wraps tightly around Rohan's, Bram's thick fingers holding Rohan tight like a vice grip. Almost immediately, Bram follows on Rohan's heels, spilling into Rohan's ass until there are white ribbons dripping onto the bed from Rohan's hole.

For a second, they go still, save for their panting breaths. It takes a moment for their bodies to re-solidify. When Bram runs his hands over Rohan's chest, Rohan wakes back up, spinning around to grab his face and kiss Bram on the mouth. Bram doesn't hesitate to pull him in and kiss Rohan back, molding to him.

Rohan pulls his legs up to straddle Bram's hips and hisses like an insult, "You're so fucking handsome."

Bram swallows Rohan's tongue once more, sinking his fingers into his long hair before wrenching back to whisper, "Your ass is incredible."

Rohan bites Bram's lip, his breath huffing out of his nose. "Do it harder next time."

Bram grabs the back of Rohan's head. "Harder?"

Rohan almost whines in his throat, his face pressed to Bram's as he fights to keep his rapidly dissolving composure. "Want you to fuck every hole in my body until I can't move."

Bram pulls Rohan back into a hungry kiss, tracing Rohan's spine down to the swell of his ass so he can rub his fingers over Rohan's rim. "I'll do anything you want."

Rohan groans through their next kiss, spreading his knees wider as Bram lazily slots his ring finger back into Rohan's ass. "God, I—" Rohan inhales sharply, kissing Bram to buy himself time as these barbed words work up his throat. "Want you so bad."

Bram slowly works his finger deep into Rohan's hole, not minding in the slightest that it might be him getting this workout next. Pearl and Rohan would probably both love that.

"You can have my real name if you want it," Bram murmurs, every inch of his skin licked with heat. "Maybe you could date him instead of Bram Stoker."

When Rohan kisses him again, frenzied and breathy, it somehow feels like a *yes* to Bram's body-drunk brain.

"*Sorry sorry sorry!*" Pearl's voice cuts through the haze and both Bram and Rohan sharply pull back, turning to see him leaning onto the bed, his hands splayed out, eyes wide, skin shining in the lamplight. "Sorry, I didn't mean to let it go on that long."

Like lights flicking on, Bram and Rohan both snap out of the magnetic pull of the trance that Pearl had them veiled in.

"Did you do some magic shit to us?" Rohan demands, peeling himself off of Bram to glare at Pearl.

Pearl stares back at him, his black eyes softening, lips parting. Then, his tail begins to swish where it hangs between his legs. "I wanna touch your holes too!"

Rohan's eyes flash, a look on his face like he bit down on something unexpectedly sharp. He crosses his arms in front of his chest, turning his head away from both of them, mouth puckered. "Look, I wasn't exactly planning on that."

Bram sits up, guilt prickling down the back of his neck. "I, uh—"

"It was *so sexy*, please!" Pearl hops onto the bed, wrapping his arms around Rohan's neck and kissing his face. His voice is rich and full once more, nurtured by a decadent meal. "I really want to touch it, it looked fun and I've never seen a human do that before, please Rohan!"

Rohan's chest slowly expands as he breathes in deep, his fingers tightening over his arms.

"We could do it at the same time." Pearl lowers his voice to a stage whisper. With his pink-brushed cheeks, he looks well and truly drunk.

"Bram and I could fill up all your holes all at once and I bet it would feel *amazing.*"

"Alright, alright, *fine,*" Rohan snaps, red once more. "Fucking relentless."

Pearl hugs him tighter, immediately diving his hand between Rohan's thighs. "Show me."

"Slow down," Rohan scolds, snatching his wrist.

Pearl nods over and over, and Bram feels the warmth returning to his chest.

"You want the pillows?" Bram asks quietly.

Rohan's gaze cuts to his, embarrassment bristling out of him. "Back up," he answers, voice clipped. "Sit there and I'll show you."

Bram does as instructed, pressing his back to the wooden headboard. Rohan slinks down in front of him, pressing his back to Bram's chest as Pearl eagerly crawls up between Rohan's legs.

When they all do it together, there's a different kind of feeling that works its way up their spines. With Pearl and Bram each fingering the two matching holes beneath Rohan's cock, there's nothing left to be embarrassed about. Rohan's head goes slack on Bram's shoulder, his legs frogged up beside him, every breath a velvet gasp.

"I love humans," Pearl says, his eyes wide as he gently works two thin fingers into the tunnel of nerves in Rohan's body.

"You're so cute," Bram tells him, watching Pearl's massage Rohan's hole, his own finger twice as thick in the other pocket of softened flesh.

Rohan moans into Bram's neck as liquid heat pools in his abdomen. "Swear to god I'm gonna fuck you by the end of this week," Rohan threatens, voice full of breath.

Bram pulls his finger out, tracing down Rohan's balls and over the soft skin beneath. Rohan's knees tense, and Pearl grins.

"He likes that," Pearl says.

Bram rubs his finger along the bridge of skin leading to Rohan's hole, and they both hear his breath catch, his back arching against Bram.

"*Jesus,*" Rohan grips Bram's thigh.

Bram smiles, reaching for Rohan's face so he can kiss the next gasp from his lips. Pearl takes the cue, snaking his tail up against Rohan's ass to tease him. Rohan jumps, rewarding Bram with a deep moan rumbling across his tongue.

"Don't worry," Pearl says, leaning up to whisper. "We can get Bram back later."

Rohan and Bram both turn to look at Pearl, Rohan panting hard, his angled face still flushed, his hair a streaming mess. Bram keeps his wide face nuzzled to Rohan's cheek, staring at Pearl with one eye like he's hiding behind Rohan, his pretty brown gaze warm with affection, his black hair sticking out from all of Rohan's pawing.

Pearl's entire body perks up, anticipation filling his lungs as he stares at these handsome men waiting for him.

"I think you're the one who needs a lesson next," Rohan says to Pearl.

"You know that's what he wants, right?" Bram murmurs.

Rohan looks at Bram, a tired smile crossing his lips. "We can't surprise him with anything, can we?"

"No," Bram says. "I don't know how to trick an incubus."

Pearl can hardly breathe through his own excitement. "It's a well-guarded secret."

"Guess we'll have to force it out of you," Rohan says, grabbing Pearl's arm.

"I know how to get info out of stubborn people," Bram adds, twisting Pearl's tail around his hand.

Pearl gladly falls into their grasp, pulled in deep between the rich scents of their desires, no longer held back by thick walls but nestled safely in the mouth of their lust.

RAM

When Ram draws the portal to the human world, he tells himself he is prepared for anything. After countless conversations with his father about reckless behavior and childish attachments, Ram is sure he has thought of everything to pave the way for a successful rescue mission. He even sports a protective layer of clothing around his hips just to keep himself better defended this time.

Every time he thinks about that damn red-haired human kneeing him in the crotch, a twinge of phantom pain twitches through each shaft of his cock. He will not be caught unawares a second time. He will be patient, cunning, and ruthless. These humans won't know what hit them. They will rue the day that they stole his most precious cub from him.

Ram: full fledged incubus, and former owner of Pearl (aka Angel). After Pearl ran away from home, Ram swore to return his stolen cub and resume their teaching, only to discover that Pearl had been kidnapped by very experienced human thieves who were not to be taken lightly.

As Ram finishes the chalk outline around himself, tearing between his world and theirs, his being is swallowed up in black voidlight, and he lays a hand on his father's mace.

"Ah, there you are."

Ram stiffens at the sound of a cool, dry voice.

Inside the darkened garage, a human sits on a folding chair, one leg crossed over the other. He pushes his glasses up his nose with a black-gloved hand and rises up to stand across from Ram, a small gun held at his hip.

"Don't try anything," the man says, quietly. "I've been told you have a particular weakness to—"

Immediately, Ram surges forward, drawing the marble mace, but before he can connect, a sharp pain sinks into his bicep, and the human vanishes from sight.

"Chemicals," the human finishes.

Ram wheels around to face the man, the outline of his neatly buttoned, dark blue, three-piece suit beginning to skew in Ram's vision. Breathing hard, Ram rushes forward, attempting once more to use brute strength to subdue this scrawny human, but to no avail. The human easily vanishes from his sight, practically dancing out of Ram's path as another stinging dart lands directly in Ram's neck.

Furious, Ram rips the dart out, snarling at the blurring shape of the man in the blue suit with the slicked-back hair and the thick-rimmed glasses. Ram takes one more step toward the wavering sallow color of the human's face before his entire body sags with some unknowable weight, and then he is on the floor.

Pulling his glasses off his face, Lee regards the unconscious incubus sprawled out on the floor in front of him, and kneels down by his black bag to fish out a length of rope. He had almost hoped it would be more difficult to capture this beast, but Pearl's instructions were clear, and incredibly spot on.

Leandro "Lee" Baladin: former nurse practitioner and recently appointed second-in-command to Bram Stoker, leader of the Southside Vampires. Lee is a jack-of-all-trades, and takes his station very seriously.

Following the drawings Pearl made for him, Lee takes the chalk from Ram's hip pouch and creates a "binding lock" to keep the incubus in place. Next, he ties up Ram's thick arms and ankles, and sets out a bottle of water, a plastic bag, and his personal knife roll.

Sitting back down on his folding chair, Lee pulls out a crustless peanut butter and jelly sandwich from the blue-and-white cooler, leaving the two rice balls for later, and waits for Ram to wake up.

Fifteen minutes later, the incubus groans, his massive tail twitching across the floor. As soon as the tip—scarred over into a nub, just as Pearl said it would be—touches the edge of the binding lock, something like static crackles through the air, and Ram jolts back from it.

"What—" Ram tries to pick himself up from the floor, struggling against the ropes tied around him. "What have you done?"

Lee takes a breath, preparing for the next part of this confrontation. Pearl, Bram *and* Mr. Rohan all warned Lee about the power of the incubus's trance and what it can do to a human mind. Conjuring up one's deepest and most vulnerable desires to wield against them, painting an elaborate illusion to lull someone into a lustful frenzy.

"Mr. Ram, it's a pleasure to meet you," Lee says, folding his hands into his lap. "I apologize that we can't meet each other on equal grounds, but you can understand why I had to take measures to protect myself."

Ram bares an impressive set of teeth at Lee, definitely an enlarged set of incisors in that mouth. *"You will regret this, human!"*

Lee nods. "Of course I will. I've been quite good at separating my private and personal life for some time now, but you are a special case."

The incubus with pitch-black eyes and brown-and-pink mottled skin snarls at Lee from the floor. Pearl mentioned that incubus like Ram often shave their heads, associating long hair with the succubus playbook. "Return my mace and chalk immediately."

Lee does not move. "You understand why that would be an incredibly stupid move on my part, right?"

The incubus only growls back, painstakingly hoisting himself up to sit on his knees and glare at Lee. His body is built on a massive frame that could easily crush a body like Lee's.

"I can see you're not feeling very compliant right now," Lee says. "I'll wait for you to settle down so we can talk."

"How about I rip open your—" The incubus heaves, his horned face going ashy as nausea stirs in his belly. "Your...hh...*hah.*"

Lee rises up, plucks the plastic bag from the floor, and holds it up for the incubus to begin puking into. Thick black bile fills the bag like oil, and Ram gives a shuddering breath after it leaves him.

"You fucking humans and your fucking chemicals," Ram pants, his mottled skin rapidly losing color. "You never fight as proper beasts."

"My boss fights like you," Lee responds, tying the bag off and setting it behind his chair to incinerate later. "He respects a fight, and a fighter. He takes pride in the abilities of his own body. It's quite a sight to see, although I'm guessing you'd rather not remember getting bested by him and your former student."

"It was that damn red-haired human with the chemicals, that was the only reason they were able to get the better of me!" Ram insists, scraping up whatever dignity he can. "And they did something to brainwash Shining Star as well! Hardly a fair or honorable fight. And *you*." Ram narrows his black eyes, no whites left in them. "You did not even try to lay a hand on me. A shameful ambush and rotten chemicals to reduce my strength. You could never call yourself a warrior."

"I don't," Lee tells him, holding his arms behind his back as he looks over his captive. "I am the lieutenant to Bram Stoker. I wear many hats, but *warrior* isn't one of them. What I do is clean up the kinds of messes that the rest of our organization, or the general public, would be better off without ever having to see. Right now, Mr. Ram, you are one of the messes I am responsible for."

Ram's ragged breathing deepens, and he lifts his head up higher. "You are the ones who stole from me."

"That's not how Pearl tells the story," Lee replies, head tilting to the side. "Sorry, you know him as Shining Silver Starlight."

Ram's tail coils toward his body.

"Your former student came to Bram Stoker willingly," Lee says. "There was no theft involved. Pearl, *formerly known as* Shining Silver Starlight, is officially under the protection of the Southside Vampires, and as such, when *you* attempted to kidnap Pearl from inside Bram Stoker's own home, Mr. Ram, you made yourself an enemy to Bram Stoker, to the whole of the Southside Vampires, and most importantly, to me."

Turning to his folding chair, Lee takes up the knife roll, untying the leather straps so he can unspool the contents inside.

"The Vampires don't tolerate leeches, Mr. Ram," Lee says, scanning over his options.

Heat rises up through Lee's legs as he studies the edges of his tools.

"You hold a position of submission," Ram says. "Servant to another who orders you to unsightly tasks."

The fine, clean edge of the scalpel, the tight serration of the hunter's knife, the long, thin edge of the butcher's blade. Lee sees himself in the reflection of the silver.

"Work like yours does not allow for very much companionship, does it?" Ram asks, the quality of his voice changing from abject hostility, to pliant curiosity.

"No, it does not," Lee answers, touching the opened mouth of the pliers. "I made my peace with that a long time ago."

"It is cruel to ask a man to suppress his desires just for the sake or convenience of another," Ram says, his voice like billowing smoke as it crawls up Lee's neck.

"I wasn't asked to suppress my desires," Lee murmurs, setting the tip of the screwdriver against his nail.

The first layer of the incubus's trance induces arousal in the subject. If there are no other bodies present, it is easier to anchor the subject's focus on the incubus themself, in order to stoke the fire and keep the subject open to possibilities.

"And yet you lack something." Ram's voice is far more sultry than it was before he began his prying. All the anger and self-righteousness have vanished, replaced with a smoldering purr that rolls over Lee like warm water.

"That might be true," Lee says, fondling the edge of the wooden mallet. "It has been a long time since I indulged."

Lee can feel the quick spread of arousal licking up his thighs.

The second layer of the incubus's trance heightens the subject's need to seek an outlet for the growing lust. The subject will begin to lose interest in anything that does not bring them pleasure, becoming more suggestible to distraction, more forthcoming with information.

"What is it you want from me, human?" Ram asks. "It is only the two of us here, is it not?"

"Yes," Lee answers. "Pearl gave us all the information about how your portals work, the most likely places you would come through. I narrowed down the best option for you, and made sure to wear the charm Pearl made for me to conceal my presence, so I could get the jump on you."

Lee reaches into his breast pocket, removing a small pouch of silk. Ram instantly recognizes Pearl's—*Silver Starlight's*—scent in the air. There is no doubt that his hair is in that pouch, tied into a knot and dipped in blood.

"You forced him to make that for you?" Ram asks, his sultry performance faltering.

Tucking the pouch back into his pocket, Lee begins removing his dark blue suit jacket to hang on the back of his folding chair. "We haven't forced him to do anything. Pearl helped because he wanted to make sure that we made it perfectly clear to you that Pearl has no intention of ever returning to your world."

"Ridiculous," Ram spits back at him. "I hold something of great value to Silver Starlight. If my Starlight has any hope of getting it back—"

"He doesn't care about his voice," Lee says, calmly rolling up the sleeves of his dress shirt. "Pearl appears to be quite happy in the care of Mr. Stoker and Mr. Rohan. They keep him well fed, as I understand. Well enough that Pearl can even speak on his own for short periods of time. It doesn't bother him to be mute."

Ram glares at the human named Lee as he reaches into the fabric roll to pull out the needle-point knife. His lips part, the slightest hint of blood beneath the skin of his sallow cheeks.

"He recorded a message for you," Lee says, pulling out his cell phone. "I thought it would be unnecessary, given how obvious it is that Pearl helped me. But now I'm starting to think that even if I did play that message, you wouldn't believe it was real."

Lee looks at Ram, his green eyes wide with sudden interest as he grips the handle of the knife. The moment Lee places the tip of his brown dress shoe past the border of the binding lock, Ram immediately clenches his hips, attempting to lash out with his tail, but nothing happens. Lee approaches him, the skin of his face beginning to tic as though he's fighting to keep his expression calm.

"I numbed your tail while you were passed out," Lee says, planting his foot beside Ram's leg. "It should be in full effect by now."

Ram stares up at this human named Lee, the adrenaline clearly coursing through his veins, the desire pulsating inside his body.

The third layer of the incubus's trance severs the subject's connection from their better judgment, allowing the pursuit of deep, buried, or forgotten desires.

As shadow drops over the empty garage where the two of them are holed up, Ram tries to pull against the ropes binding him. For the first time in a very long time, there is fear igniting through his blood. This human is not like any other Ram has encountered. This is exactly the kind of human that led to the paired fledgling training system that everyone must go through. It is always safer to hunt in pairs, and it is always safer to prey on couples who can fixate on each other, not the incubus who wishes to feed off of them.

Before Ram can take hold of the illusion and tailor it to the human named *Lee*, the lights reset. The abandoned garage does not paint over with some imagined bedroom. There is no illusion at all. Ram stares wide-eyed at Lee, his skin prickling with sweat.

"What's wrong?" Lee asks. "I thought you'd pull me under your spell by now."

"I did," Ram mutters, his booming voice reduced to a fizzle.

The human crackles with excitement, his breathing deepening, his skin flushing with blood. The scent coming off of him carries the tang of iron.

"Can you tell?" Lee asks, electric green eyes piercing through Ram. "I've been looking forward to this."

Panic seizes Ram's spine as images flood his mind—the human's desire for *him*, studied and cataloged, picked clean apart. Blood, bruises, broken bones, screams of pained ecstasy, gasping for air, grasping for consciousness.

Just as Ram tries to drop his head and shove his horns into this human's fleshy body, Lee grabs his leftmost horn, wrenching Ram's neck back.

"Ah, ah, ah." Lee raises that needle-point knife to touch the column of Ram's throat. "Pearl warned me you get jumpy when you're cornered."

The metal is cool against Ram's skin as Lee slides the point up to touch the artery pounding in Ram's neck.

"You seem to share the basic anatomy of a human," Lee says, the leather of his glove pulling at the skin covering Ram's horn. "The major differences appear to be in these extra features, the horns, the tails, the wings. That, and your ability to feed off desire instead of food. I'm guessing that's why you're so weak to chemicals. Your bodies weren't made to process complex substances."

"Would it not be more desirable for you to lay with me?" Ram asks, his breath short, fear beating through the cage of his chest at this clinical talk. "Then you could see the body you wish to study in its natural form?"

Lee's pale pink mouth twitches toward another smile. "Oh, I'm very curious about that as well, Mr. Ram. I'm curious about all of you. Your blood appears differently than a human's under a microscope. You share qualities with plant life. You must absorb desire passively like sunlight."

When Lee takes another breath, it seems to rattle in his throat like an ill-fitted pipe.

"Am I feeding you now?" Lee asks, bloodlessly drawing the knife down Ram's throat and into the soft hollow at the center of his clavicles.

Ram doesn't want to admit it, he does not want this human's lust inside him, but every breath he takes is laced with rich, potent, dense desire that buzzes beneath his skin, easily filling the gouges taken out of him by the chemicals and the failed trance.

When Lee slices a delicate line into the skin of Ram's chest, Ram bares his teeth at the sting of pain. Raising the knife tip, Lee feeds himself a drop of translucent, red blood.

"Incredible," Lee breathes, and Ram can feel the opening of his capillaries, the increased flow of blood, the shift inside Lee's hips as he stiffens in his suit pants.

"You *have* been suppressing yourself," Ram says, horror and awe like water and oil in his mouth.

"I prefer to call it professionalism," Lee says.

The knife comes to rest on Ram's lips, one twitch away from slicing into his mouth.

"What do I taste like?" Lee asks. He holds Ram's chest against his own hips, the spreading warmth of his erection bleeding into Ram's skin through the finely fit clothes. "Am I too rotten to eat?"

Ram tries to remember his own training from so long ago. His former owner had always warned him about the dangers of hunting alone. Sometimes, a human is more than one incubus can handle. Sometimes humans have dangerous desires that are better left contained.

As Lee draws a droplet of blood from Ram's pale lips, the knife dimpling the splotch of pink skin across his jaw, Ram feels Lee's cock swelling against his chest. The strength and depth of the arousal pouring off of Lee is almost enough to blot out the pain from the knife. The look on this human's face confounds. He watches the gathering droplet of blood as though it contains a universe.

Ram stiffens when Lee grips his horn tighter and licks Ram's split lip, hot breath puffing over Ram's skin, deep hunger opening up inside the human's body like a fissure. He startles when Lee forces them into a kiss. A bloody tongue fills Ram's mouth, and a massive spike of lust hits him almost as swiftly as the chemicals.

Has he ever been kissed with a need this great? Entirely directed at *him*? Not a human disguise he wears, nor a performance put on by him and Shining Starlight, but Ram in his real body?

Lee breaks off with a harsh breath, narrowing his eyes. "Who brings a *mace* to a fight with humans? It's ridiculous."

Ram's blood stains Lee's lips, his harsh words sap the confidence from Ram's skin, and yet, the human's desire for him is only growing. Lee trails the tip of the knife down the curve of Ram's chest, quickening Ram's breath as he waits for another burning slice.

"Pearl told me you all regularly trade with humans," Lee says. "You should know better by now."

A cut opens up across Ram's cheek, the knife flicking impossibly fast. Ram doesn't mean to gasp, but the pain blossoms so quickly. Lee rakes his gaze over Ram's face, an all-too-familiar disappointment dripping from the human's expression—a cold calm that thinly veils the capacity for violence.

Ram's father looked at him exactly like this when he returned home, wounded and alone, the first time. But his father did not take a knife to Ram's face, and he certainly did not exude so much lust that it completely eclipsed every other feeling in the air.

"Did you not think this through at all?" Lee asks, the edge of the knife coming to rest against the length of Ram's throat.

Ram startles when his own cock throbs between his legs, heat pulsating through each appendage.

"Of course I thought about it," Ram snaps. "But humans are not usually so—"

Another cut across the meat of his shoulder.

"*Excuses.*" Lee's voice is all breath, his pupils fully dilated, eclipsing the green of his irises.

Ram's cock stirs, blood rushing through his body as he stares, wide-eyed at Lee.

"I know your type," Lee says, punctuating his words with another shallow cut across the thick slab of Ram's breast. Ram gasps at the stinging pain, such a light wound, but he is acutely aware that he has no control over this man with unseen tricks up his sleeve.

Lee presses his cock against the center of Ram's chest. "Traditional. Honor-bound. Probably trying to impress your father."

Ram swallows, the quiet volatility of Lee's presence prickling down his back. Did he reverse the trance somehow? Is Lee now able to read *Ram*? No, that's impossible.

"You're so wrapped up in your own self-image as a man who solves problems, you can hardly see all the problems you're causing with your own carelessness," Lee says.

Another flick of the knife across his bicep steals Ram's breath.

Ram's twin stems are slowly but surely stiffening in his pants, the confusion of adrenaline and pain and fear and *awe* mixing into a deadly brew.

"Tell me I'm right," Lee says, his gaze practically shaking as he fights with his own arousal. Every word he speaks, every droplet of blood answering the knife, only makes Lee harder as he rubs himself against Ram's beating heart. His hand is still barnacled to Ram's horn, the leather of the glove creased tightly around each knuckle.

"You..." Ram's voice is much too quiet. "What *are* you?"

Lee's mouth tics into a quarter of a smile, only the corner of his lips betraying a manic glee. "I'm just a man who knows what he likes."

Ram swallows reflexively, his body and his mind rearranging themselves in the presence of someone so effortlessly in control of himself.

"Let's find out what *you* are," Lee whispers. He steps back, releasing Ram's horn to allow some space between their bodies, only to set the delicate tip of his knife against Ram's left nipple. Ram's breath sucks into his lungs as his skin prickles, no pain yet, but the mere presence of the metal has him bracing. *He can no longer read Lee's desires.* The aborted trance has turned Lee's mind to impenetrable shadow, and Ram has no clue how far this human will push things.

"I'd keep that breathing steady if I were you," Lee says, gaze fixed on Ram's chest. "Wouldn't want to cut you by mistake."

Ram tries to wrangle his breath back to normal, but the soft pad of a leather-clad fingertip on his right nipple only makes it more difficult to stay calm. Both his nipples swell to attention with such light pressure. As Lee swirls his finger around in a small circle against Ram's flesh, he presses the flat of the blade in closer. Sensation billows inside Ram's chest at the small bit of pressure, and if it weren't for the knife, he'd want more. The topmost root of his cock strains against his pants at the maddeningly slow manipulation.

"Seems incubus have similar erogenous zones," Lee mutters to himself. "How do you breed?"

His thumb and middle finger lightly pinch the hard bead of Ram's nipple, and Ram gasps again, ashamed at how quick he is to rise to these tiny gestures.

"Is it only human semen you consume? Or is there some other process you have to go through to mate with one of your own?" Lee asks.

Acutely aware of the knife dimpling the flesh of his nipple, Ram attempts to get his voice to answer him.

"Fertility occurs in cycles," Ram answers, his face warming up at this strangely intimate-yet-cold talk. "We do not feed while we're fertile."

"Like going into heat?" Lee asks. "Is your hunger suppressed or do you just choose not to?"

"It is suppressed," Ram answers, hearing himself divulging the inner workings of his own people with no resistance, yet he can't stop himself. "We feed on humans until the cycle begins, so that we may be full enough to complete the cycle without needing to visit this world while vulnerable."

Lee makes a humming sound in the back of his throat, slowly and carefully drawing the knife across Ram's nipple, somehow avoiding drawing any blood, but Ram feels every centimeter of the blade.

"A parasitic species," Lee says with a sort of awe in his voice. "A body designed to take any kind of human fluids without harm to you, but vulnerable to your own body's needs." He licks the inside of his bottom lip, the slightest bit of pink flesh visible in his open mouth. "Fascinating. I imagine you're very hungry by now."

Ram is *starving*. Even with Lee's lust pouring off of him like thick smoke, Ram's body is depleted, vibrating with adrenaline, teetering on the edge of panic.

"What feeds you more?" Lee asks, spreading his gloved hand over Ram's chest. "Desire or cum?"

Ram swallows again and he hopes it isn't obvious how deeply he thirsts. "Solid food provides more sustenance."

"According to Pearl, the primary difference between an incubus and a succubus is how you eat. Succubus are more adept at absorbing fluids from within the cavities of their bodies, and incubus are more adept at absorbing fluids through their skin."

Ram doesn't deny him, a new curiosity brewing as he wonders if this human will let Ram fuck him just to keep Ram alive.

"But he also mentioned that you can all feed both ways, and that the difference in absorption rates is often negligible."

Ram's heart pounds. All this talk of feeding is only making him hungrier. The scent of Lee's unreadable desires fill his nose and his swiftly emptying mind. He would like to fuck this human, to feel hot cum sprayed onto his chest, softening his skin, filling the void in his body—to reassert his control over this situation.

Lee's gaze drops like a stone onto Ram's hips. Slowly, Lee kneels down between Ram's thighs, the tightly fitted material of his dark blue suit going taut around the human's hard cock.

Ram's stomach clenches at the knife's edge coming to rest against the generous bulge in Ram's pants.

"Easy," Lee cautions as he reaches for the buttons over Ram's abdomen. "No sudden movements now."

As he peels down the fabric from Ram's hips, the friction of the thick material against his taut cock is enough to steal Ram's breath. He wishes he weren't so damn hard, but as Lee exposes his split root, he can't help the bit of pride when Lee's brow quirks.

"Pearl also mentioned you're rare even amongst your own kind," Lee says, his voice quieting down as he studies Ram's twin cock. Lee's nostrils flare as he breathes in the sharp scent of Ram's skin, sweat, and gathering lust. "A high value incubus with an important father. You must be a very desirable partner in your own world."

Ram can't help puffing up at the implication.

"A shame you managed to fixate on the one person who doesn't want you," Lee says.

Embarrassment slides in like another knife as Lee brings his right hand to his mouth and bites the leather, loosening its hold on his fingers until he can unsheathe his bare hand.

"Shining Star will return to me eventually," Ram insists. "I am the owner of—"

"His voice, yes," Lee responds mildly, touching the engorged upper head of Ram's cock. "Pearl told us that he'd rather be mute in this world than have a voice in your world. Not that it's stopping him, of course."

Lee threads his bare fingers between Ram's stems, driving the breath from Ram's chest at the unbearably light touch against his heated skin.

"He's already begun learning sign language with Mr. Stoker and Mr. Rohan," Lee says. "Pearl is quite self-sufficient. He never really needed you to begin with. You, on the other hand, seem to have convinced yourself that you need him."

Ram fights back a moan, his breath leaving him in a shuddering sigh as Lee lifts his stems as if to inspect them like goods for sale.

"Do you come from both heads?" Lee asks. "Or is one just for show?"

Trying to hold onto his composure in this man's presence is like withstanding a flash flood with his eyes open.

"There is an easy way to find out," Ram says, feeling his own petulance growing. "Although you may not be able to accommodate my size. Humans do not stretch as easily as succubus do."

"No, we don't," Lee agrees, his gaze cutting to Ram's. "But you'll have no problem taking me."

Ram's eyes widen as he holds the unblinking gaze of a predator for a few silent seconds that beat through his chest like a hammer. How did Ram let this happen? He can practically hear his father shouting at him from the other world, demanding to know where Ram's stupidity came from.

Maybe his father was right. Maybe Ram should give it all up—Shining Star, his work as an instructor—and return to his position guarding the trade routes between worlds.

Lee shoves Ram to the ground so easily, pouncing on him like a cat. He is so much thinner and smaller than Ram, but what Lee lacks in power, he makes up for with exquisite timing and understanding of his opponent. As Ram's back and shoulder hit the ground, the concrete biting into his skin, he realizes just how much Lee has gleaned about him. This man appears to be an expert in his field, terrifyingly efficient, confident, controlled—everything Ram has failed to be over the cycles.

Lee moves unbelievably fast when he wants to. He and Shining—*Pearl*—have that in common, but where Pearl would run and hide, or tease and distract, Lee meets Ram head on. Sprawled on his side with his knees bent toward his chest, Ram can only feel the lack of his tail at the base of his spine as a sharp tug on the muscle sends a wave of heated arousal down his legs. His hole is being exposed beneath his tail, Lee's knee pressing against the back of his thigh to keep Ram folded into place.

The sound of clothes rustling, a zipper and a belt hastily undone, has Ram flailing in his ropes.

"Greedy humans!" Ram bellows. "Taking whatever you want!"

He cannot *stand* the ringing anticipation seizing his hips, echoing through his legs and belly with Lee on his knees behind him.

"Says the fucking parasite," Lee hisses back, taking his cock out from his suit pants.

Ram *shudders* at the press of heated flesh against his ass—gathering slick lining his walls.

Lee groans deep in his chest at the wet hole clenching around the head of his cock.

How long has it been since he did this?

Ram throws his head back, teeth grit as panicked pleasure sinks into his muscles.

Lee quickly forgets about reducing the friction of the floor against his suit pants as he grips Ram's thigh and shoves his cock into Ram's ass. Even with Ram writhing around on his side, it's easy for Lee to push past his clenching rim, and he grips Ram's haunch to steady himself on his knees. There's not enough movement, so he slices open the ropes around Ram's ankles, abandoning the knife on the floor to grip Ram's thigh and wrench it up higher. At first, the fluid inside Ram was barely enough to coat Lee's cock, but when Lee slowly pitches his hips to test how deep he can get, more wetness rises to meet him, welcoming him in.

Ram's back arches, his arms flexing as the ropes go taut around his wrists. Every one of the cuts Lee opened up on him sings with pain as Ram's ass relaxes at the first cock he's taken since he graduated out of his fledgling training. This human is not overly impressive in size, but he wastes no time, immediately sinking deep enough that his hips press against Ram's ass. He hoists Ram's thigh up against his chest just to make more space for himself, and the humiliation of it is just as powerful as the pleasure it incites.

It only takes a short burst of movement before Ram's walls are soaked and sucking Lee's cock deeper, but he bares his teeth all the while.

"*Greedy—wretched—humans!*"

The fury on Ram's face does not match the taut skin of his split cock, flushed and dripping onto the cement. A dark blush has begun spreading across Ram's chest. Lee is almost surprised at how tight Ram is around him, a delirious clenching pressure on his shaft that pushes Lee to go faster, ignoring the hard floor biting into his knees. He almost forgets to pay attention to Ram, pleasure snaking up Lee's spine from the head of his dick.

"*L-Let me go!*" Ram pants, his low, rumbling voice turned to a breathy, desperate plea.

Lee does not release him, gripping Ram's thigh as he fucks Ram harder, his adrenaline carrying him weightlessly through the rhythm. Ram's black eyes are peeled wide, his mouth hanging open as he gasps for air. His mottled skin has a dark flush from his head to the middle of his chest as his back arches into a half moon.

"No, no, no, *no—*"

Ram's ass cinches down on Lee's cock, wresting the breath from Lee's lungs while Ram's voice devolves into a ruinous moan. Ram throws his horned head back and comes on the concrete floor in a thick mess, both cockheads spurting uncontrollably while Ram's massive body contorts into a taut slab of stone.

Lee tries to maintain his control but Ram's ass is hot as a fever and perfectly slick. The thought crosses his mind to pull out now while he can and deprive this incubus of a full meal, but he wants this proud fool to feed off his cum and know that it was Lee who depleted *and* replenished him.

Ram's body thrums with the overabundance of desire pouring into him. He can barely think with this human's modest cock filling his ass. Ram's old owner used to chastise him for being too selfish in bed. *It's not enough to have size,* they would say. *You still need to know how to please others if you want to be a real incubus.*

Aftershocks of overstimulated pleasure roll through Ram's muscles and nerves as a human half his size takes him to pieces. He should have listened to his teacher, to his *student.* He should not have come to the human world today.

The human named Lee comes inside Ram, hot fluid soothing Ram from the inside like the first breath after drowning. Lee huffs quietly, his hips slapping against Ram's ass, almost no change to his demeanor, just a note of relief in his sighing breath as he finally empties his balls and goes still again.

Immediately after, Lee rises back to his feet and fixes his clothes. He gathers the knife as Ram's entire body pulses with pleasure and pain. Ram's eyes slide shut as he begins to absorb the food offered to him, the haze of a desperately needed meal setting in, an—

"Ah!" Ram yelps at two more cuts, quick and clean, sliced into the cheek of his ass.

"There," Lee says, only breathing a little harder as he stares down at the L-shaped cut on Ram's haunch. "So you don't forget who did this to you."

Ram goes slack against the concrete, panting as his skin rings with the cutting pain and the echoing pleasure. Humiliation and shame feel like an afterthought. Ram's mind is drenched in a syrupy haze, but he can't take his eyes off of Lee. He *can't,* or else he'll be taken by surprise again. He watches Lee stand up, returning to his supplies to remove his remaining black glove, then rinse his hands with a bottle of water. Shortly after, he snaps on a pair of thin, white gloves and begins to remove new tools.

"What more do you wish to inflict on me?" Ram asks, his voice thick, tongue heavy with exhaustion.

Lee approaches him, his gaze on a plastic bottle of clear fluid. "Stay still."

With the same deftness that he cut open Ram's skin, Lee begins cleaning every open wound and applying bandages where necessary. Ram is too tired to do anything but lay there, a strange and unwelcome feeling worming its way up through his belly.

He does not want to like *any of this.*

"As I see it, you have two options," Lee states as he cleans the cut on Ram's ass. "Return to your home, sick and wounded and empty-handed for the second time. Or."

He drags out the sound as he un-peels the last bandage.

"You willingly return to my home where you will agree not to cause trouble, and I can feed you until you're back to full strength."

Staring down at the wounded incubus with cum still wet on his hole, Lee crosses his arms and waits. He wasn't expecting to get so carried away, but he supposes that's the power of these creatures. Effortlessly loosening the lid on desire and control is their purpose.

"How are you...so calm?" Ram asks, his black eyes threatening to slide shut again. "I have not met another human who could so easily channel their own desire."

Lee shrugs. "I told you. Professionalism."

Ram closes his eyes again, sighing heavily.

Lee kneels down behind Ram, finding the ends of the rope to loosen the knot he tied around Ram's wrists. "I'm right about the father, aren't I?"

Ram's shoulders tic and he turns his face away from Lee. It's as good as an admission of guilt.

"Well, then," Lee says, pulling the rope free to wrap around his shoulder. He stands up, peeling off the latex gloves, and offers a hand to Ram. "I think the correct choice is obvious."

Ram slowly rolls his shoulders out, pulling his arms back to his front, resisting the urge to curl up into a ball.

Lee waits, silent and still, until Ram turns to him with a sheepish frown, and takes the offered hand.

"I will need a lot of food," Ram warns, though his voice is much quieter now. "To repair the damage you have just done."

Lee braces himself for the weight of the creature nearly twice his bulk as Ram hoists himself back up to his full height. He towers over Lee, his thick tail slowly regaining feeling as he flicks it up off the floor.

"I'm confident we can work something out," Lee tells him.

Ram can feel Lee's desire gathering against his skin, sharp as a knife held harmlessly against his pulse. A shiver runs up his spine as Lee eyes him, calm as ever. In the same breath, that lustful knife recedes as though it was never there.

"If you're lucky," Lee says. "Perhaps I'll teach you a thing or two about control."

THE END...?

▲▲

ABOUT

GEM is a scholar of inter-dimensional beings with a particular interest in documenting the interactions between humans and incubus. He strives to present the fullest truth in all its wet, glorious detail. He holds lessons for humans about the beings that share their world on his website.

This book is a passion project that was only able to be made through the wonderful support of readers like you! You can find more stories by FRICTION PRESS on itch.io. Please consider supporting works like this! And don't forget to tell your friends.

subscribestar.adult/friction-press
friction-press.itch.io

This story was edited by Beleghir.

beleghir.dreamwidth.org

This book was formatted and proofread by Subvertebra.

linktr.ee/subvertebra

If you found yourself unfamiliar with the muffing described at the end of this book (when Rohan puts everyone's fingers in his balls), I recommend reading the zine "Fucking Trans Women" by the late Mira Bellwether. You don't need to be a woman or even trans to find beauty in the way people take pleasure in their bodies.

GALLERY

PUCK

fastpuck.itch.io

bsky.app/profile/fastpuck.bsky.social

CYBORG NACHTE

bsky.app/profile/cyborgnachte.bsky.social

INT. COVER
PG. 176, 177

PG. 178, 179

MALEVOLENT
← LUST AURA
THE
ACTUAL
INCUBUS
↓

THANK YOU FOR READING!